Raves for *Twisted Creek*

"Absolutely delightful."
—*New York Times* bestselling author
Catherine Anderson

"A wonderful, character-driven tale."
—*Romance Reviews Today*

"Will weave its way around the reader's heart."
—*New York Times* bestselling author
Debbie Macomber

"A moving story."—*Romance Junkies*

BA
BAKERY

Praise for

Twisted Creek

"*Twisted Creek* will weave its way around the reader's heart. Compelling and beautifully written, it is exactly the kind of heart-wrenching, emotional story one has come to expect from Jodi Thomas."

—Debbie Macomber, #1 *New York Times* bestselling author

"Jodi Thomas is a masterful storyteller. She grabs your attention on the first page, captures your heart, and then makes you sad when it is time to bid her wonderful characters farewell. You can count on Jodi Thomas to give you a satisfying and memorable read. *Twisted Creek* is absolutely delightful."

—Catherine Anderson, *New York Times* bestselling author

"Thomas sketches a slow, sweet surrender, keeping the tension building to a rewarding resolution in this unsentimental, homespun romance." —*Publishers Weekly*

"*Twisted Creek* is a wonderful, character-driven tale that tells just what a family can be, even if it's made up of a bunch of lonely friends . . . Romance blooms slowly, but for two nearly lost souls, it's rewarding when it does . . . As usual, Jodi Thomas kept me up way later than normal! *Twisted Creek* could be anywhere, but Ms. Thomas makes it uniquely Texan with her wonderful characters and great dialogue. This is another thought-provoking novel to add to your Jodi Thomas collection." —*Romance Reviews Today*

"Romantic suspense and sweet women's fiction are an unlikely combination, but in *Twisted Creek*, veteran storyteller Jodi Thomas makes the pairing work quite well. Allie's love for her aging grandmother is sensitively portrayed, while her blossoming relationship with Luke simmers unforgettably in the background. This is a moving story about overcoming hardship and bitterness and about being brave enough to make a happy ending—no matter what it takes."

—*Romance Junkies*

Rewriting Monday

JODI THOMAS

BERKLEY BOOKS, NEW YORK

THE BERKLEY PUBLISHING GROUP
Published by the Penguin Group
Penguin Group (USA) Inc.
375 Hudson Street, New York, New York 10014, USA
Penguin Group (Canada), 90 Eglinton Avenue East, Suite 700, Toronto, Ontario M4P 2Y3, Canada
(a division of Pearson Penguin Canada Inc.)
Penguin Books Ltd., 80 Strand, London WC2R 0RL, England
Penguin Group Ireland, 25 St. Stephen's Green, Dublin 2, Ireland (a division of Penguin Books Ltd.)
Penguin Group (Australia), 250 Camberwell Road, Camberwell, Victoria 3124, Australia
(a division of Pearson Australia Group Pty. Ltd.)
Penguin Books India Pvt. Ltd., 11 Community Centre, Panchsheel Park, New Delhi—110 017, India
Penguin Group (NZ), 67 Apollo Drive, Rosedale, North Shore 0632, New Zealand
(a division of Pearson New Zealand Ltd.)
Penguin Books (South Africa) (Pty.) Ltd., 24 Sturdee Avenue, Rosebank, Johannesburg 2196,
South Africa

Penguin Books Ltd., Registered Offices: 80 Strand, London WC2R 0RL, England

This is a work of fiction. Names, characters, places, and incidents either are the product of the author's imagination or are used fictitiously, and any resemblance to actual persons, living or dead, business establishments, events, or locales is entirely coincidental. The publisher does not have any control over and does not assume any responsibility for author or third-party websites or their content.

REWRITING MONDAY

A Berkley Book / published by arrangement with the author

PRINTING HISTORY
Berkley edition / April 2009

Copyright © 2009 by Jodi Koumalats.
Interior text design by Kristin del Rosario.

ISBN: 978-0-425-22694-0

BERKLEY®
Berkley Books are published by The Berkley Publishing Group,
a division of Penguin Group (USA) Inc.,
375 Hudson Street, New York, New York 10014.
BERKLEY® is a registered trademark of Penguin Group (USA) Inc.
The "B" design is a trademark of Penguin Group (USA) Inc.

PRINTED IN THE UNITED STATES OF AMERICA

10 9 8 7 6 5 4 3 2 1

Chapter 1

Bailee, Texas
Population 15,007
Thursday, March 20, 2008

Dust battered the side of my rusty Saturn as I counted out the money I had left in my purse before going into the bakery for another one of Lorie's home-cooked meals.

Two hundred forty-five dollars and some change. "The great Pepper Malone has tumbled," I murmured, as if my life could be summed up in a headline.

I had enough to drive to Dallas and stay a week in a cheap, very cheap, motel while I looked for a new job. Enough to make it back to Chicago and face the music. Enough to hide out here in Bailee, Texas, for a month or more.

The choices were like trying to pick a roommate at an alligator refuge. I managed a grin and decided this time my rushing-in-like-a-fool attitude might get me hurt.

Closing my eyes, I fought back tears. I wasn't strong enough to start over in Dallas with no friends, no family, and no job. Or brave enough to face what I'd done in Chicago.

In the newspaper game they call it "co-oped" when a reporter gets too close to a story, and under the covers was definitely too close. Chicago was not an option.

I stared out at the dilapidated town square of my mother's hometown. It might as well have been named Nowhere, Texas, instead of Bailee. Even the statue of the Civil War soldier looked like he would evacuate this dusty huddle of buildings if he got the chance. The place didn't just look like progress passed it by; progress hadn't bothered to glance in Bailee's general direction.

Huge hundred-year-old elms, bent by the constant winds, lined Main, reminding me of skeletons tossing their useless bones in the street.

One question kept circling in my mind. Was I desperate enough to stay here? I was a gypsy bred on bright lights and traffic fumes. I needed Starbucks for breakfast, McDonald's for lunch, and sushi for dinner. I felt like a space traveler bounced to an unknown planet where chicken fried steak came even as a sandwich and the two Main Street traffic lights started blinking after nine. I should have tested the air here before I opened the hatch. This place could be toxic to my health.

Two hundred forty-five dollars and some change. Not much to show for ten years on my own. I wasn't counting the three broken engagements or the dozen or so apartments I'd called home since college. I blamed my lack of nesting skills on my job as a reporter, but then even Superman and Lois got married.

I felt older than thirty-one and broken deep in my soul, but I knew I had to fight on because fighting was all I'd ever truly been good at. My mother said once that I'd been born fist flying at the world and somehow I'd never stopped.

This time, I had to use my brains. I had to disappear long enough to lick my wounds before I came out fighting again. Nowhere could be better than here in a town even the interstate skipped.

I shoved the money back into my wallet and headed into the bakery for a meal. Today had to be the day I turned this trash heap of a life into something. Today wasn't the end of me. It was the beginning.

A few minutes later, I crossed my eyes and tried to concentrate on the words scratching their way out of the old jukebox in the corner. "Clowns to the left of me, jokers to the right . . . here I am stuck in the middle . . ." Stealers Wheel was belting out my theme song right here in the Lone Star Bakery.

At least I thought that was the name of the place. The sign outside only read BAKERY and the menus read MAIN STREET CAFE, but LONE STAR was written six feet high on the back wall. The place looked like the product of cross-breeding eateries. A bakery counter and cake-lined window. Diner booths along two walls. Cracked red vinyl stools near the back that had faded and peeled into what looked like an art project.

If I was starting over, Bailee was as close to virgin soil as I'd ever find to plant myself, but the bakery didn't much resemble the Promised Land. Though the counters were clean and tiny bells chimed whenever someone opened the door, the décor was definitely neglect.

Maybe this place had evolved from one name to another, as most people in the South tend to do. When born, I was called by both birth certificate names. "Look at dear little Patricia Anne." Then somewhere around four, after going through a few not-so-sweet baby names like *Stinky* and *Messy*, it shortened. By the time I was in school my name had morphed into abbreviations like *P.A.* or *Pat* or *Patty*. In college, I settled on what felt right: *Pepper.* Pepper Malone. The handle fit and looked great as a byline.

The music played on with no one listening except me. I took the only empty stool available. After ordering, I read through the same newspaper that had been on the counter yesterday and the day before. The *Bailee Bugle.* A weekly of surprising quality in a place where hard news never happened.

My food arrived as I made it to the want ads. I wasn't surprised to discover no listings under *Jobs.* Why bother; in a town this size, everyone knew who was out of work and who needed help.

I glanced around while I finished off my chili pie, the only meal within my budget. Clowns to the left, hicks to the right, I decided. This place could have been used to study the layers of human evolution. One man in the corner was eating his meat loaf with a spoon. Another looked so dirty he must be dusting the area around him with dirt as fine as powdered sugar.

A kid of about thirteen was catapulting sugar packets toward a table of high school girls. No one seemed to notice him, including his targets. I gave him a raised eyebrow and he answered back with one finger, blowing my belief that Bailee, Texas, might be a clone of Mayberry.

Two cheap-suited lawyer types at the first table were arguing over something no one cared about but them. Neither looked like he was listening to the other, just waiting for his turn to talk. As their disagreement rose in volume, the crowd compensated.

I shook my head. These locals, rough and loud, were nothing compared to the thugs who suggested I leave Chicago two weeks ago after my last article hit the stands. I still bore the bruise on my arm of what they thought of my work. They had to be the bottom-feeders of mankind. I don't think they even heard one word of my explanation, even though I was yelling at them as they helped me to my car.

I grinned as the baker passed. I may have crossed paths with the worst of mankind, but Lorie Fuller, the owner of this place, had to be near to the best. In the two days I'd been in Bailee, she had learned my name and welcomed me likc an old friend each time I came in. She looked to be in her late thirties, overweight by fashion standards, and was blessed with honest brown eyes.

She worked her way toward the long corner where I sat between a guy who looked at me as if he thought he'd seen me on a wanted poster and a middle-aged woman with shopping bags cluttered around her feet, making her look like a nesting chicken.

The shopper hadn't noticed me at all. I had a feeling the man missed little in his surroundings.

Sweet Lorie Fuller refilled iced tea glasses as she moved between crowded tables. If I'd been blind I would have smelled her coming, all warm yeast breads and ginger. With her short, curly hair, white apron, and round face she could have been the model for the baker in a children's picture book.

"Morning," I said with a quick nod and doing my best to fit in with the crowd.

She glanced at the old schoolhouse clock over the door. "Almost afternoon, Pepper." As she neared, she added, "I knew you'd think about what I said."

"I haven't . . ." There was no use finishing; the baker turned into a fortune-teller before I could say another word.

"Now, Pepper," she whispered as she slid a slice of buttermilk pie across the counter that I knew would not be on the bill. "You got to go across the street and apply. It's the only job for you."

I looked at the newspaper office thirty feet away and

didn't bother to disagree. "I know. I thought I'd put it off until I was actually starving." That gave me until the middle of next week sometime if I limited my diet to chili pie and stew and gave up hair care products.

I'd told Lorie I came to town to check out my inheritance. My mother mentioned, when I called her in L.A. and told her I was leaving for parts unknown, that my great-aunt had willed me the family home in Bailee. She forgot to mention it was a trailer parked out on a road so neglected that nature had taken it back.

Which turned out to be the second problem with the information. The first one being that dear old Aunt Wilma Davis was still alive. I found her recovering in the local nursing home from a broken hip, but very much this side of death's door and looking forward to getting back to her little aluminum cottage in the weeds.

Lorie leaned on the counter. "You got a good shot at the job," she encouraged, as if I'd known her longer than since Tuesday. "If you don't go today, you'll have to worry about it all weekend 'cause he'll never have time to hire you on Friday. There's a sign in the window, so you know he's looking for someone."

I smiled. It's hard to stare into sunshine and not feel warm. If Lorie could bottle her kind spirit, the whole world would crave it. "I guess I could just see about it."

The shopping lady to the left shouted, "Somebody better do something about that boy over there before he drives me nuts."

I forgot about my job hunting and looked, along with everyone else, at the chubby kid still tossing sugar packets. He'd decided to rip the pack open so sugar scattered as it flew across the room.

Lorie frowned, but didn't move.

The bag lady reached behind me and poked the man

on my right. "You should do something. You're a lawman, aren't you, Luke?"

He was tall, dark, and well built, and I noticed that he wore a band on his left hand. He might have been an off-duty cop, but he definitely had *married* written all over him. Some men have that look, or maybe it's a nonlook. They'll smile back at you, maybe even open the door for you, but you know they're not interested in even window shopping. Luke wore *already found happily ever after* like invisible armor.

"Not my jurisdiction," he whispered behind my back, as if not wanting to draw attention. "I just handle problems out at Twisted Creek."

The lady with the bags frowned. "Do something, Luke!"

"I *am* doing something," he answered. "I'm eating lunch."

She nudged him again.

Luke placed his sandwich down and swiveled on his stool. "Border Biggs," he said in a low voice that seemed to echo off the walls like rumbling thunder. "Stop doing that. You're driving Mrs. Potts crazy."

The stout kid slowly leaned forward, half out of the booth. "Or you'll what?" He smirked. "Arrest me for tossing sugar?"

"No, I'll just shoot you."

The jangle of the bells on the door did nothing to soften his words.

A huge man in a brown county sheriff's uniform entered the cafe. He pulled off his hat and studied the room, but only silence met him.

Luke picked up his sandwich and pointed toward Border Biggs. "Glad you're here, Deputy Toad. This kid's been acting up. Would you shoot him? I'd like to finish eating before my wife buys out the dollar store."

I watched the law officer named Toad take a few steps.

His wide smile reminded me of an alligator. "Ever'body knows I quit carrying a gun when I learned to kill a man with my bare hands." He wiggled his fat fingers. "Which kid did you say was acting up?"

Border Biggs's eyes widened. He'd been prepared to bother everyone, but not to face down a mountain of muscle and fat wearing a badge.

Lorie moved out from behind the counter. She stepped in front of the boy's booth, grabbed the sugar tray, and bopped the kid on the head with a huge wooden spoon.

Border dropped into his seat. "Child abuse!" he yelled.

Next to me, Luke turned back to his sandwich.

The deputy stood in the center of the room and asked, "Did anyone see any abuse?"

People went back to talking among themselves. Apparently I was the only one who saw anything, and I wasn't planning to say a word. For all I know, they shoot outsiders who interfere with the law and sugar tossers.

I suddenly realized that I had made my decision: I was staying. For now.

Lorie, the baker turned fortune-teller turned mind reader, refilled my coffee and whispered, "Go over there right now before you change your mind, Pepper. Take the job."

The thought of sitting all day in a singlewide with Herbert, Aunt Wilma's one-eyed cat, and her John Wayne bobble-head collection was more than I could bear. Visits to my great-aunt, who only talked to me between bingo games, didn't sound much better. This was the only job open in town and I was more than qualified.

"He'll be in there alone," Lorie added. "He always takes his lunch alone."

Michael McCulloch, I almost said aloud. The resident Monster of the *Bailee Bugle*. Grinning, I thought, *Why can't this town have a monster? It has a toad for a deputy.*

I stood, paid my bill, and squared my shoulders. Yesterday at breakfast I'd asked Lorie if there was any chance the opening at the paper was still available. The sign in the window had been there so long it had faded.

"Give it a shot," Lorie said. "What have you got to lose?"

I walked out of the café figuring half the folks inside were watching me. Dust whirled around me as I crossed the street. The shadow of the three-story courthouse, a half block away, already crept down Main. Half of the angled parking slots were taken by pickups, some so old they were in danger of being turned into front-yard flowerpots any day.

Bailee reminded me of one of those towns in black-and-white horror movies where aliens land and kill off most of the people before anyone in the state notices. It was big enough to have a newspaper, a high school, two car dealerships, and a dilapidated movie theater, but not so large that folks couldn't spot a stranger.

I'd never lived in a small town, but I remember my mother telling about how, when she was young, everyone piled in cars at night and circled Main, turned off at the swimming pool and drove down the highway to the Dairy Queen, then circled back, made the drag again before parking for a while on the grain elevator lot.

I could see the tall rusting towers at one end and the turnoff to the drive-in at the other. No wonder Mom ran away to Fort Worth when she was seventeen. She'd never really stopped running, either. About the time she got a house decorated it was time to move. If she didn't have a cell phone, I'm sure I would have lost track of her by now.

The thought crossed my mind that if she'd stayed here, I might not be afraid to fall asleep at night. I might not always feel the desire to double up my fists, ready for a fight.

Opening the door to the *Bailee Bugle*, I stepped inside. After all that had happened to me in the past month, I didn't much care if Michael McCulloch was a fire-breathing dragon. He'd give me a job or eat me. Either way, I'd put off going home to hairball-hacking Herbert and watching endless old westerns until dawn.

Chapter 2

Bailee Bugle
12:25 P.M.

A rush of wind joined me as I walked in, scattering papers as I moved to the front desk and rattling what sounded like a hundred flyers along a long bulletin board.

A tall man in his thirties stepped out of the first office off the main room.

While he crossed the open space between his office and the long front desk I looked around. This place looked like it belonged in a museum. The perfect example of a 1940s press room, right down to the flyers whirling in the wind.

"Sorry." I slapped at flyers, realizing I was adding another level of chaos to the disorder.

He smiled. "It doesn't matter. Rustling paper has been the doorbell around the office for as long as I can remember."

Picking up a pencil in his left hand, he asked, "What's the address you're looking for?"

"Address?"

His tolerant smile seemed to tell me that he already knew the rules to the game, so I could stop playing. "Strangers in town always stop by here for directions. I've thought of adding *Tourist Information* beneath the *Bailee Bugle* sign painted on the windows."

I decided to play along. "What makes you think I'm lost?"

"Lady, you got 'city girl' written all over you." He pointed with his pencil. "Designer purse big enough to be an overnight bag. Cell phone case strapped to the handle. Nails painted like Neapolitan ice cream and"—he leaned over the counter—"high heels tall enough to put you eye-to-eye with me. You definitely aren't from around here."

I dug in my bag, fully aware of him watching me. "I'm five ten," I said before he asked. People always asked. I'd never figured out why. Couldn't they see for themselves that I was tall? The question always made me want to ask their weight.

"Six three," he answered, as if we were introducing ourselves.

This couldn't be the Monster of Bailee, Michael McCulloch. This must be his cousin, the village idiot.

He shifted, less sure of the game. "May I help you?" he said, more formal this time.

I pulled my portfolio out of the bag and pressed one corner flat.

"I wouldn't have taken you for a salesman," he said. "But I can save you some time. Whatever it is you're selling, we're not buying."

I looked up at him and said as politely as I could manage, "I'd like to speak to Mr. McCulloch."

"I'm Mike McCulloch, but I'm still not buying. Sorry you made the trip for nothing."

I studied him. He wasn't what I'd expected. I'd guessed he'd be older, bald, and potbellied. At the very least, he should have worry lines permanently indenting his forehead. This guy didn't look like he even worried about matching his socks.

He dropped the pencil back on the counter. "You might save gas by calling next time before you come." He turned back toward the front office.

"I'd like to apply for the opening you have posted in the window, Mr. McCulloch." I blurted the words out before I lost my chance. "I'm Pepper Malone." I pointed to the yellowed paper at the corner of his huge window.

"You're kidding. This has to be a joke." He returned to the counter. "You look like you might be able to spell, which leaves you more qualified than anyone who's ever held the reporting job here."

"I can spell." I grinned at his surprise. "And I'm not kidding. I've got a journalism degree from Rice, eight years' experience at the *Chicago Sun*. And—"

"Stop right there." Mike shook his head, and any order his hair had once claimed vanished. "You're way too qualified to write obits and weather, and we don't have enough news around here to offer you anything else. I'm sorry."

"You're not giving me a chance?" I opened my portfolio and prepared to fight. "I'll have you know I've worked—"

He held up his left hand in surrender. "Trust me, Miss Malone, you don't want the job."

I tilted my head and stared at him. He offered no made-up reasons and pretended no false importance. I was used to fighters . . . and liars. I didn't understand this kind of man any better than he understood me. "How much does it pay?"

"Three hundred and seventy five a week, and you use your own car and gas on assignments."

"I'm worth five times that."

"I'm sure you are. I should have listed the salary on the post. You wouldn't have bothered to cross the street."

"You saw me?"

"I see pretty much everything in this town," he said with no false pride. "Plus, you're hard to miss, lady, with that designer coat and candy-apple-red smile. You've got a way about you, like someone not afraid to storm the walls of any fortress. I'll bet you're a great reporter."

"I am," I said, "and I'll take the job."

He grinned as if calling my bluff. "Suit yourself. Pick a desk. You'll start right now." He pointed toward three forgotten desks. "I assume you have your own laptop. We've got a deadline in four hours."

I almost giggled. I had done a grand job of screwing up my private life, but one thing I knew I was good at was work. If he handed me rough notes I could probably fill a paper his size with copy in four hours. "I'll be right back." Without another word I headed out to collect my office bag and the half-dead pepper plant from my car.

When I returned, the editor was standing at the door to the shadowy back office. "Orrie Cleveland, come out and meet our new reporter, Pepper Malone."

I heard what must be Orrie Cleveland's chair squeak its way to the door.

"Orrie is a genius on the computer," Mike offered.

The rounded little man seemed to have had the office chair molded to his frame. Everything about him, from his skin to his hair, seemed the dull worn brown of the leather chair. He might be a genius, but he reminded me of a groundhog. He nodded and mumbled a hello before disappearing back into the shadows of his room.

Mike watched my reaction, then offered, "He's a real talker."

Without another word, he went back into the first office.

"Aren't you all," I mumbled to myself as I unloaded a bag half the size of a file cabinet atop one desk and dropped my plant on the corner, where light shone in through the windows. The plant looked like it should be in hospice, but I had a rule that I never tossed a pot until I was sure the plant was dead. It wasn't much of a life rule, but we can't all think of the great ones.

Ten minutes later I was settled in and turned to straightening all the flyers along the long desk that separated the world from the *Bugle*. Several notices were out of date. I tossed them. At the edge of the desk I noticed a midnight-blue book, a journal, looking out of place.

The wind had been flipping pages back and forth.

I glanced at the page now open. It read:

Journal Entry: How do you tell the truth from a lie when you're the one talking?

I stepped away feeling as if I'd invaded someone's private thoughts. Back at my desk, I opened my laptop. I pulled up my e-mail and realized the messages were all from Chicago. I pressed Delete. I needed to get away from what I'd done. Maybe if I didn't think about how dumb I'd been, Chicago's problem would go away.

Five minutes later, when I looked up, Mike McCulloch was coming toward me. "Settled in?" he asked, then without waiting for an answer, he said, "I'll have your first assignment in a few minutes. I thought you might want to look over some back issues." He dropped the papers on my desk and went back to his office.

As I pulled the papers he'd given me closer, I noticed the blue journal was missing from the corner of the desk.

If it was McCulloch's, he'd suddenly become a great deal more interesting than I thought he was. Beneath that easygoing shyness lay turmoil.

And in that, I found something in common with him.

Chapter 3

Bailee, Texas
Population 15,008

I used my sleeve to polish the nameplate as I moved my things around on the beat-up old desk. I'd dumped the plate in my office bag along with everything else in my cubicle when I left Chicago. Like a carpenter caressing his tools, it felt good to think of working again. Writing had always been my center, my focus. The one time I'd slipped and concentrated on something . . . correction . . . someone else, I'd almost lost everything, including my sanity.

Never again would I mix a story and my life together.

Glancing around the dull office, overdecorated with mahogany and dust, I reconsidered the sanity part. This place was part museum, part junk store. An old Underwood typewriter sat on one of the desks. I hadn't seen one of those in years. McCulloch's office was at the front. Orrie Cleveland's cave at the back. A sign blocked the glass top of his door. It read, DON'T BOTHER ME. I'LL FIND YOU IF I NEED YOU.

All other desks were in the center of the main room. Guessing from those that looked occupied, I'd say the paper had three more employees besides Michael and the antisocial groundhog.

I walked between the desks, studying each.

An older woman with no children must be first—no pictures, a cat tape dispenser, and a box of Kleenex placed between her and the rest of the world.

A younger man, I think, must be at the next desk—forgotten CD player on one corner. Probably replaced by an iPod. Papers scattered in poorly organized files. Watermark stains the size of cola bottles on the right side of his station.

And the last desk. I'd guess an old man—one picture of a woman dressed like she belonged on the cast of *Happy Days*. No computer. One highball glass filled with sharp pencils and a hook on the wall at just the right height to hang a hat.

While I was praising my detective skills, I turned toward my new boss.

I could see McCulloch in his office thirty feet away. He was doing his best to ignore me. Maybe he was simply waiting for me to come to my senses and leave.

With nothing else to do, I turned on my laptop and began writing his profile. Tall, but well proportioned. A little on the thin side. A runner's body, I thought. In need of a haircut and clothes bought in this decade. Favors his left hand. One of those men who could be good-looking if he tried. Judging from what I'd witnessed, he never tried.

Not exactly the profile of a monster. But then, I'd proven a failure at recognizing monsters.

The front door opened. A gray-haired man in a fedora strolled in. He made it all the way to his desk and hung up his hat before he noticed me. Then he simply smiled and nodded once. Pure Southern charm.

From the stains on his cuffs and the sadness in his eyes, I added *widower* to his fact sheet.

Before I could introduce myself, I heard the high pitch of a woman's scolding coming from the back. A few seconds later a frail creature rushed through the opening and into the great room. Bone thin, she wore a plaid wool skirt that she'd probably had since high school many years ago.

A young man of about nineteen carrying a box of paper followed her.

Bingo, I almost yelled. I'd got them right.

The woman stopped in the middle of her orders to the kid and stared at me as if I were a frog occupying a chair. Her smile was forced over lips as thin as her penciled-on eyebrows. "May I help you?" she inquired.

I smiled a bit too enthusiastically and took a step toward her. "Hello, I'm Pepper Malone. I was just hired."

The woman ignored me and turned to the old man. "I didn't know about this. Did you, Webster?"

He shook his head. "Nope, but I'm not on the 'to tell' list, I guess." He winked at me. "I'm Webster Higgins, but some folks call me Web for short. I handle the ads. It is a pleasure to meet you, Miss Pepper Malone."

I shook his hand without letting the woman out of my sight. Her territorial stare left no doubt how she felt about me.

After Webster turned loose of my hand, he added, "And this lovely creature is Audrey Leland, our bookkeeper and office manager. We couldn't run the paper without her constant guidance."

Audrey, who I guessed to be nearing fifty, blushed. She truly blushed, then with a twitch of a smile took my hand.

"I am the bookkeeper, but I also write the social page, so I'm also a reporter." She pulled away quickly as if I might have germs. "If you are newly hired, there will be papers to fill out. Forms to file. You do have a copy of your social security card and a picture ID, I hope."

"Of course." I found it interesting she didn't take my word. She'd check a second source before stating anything as a fact. A born journalist.

"Then"—her lips thinned into a smile—"welcome. We can sure use another hand around the place."

The young man, stout with muscle, took my hand next. "I'm Bob Earl," he said without tossing in a last name.

When he raised his gaze to mine, I saw a blankness in his stare and understood why no one in the office had bothered to stop him from putting his drinks on the old wooden desk.

Michael McCulloch finally ended the greetings by yelling simply, "Malone!"

I fought the urge to yell back, "What?" but decided to be nice at least my first day. Grabbing my notepad, I hurried to his office.

He didn't bother to look at me. "Go over to Gray's Funeral Home and see if he has any pendings."

I wrote down *Gray's—pendings* and looked up. The back wall of his office was a ten-foot-square gun rack with more weapons than I'd ever seen outside the gun show I covered once as a cub reporter.

"You hunt?" I managed, thinking that sounded much better than *How many things have you killed lately?*

"No," he answered, without further explanation. He shuffled through papers on his desk. "While you're out on that end of town, double-check the times at the sale barn next week."

I wrote down *times—sale* without having any idea what he was talking about.

"What else, Chief?"

He finally looked up. "Don't call me Chief."

Before I could ask him what I should call him, he snapped, "Any questions?"

"Nope." I flipped my notepad shut.

"Good," he said without smiling. "Be back in less than an hour. I'll have copy for you to write from the counties reporting in."

I walked out, wondering if the real Michael McCulloch was the man I first met or this boss he'd turned into the minute I'd moved in. I couldn't tell if he was looking for a reason to fire me, or if he simply didn't care. The easy manner had vanished. Strange man to run a paper.

On my way out I caught sight of the midnight-blue journal tucked between two style books on a shelf. Too bad I hadn't read more than one entry.

As I collected my purse, I whispered to Webster, "Where's Gray's?"

"North road out of town," he whispered back. "Talk to the secretary, Peggy. She's the only one who'll know what's going on. Double-check all the funerals scheduled, times, dates, places. We got three cemeteries, you know."

I didn't know. "What's the sale barn?"

His smile was kind. "Last barn on the same side of the road as Gray's place. About a half mile out of town. Rodeo grounds next to it."

I thanked him, but before I could leave, he added, "If you're wanting times, go inside. Don't ask the boys riding in the corrals. They'll lie to you for the fun of it."

Grabbing my keys, I was almost to the door when Audrey said, "Park behind the building. We'll keep that door unlocked until you get back. It's a lot safer, less dings from those pickups parked on Main."

I walked across the street to my Saturn and climbed in. As I slid on my sunglasses, I noticed McCulloch watching me from his window.

He'd told the truth; he could see most of what happened in Bailee from his vantage point. A strong man, watching, recording, even influencing everything that happened around him, yet somehow I got the feeling he was the one caged.

Chapter 4

Bailee, Texas
Population 15,007

I drove into the funeral home parking lot behind a hearse and watched until they unloaded the newest customer before I walked around to the front of the place. I'd just decided to stay in town and someone else had checked out. Census still accurate.

The smell of carnations greeted me at the door. It might be a cold wintry kind of day outside, but in the parlor of Gray's Funeral Home it was misty summer twilight. All the shades were at half mast and a soothing hue of fleshy beige melted over everything from carpet to drapes.

Note to self: Don't let them bury me in beige.

I hated funeral homes. I couldn't think of one good time I'd ever had in one. My father died when I was seven. All I remember about the funeral was sitting at the end of a pew watching kids play in the snow outside while their parents paid respects. I think I must have wished I could have crawled up in my daddy's arms one more time to feel safe and warm. If I didn't wish it then, I'd wished for it a hundred times since.

My mother's mourning period lasted three months before she married her boss from the lumberyard and sent me off to a "not so grand" boarding school. I was the only girl there who lived less than fifty miles away from home and still didn't get picked up on weekends. Except for phone calls and quick lunches when she came into town, I've pretty much been on my own since. Sometimes, I swear, when I call her, she has to think for a moment before she remembers who I am.

I remembered people saying that it would be a while before my life got back to normal after my father died. They lied. It never had.

"May I help you?" a lady in beige whispered. She had to be the original cookie-cutter mold for sweet little old ladies.

I forced a smile. "I'm a reporter with the *Bailee Bugle*. You must be Peggy."

She looked as if I'd said something funny. "I am, dear, but I've already typed up the facts. I was about to e-mail them to Mr. McCulloch. We lost dear Alma Weatherly today. Heart failure, poor thing. If she'd just lived one more week she would have made it to ninety-four. But, oh well, God's time."

I thought about suggesting that dear Alma Weatherly had been hiding out from God for quite a while, but I didn't know if this babysitter-of-the-newly departed would get my humor.

I collected my information about Bailee's newly departed and almost ran out.

Half a mile down the road I stepped into a place I discovered I hated more than funeral homes. Sale barns!

The smell of manure drifted on the damp air as I walked

inside the metal building. The barn walls rattled as the wind pounded to get in. I could almost feel the odors clinging to my skin, thick as cold sweat. Following the only bright light in the place, I made my way upstairs to a small office.

Two jeans-clad secretaries welcomed me and told me the same thing the beige lady had. They'd been about ready to e-mail the facts to the paper.

One cowgirl, with tiny dangling boots for earrings, asked me about Mr. McCulloch. The other poked her and giggled as if they weren't fifteen years out of high school.

"He's fine," I answered. "I only met him thirty minutes ago."

"Is he looking well?" the woman pushed. "I mean, he's not sick, is he?"

Her partner chimed in. "We're just asking because we'd hate it if he were ill. The paper's real important to everyone around these parts."

I stared at the two leftover rodeo queens. "Has he been ill?"

Both shook their heads.

The one with the boot jewelry added, "Mike's like a ghost around here. It's as if Mike and Dave McCulloch both died that rainy night ten years ago."

The other one looked like she might cry. "There was no doubt they was brothers even if Mike was thin and Dave heavier. Mike was quiet, a loner, you know. Dave never met a stranger. Mike kind of drifted in and out of places, but Dave, now he was the life of every party."

Boot Earrings agreed. "There was nothing Dave wouldn't try. Mike was more like his shadow when they were kids."

I thought about asking what happened to Michael's brother, but somehow I felt like I'd be prying. He had a right to his private life. "I'll tell him you asked about his health," I said.

"Don't bother." She shrugged. "I'll ask him myself when I see him. In a town this size, nobody can hide out forever."

I figured McCulloch must have sent me to the two worst places first, hoping I'd quit. He'd also sent me out for no reason. He had to have known they'd be e-mailing the information in.

What kind of man hires a reporter, then tries to get rid of her minutes later?

On the way back to the paper, I passed the Shades of Time Nursing Home and decided to stop by and visit my aunt Wilma. She was my grandmother's sister. She'd never married, or lived anywhere but Bailee that I knew about. But then my mother was never loose-lipped about any of her relatives. For all I knew Wilma had hitched her trailer to the circus wagons in her youth.

Maybe if I could catch her between bingo games, I could ask a few questions about her and about this town.

Aunt Wilma was sitting in a hallway lineup of wheelchairs when I walked in. She'd advanced to a walker since yesterday, but from her frown, she preferred to be pushed in a wheelchair. As usual, she showed little interest in seeing me.

"How's the cat?" she asked when I got within yelling distance. "Didn't come to tell me he died, did you?"

"Herbert is fine," I said. "How are you?"

"Ready to go home, but they won't let me. Tell me I need rehab. Who knows how long that will take? Once they get you in these places, they tend to try and keep you for no good reason that I can figure out."

"I'll ask when they think—"

She didn't let me finish. "I can ask them myself, but you

can tell them it's cold in here. You'd think for what this rehabilitation is costing me they could turn on the heat."

Nodding, I took the chair next to her. I could see why no one in the family ever came to visit her. My mother always said she wasn't close enough to her family, but a thousand miles seemed close enough to this one. If I didn't get the subject changed fast, I had a feeling she'd complain about everything in her world.

"Aunt Wilma, could I ask you a question or two about Bailee?"

She looked at me as if I were a secret agent for the IRS.

"I took a job writing for the *Bugle* while I'm here. What can you tell me about Michael McCulloch?"

She leaned back in her chair. "He's fourth generation. That paper's been in his family for almost a hundred years. The first McCulloch was quick to defend his editorials at gunpoint, from what I hear. The second, Benjamin, I think I remember his name being, went off to World War I and reported back to the paper every week. When he came home he had to fight union organizers as well as the KKK. The next one, Mikey's father, was my age. He never missed more than a day or two of work in forty years. If I remember right, Clark McCulloch died at his desk."

"What about . . . Mikey?" I asked.

She looked at me for a long moment before saying, "He's like everybody else in this town. He'd like to rewrite a part of his past."

"What part?"

"That's for him to say," she said as the cafeteria doors opened for the afternoon session of bingo. "You make him a good hand, girl. He don't need no more bother coming into his life."

Nodding, I decided I had more questions after talking to her than I'd had before dropping by. If I squinted real hard I could see the look of my mother in her. That would have made my mom furious. She's spent thousands trying to look like someone else's relative.

Aunt Wilma pulled herself up with a tight grip on the walker. "Since you got a job, you got money. Buy Herbert some of those chicken fingers at the Dairy Queen. Just give him one a night. Any more and he'll think he's living the high life."

"With or without gravy?" I couldn't believe she wanted me to buy the cat takeout.

"With, of course. It comes free. No sense wasting it." Turning away, she lifted her walker and plopped it down six inches in front of her, then shuffled her feet toward it. With a steady *clomp*, *swish*, *clomp*, she left.

I watched her go, wondering what moment in time she'd pick to rewrite. She was bitter, and cold, and poor. Maybe she knew the turning point, even chose it. Maybe she'd just drifted here.

As I walked back to my car, I felt a chill go all the way to my bones. The wind had turned colder, blowing now off the rocky hills from the north, but it was more than that. This place was seeping into my soul, and I couldn't help fearing that somehow I was at one of those invisible turning points.

Chapter 5

Mike watched Pepper Malone all afternoon from the open door of his office. She knew the job. He'd never seen anyone write copy faster. She also had no fear of him or anyone else. She'd stormed back from the funeral home, gone straight to her desk and written the stories, then flopped the finished copy in front of him and asked why he'd wasted her time and gas having her drive out north of town.

He'd been so unprepared for the challenge, he'd said the first thing he could think of—that she needed to know where everything in town was—but he had a feeling she didn't swallow the answer whole.

Most of the afternoon, he'd had her taking the calls and e-mails from regional reporters. Since that was usually his job on Thursdays, he had nothing to do but look busy and watch her. He could never remember seeing a woman so tall who seemed so graceful. If she ever smiled, she might be pretty, but the way she tackled work it would probably be summer before that happened.

Caring what was going on in the big room outside his door was new to him. The conversations were usually only background noise while he worked. Audrey complaining about pretty much everything, Webster telling Bob Earl about the big cities he'd seen in his years away from Bailee. Bob Earl asking Audrey to explain one more time something he'd known how to do the day before, but forgotten. And, once in a while, Orrie Cleveland yelling that he needed more info from Webster about an ad. The office wizard did a great job of putting everything together, but had no social skills. If Orrie Cleveland had even acknowledged Pepper past the nod of an introduction, Mike hadn't heard it.

Mike cared about the people who worked for him, but they didn't know him. If they saw inside him, Mike knew they'd all be surprised at how out of place he felt. His life, his work, his responsibilities were here, but his dreams were somewhere else. For as long as he could remember, he'd wished for another life. A life he saw on the rare misty morning that lay just beyond the Bailee city limits, when he allowed himself to wish.

In this town, folks seemed to think McCullochs were born to be editors, and with the job came the title of Mr. McCulloch. He'd been *Mikey* in grade school, *Mike* or *Michael* to everyone after that, until the day he stepped into his father's shoes. He'd been twenty-five when his old man died, but that day it seemed like he aged a decade. In the same suit he'd worn to his father's funeral the week before and his brother's funeral a month before that, Mike unlocked the *Bugle* doors and became Mr. McCulloch.

If he were being honest with himself, he didn't hate the job. It just didn't fit any better than that black suit had.

Dreaming about what might have been in his life was just a waste of time. This was his reality.

When Pepper jumped up from her desk for the fifth time in less than an hour, he bumped his knee trying to swivel around before she looked over and caught him watching her.

"Chief," she called as she took long strides toward him. "I can't make sense of this one at all. Where do you get these regional reporters, from the *Mars Tribune*? The last one had to tell me about her grandkids before giving the crop report, and you're not going to believe this one."

He tried his best to look like the interruption bothered him. "Is it from Carol Bonham over near Turtle Crossing?"

She looked surprised. "You guessed it."

He frowned. "Carol has sent in news from around her area for years, but she wants to write hot romance novels. Sometimes she gets a little carried away."

"Carried away!" Pepper snapped. "She described the lightning as 'ejaculating from a wall cloud.'"

Michael looked away as he fought down a smile. He could hear old Webster laughing and would bet Audrey had already darkened a few shades of red.

"It just needs an edit," he finally managed without looking up at Pepper Malone. Next time, he promised himself, he'd hire a reporter with shorter legs. That would give him more time to think before she got to his office.

"It needs burning," she corrected, and marched back to her desk.

He heard Webster ask if he could see the whole article.

Pepper offered to let him edit it. She must have passed him her laptop because for the next several minutes Mike heard her explaining how her editing program worked.

Webster sold the ads and handled the camera work

other than sports. He worked when he wanted and was paid on a percentage. Mike had a feeling Webster hung around because he didn't want to go home alone. He sold ads from a briefcase propped on a table at Lorie's bakery.

The old man had grown up in Bailee so he knew folks even though he'd left town in his thirties. Mike had heard that Webster left because his wife had been ill for so long before she died that he'd lost his job taking care of her. When he'd walked into the newspaper's office four years ago, Webster had simply said he was retired and thought he'd like to try working for a newspaper.

Except for Audrey and Orrie, everyone who worked for the *Bugle* did so part time. Mike liked it that way. People didn't feel so connected to him at twenty hours a week and no benefits.

So why had he hired Pepper? She was like fresh air in a stagnant room. She'd be good for the paper. Maybe she'd even be good for him.

"Weather's getting worse." Webster's voice carried into Mike's office. "There'll be rain coming before dark."

Bob Earl studied the clouds. Orrie Cleveland slammed his door and darted out the back.

Mike had once thought Orrie Cleveland might have the same disease as the Wicked Witch in Oz, where she melted if water hit her. Orrie left early if there was any chance of rain and limited his bathing to once a week.

"It's a quarter to five. I say we close up before the rain hits." Audrey was already shutting down her computer. "I got my canasta meeting tonight."

Mike turned to watch as his troops began to evacuate. Webster reached for his hat. Bob Earl put the comic he'd been reading in his backpack, then made his rounds to empty the trash, his last duty of the day. That had been his first job at the paper and the only one he never forgot to do.

Pepper hadn't moved. In fact, she didn't look like she'd heard the call.

"We all leave together." Audrey leaned toward Pepper. "Except Orrie, who goes and comes whenever he feels like it. I've given up even speaking to the man. When I walk near his door he yells, 'What? What? Go away.'" Audrey made a face. "Last week when I asked him how he was doing, he told me, 'Forecast unknown.' Can you imagine that? He never gets it that we all leave at the same time."

"I'm not finished," Pepper said with a small wave of her hand. "See you tomorrow."

Audrey looked frustrated. "We're all going together," she repeated.

Mike almost laughed out loud when Pepper looked up and said simply, "Why?"

He'd wondered the same thing since the day he became the editor. Audrey, the bookkeeper for twenty-four years, had announced closing time from that day on.

Audrey always talked fast when she was irritated. "I guess you can stay if you want to, but you'll have to lock the door behind us, and I can't clock in hours I'm not witness to on your time sheet."

"Okay," Pepper answered, too lost in her work to even notice that the bookkeeper was upset.

Bob Earl waited at the front door until Audrey walked over, said good night to the boy, and locked it behind him. Webster, carrying his battered briefcase and hat, left by the back door. The bookkeeper stood in the doorway waiting for Pepper.

"The door, Miss Malone," Audrey reminded.

Pepper jumped up. "Oh, yes. Sorry."

"Be careful," Audrey whispered, loud enough for Mike to hear. "We've had trouble around here."

Pepper paused with the door open. "Trouble?"

"Someone hates the paper. We don't know why, but there's been damage. If we aren't careful to make sure the doors are locked, someone might get in and ransack the place."

Mike couldn't hear Pepper's answer, but a moment later he heard the lock click and then the tapping of her heels across the floor.

He leaned back in his chair and picked a few AP stories to put in tomorrow if they had space. The lead story about the school board looked like it was going to jump to page three. Local news always took priority. Folks could get the national news other places. Local was what sold papers.

His thoughts drifted to why Audrey's "We all leave together" statement never included him.

He looked around the office trying to see it through new eyes. A few new computers hadn't changed the look of the place. The guns on the wall, a dozen framed front pages, a huge bulletin board by the front door. Home.

The only thing fresh was Pepper Malone's desk, with her brass name-plate tag and her sickly plant. And her, he thought, leaning over her work as if her words would change the world.

She was the kind of girl he'd seen in college. Smart, stylish, and aloof. The kind who'd never give him a second look. He'd been too "small town" for them. Mike laughed. Who was he kidding? He still was.

The ringing of the phone shattered his thoughts.

"Hello," he answered without remembering to start with "*Bailee Bugle*."

"Hi, Dops." His niece had called him that since she was three. *Uncle Mike* had been too much for her, so she'd made up a name.

"Hi, Morgan," he said to the only living member of his

family. "You old enough to take over the paper yet? I'm about ready to quit."

"Very funny." She giggled. "Even if I was, I wouldn't want that old thing. It's time you stopped killing trees and bought a BlackBerry."

"So if you don't want my job, then why are you bothering me?"

She giggled again. "Some of us are going over to Marty's for some pizza. Kami's mom is driving us." She didn't give him time to say anything before adding, "I don't have much homework and we'll be back by eight."

"It's a school night."

"Please, please, please."

Mike frowned. In thirteen-year-old talk, three *pleases* usually meant there would be boys in the vicinity, even though Morgan and her friends weren't really talking to them yet.

"All right. I'll see you at eight. Try to get your math done before you go so I can check it if I beat you home, and there's money in the jar if you need extra."

"Thanks."

"What about May?"

"She's making herself a sandwich. She wants to get over to Mrs. Wilson's early because she says if you're not in the first two groups of four, you have to sit in folding chairs."

"Canasta," Mike remembered. His housekeeper was a new convert to Audrey's group.

"Right." Morgan laughed. "Maybe we need to put a curfew on her, Dops. Those parties can get pretty wild. Kami's mom says she thinks they serve wine coolers when it's not at one of the Baptist women's homes."

"Tell her to have fun," he answered. "And you too."

"I will. Love you, Dops."

"Love you too, kid."

The phone went dead, but he still held it to his ear. Ten years ago he'd thought the world had gone to hell. His brother and sister-in-law had been killed in a car accident, his father had died of a heart attack, and there was no one to take on a three-year-old to raise. Ten years ago he'd stepped out of his life to move back to Bailee. The hardest decision was the only one he never regretted: Morgan. When he saw her for the first time, she came running toward him, arms raised like he was sent to save her from the dragons. If he hadn't been planning to take her home, he would have had a time of it getting her off his neck.

She'd had a crazy mother, an absent father, and more babysitters than he could count. He took Morgan back to the old McCulloch home that had just become his and said, "We're home." She'd smiled and said, "Thanks, Dops." From that day on they were family.

Rain tapped on his window. Mike looked out at people rushing home. He noticed Bob Earl rolling up the awning at the bakery. Border Biggs, a teenage thug in a cowboy hat, was pestering Bob Earl, but he just laughed and let Border wave his arms.

Lorie Fuller would take over watching Bob Earl from now on. She even let him sleep in an apartment in the back of her place. Lorie had a sweet way about her, but Mike had seen her threaten to bar Border from the bakery more than once.

Some people said that Bob Earl was slow, but Mike thought the boy lived in his own private time zone, as though one day someone would cross over the quartz hills to the north and find a people who were all like Bob Earl. A whole town of folks who never noticed clocks or remembered details. A place where they ate dessert first and where watching clouds was a valued pastime.

Mike smiled. The people of that town would see a man from Bailee as jittery and obsessive.

"So." Pepper's voice jerked him from his thoughts. "You've had trouble here?"

She leaned against the doorjamb, her arms folded as if she were totally prepared not to believe a word he said.

"No," he answered as he stood. He'd been looking up at her all afternoon. It was time he faced her on the same level. "Audrey thinks a few newspaper machines broken into amounts to a threat. I think it was probably kids just wanting the quarters."

Pepper took a step backward as he walked out of his office but followed him to the coffeepot.

He plugged it back in, something he did every day after the others left. "Want a cup?"

Nodding, she waited for him to say more.

He handed her the first cup, thinking about how odd it was to look straight into a woman's eyes. If she ever wore five-inch heels, she'd be taller than him.

"All right, we've had a few anonymous threats," he admitted as if she'd been torturing him.

She smiled, relieved. "That's nothing new. In Chicago we had a threat come in every time the Cubs lost and we reported the score."

"That why you left? Fear of sports fans?"

"Something like that."

He drank his coffee trying to think of something besides work to talk about, but he was hopeless. He never thought of anything but work. He figured he had one level higher conversation skills than Orrie and probably no flirting skills.

Not that he was flirting with her or even thinking about it.

Mike considered hitting the side of his head to straighten his reasoning out.

Glancing at the line of windows facing Main, she finally broke the silence. "How long do you plan on staying?"

"Another hour or two. Why?"

"I don't have a key and I'd hate to face Audrey if I left a door unlocked."

He took a step toward his office. "Let me know if you leave before six. Otherwise, if you're not finished, I'll lock you in for the night when I leave."

He heard her moving toward her deşk, her high heels clicking on the hardwood floor.

"You're a tough boss, Chief," she said.

Chapter 6

Bailee, Texas
Population 15,008

True to his word, at a quarter after six, Michael McCulloch stepped out of his office and flipped off the overhead lights. "Ready?" he asked.

"Ready." I closed my computer. The storm had been battering the windows so hard I hadn't written a word in ten minutes. I wanted to call it a day, but I wasn't sure about the idea of going back to Aunt Wilma's trailer. Everyone knows Mother Nature hates trailers. In storms they were simply mobile lightning rods. And I was going to sleep in one tonight.

There weren't enough sleeping pills in town to put me out. It would be me and John Wayne movies all night . . . if the electricity stayed on. Great, now I had something else to worry about besides the storm.

Note to self: Buy life insurance and flashlights.

If the lights in the trailer went out tonight, I decided I'd drive over to the underpass at the railroad tracks and spend the night in my car.

Michael held the back door open while I turned up my collar and stared at our two vehicles huddled near the building. The back lot would be as black as pitch when he closed the door. I memorized the path I'd be running in about two seconds. Three steps off the porch, four steps down the stairs, and ten feet to my car. I could make it. If I lost my way, all I had to do was stand perfectly still until the next bolt of lightning *ejaculated* across the sky.

"Ready?" he asked as the wind tried to shove us back inside the building.

"No problem." Laughing, I took off running. "Nice night for a run."

I made it to the bottom of the stairs before he closed the door.

One step off the concrete walk, my five-hundred-dollar keyhole pump sank into mud to my ankle. I froze. Not out of fear, but in sheer panic at the thought of losing my shoe.

A second later, he slammed into me, almost knocking me down.

He grabbed me around the waist and pulled me back against him as he balanced us both upright. "Sorry," I heard him mumble like an oath. He didn't let go. "Are you all right?"

I nodded as if he could see me and leaned against him while I slowly tugged my foot free of the mud without losing my shoe. If I lost this pair of Armanis I'd have to work two weeks to replace them.

Lightning flashed. I glanced up to guess how many steps it would take to make it to my car.

What I saw thirty feet away by the trash cans made

my whole body stiffen. The light vanished, but my fear remained.

I twisted until my cheek bumped against McCulloch's face. "Someone's in the alley watching us." *Waiting for us,* my mind screamed. The rain couldn't dull the hungry stare I'd seen in the lightning's blink. The stranger had the glare of a nocturnal hunter spotting his prey.

McCulloch's grip tightened, and he shifted so that his body stood between me and the Dumpster man. My eyes were adjusting, but I didn't need another look at him. I could feel him there watching us, waiting for the right time to strike.

Michael was only a shadow beside me, but I felt his words near my ear. "I saw him, but I don't recognize him. There is no reason for him to be here this time of night. Maybe he's just a stranger passing through town or a bum searching out a dry corner."

McCulloch's words offered no comfort, but his hold was solid. Suddenly Audrey's threats seemed real, and I swore I'd go "when we all leave" next time.

"My Jeep's closer than your car." He moved his fingers down my arm and took my hand. "Stay close."

In the blackness, he twisted left and pulled me with him. Before I thought to breathe, he was opening a door and shoving me inside. My wet coat stuck to the leather seat. I barely had time to swing my legs in before he slammed my door and headed around.

Lightning popped and thunder echoed across the sky. I wiped hair from my face in the still silence that followed.

McCulloch circled the front of the Jeep. The stranger started toward us in a run, splashing water with each step like a boat running full speed into harbor.

Michael climbed in, slammed his door, and started the

engine in one fluid movement. His lights flashed bright toward the stranger, now no more than fifteen feet in front of us. I could see his eyes glaring with hate. Long wet hair hung like roots across his face.

We veered out of the parking space, losing sight of the man for only a few seconds.

When we straightened, the hunter was gone.

Michael shoved the car into reverse and swung the lights sideways, but they picked up nothing but rain.

He shifted again and bumped his way across the back lot, but nothing moved. The storm seemed to have swallowed the man whole. Framed in by the brick walls of other buildings, he'd still managed to vanish.

I leaned forward. "I couldn't have imagined him. He must still be out there."

"He's out there." McCulloch hissed the words between clenched teeth. "If you imagined him, so did I." He circled around the small lot again.

"Why would anyone be standing in the rain like that?" I knew the answer. At least I knew the only one that made any sense. "He was waiting for us." I answered my own question.

"Not us," McCulloch said. "Me."

I almost argued that there were probably more people looking for me than him, but I didn't think Donny Hatcher and the men who had threatened to end my career permanently could have gone so far as to send someone to murder me.

I choked down my worries. "Why would a bum want to meet you in the alley?" The guy could have walked through the front door of the paper any time all afternoon. McCulloch sat facing Main, framed by a huge window. He hadn't been hiding from anyone.

"If I knew that, I'd be able to find him." McCulloch pulled out of the alley and headed down Main. "This time of year the town always has drifters." Mike seemed to be forcing his voice to calm.

I leaned back in my seat and studied him, putting pieces together. "There have been more threats than Audrey and the others know about." It wasn't a question.

"A few," he answered.

"And you think that man, whoever he was, meant you harm."

"I'm not sure."

He drove with his left hand and shoved his wet hair back with his right. In the fuzzy streetlights I got my first look at his right hand. Even in the shadows I could see the flesh was twisted and scarred.

Before I could ask anything else, he swung the Jeep into an empty parking spot in front of the sheriff's office. The one-story building looked almost like a toy huddled between a three-story hotel and a bank.

He switched off the engine. "I'm going in to tell Sheriff Watson to keep an eye out for our newest resident. You can wait here if you like."

"Not a chance." I climbed out.

He took my hand as we ran up the three steps to the door. I couldn't help but notice he didn't turn me loose until we were well inside and out of the view of any windows. He didn't just think the man might be a threat. I had a feeling Michael McCulloch knew the stranger was trouble . . . big trouble.

A bald man in his sixties looked up in surprise as we clamored into his office, slinging water as we marched.

Mike nodded his greeting. "Sheriff Watson, this is Pepper Malone, my new reporter. I thought we'd better come by and tell you what we just saw."

The sheriff shook my hand and offered us a seat in true Southern style. He seemed a man in no hurry to hear bad news. When Mike began, he settled back into his chair and didn't interrupt.

"It's probably nothing," Michael finished after he'd told what we'd seen, "but I'd sure appreciate it if Toad could circle by the paper on his rounds tonight."

Watson smiled at me. "I retired last year," he said as if McCulloch hadn't been talking. "Toad, that's Theodore Morris, my sister's boy. He's the acting sheriff until we can find someone qualified for the job. He's a good boy but hates paperwork, so I fill in around here."

"I see," I wondered why he needed to tell me his history. Folks in small towns do that kind of thing. You ask them for directions and they tell you how long they've lived in town.

He nodded, reminding me of one of my aunt's bobble-heads. "Toad or one of the other deputies will circle the lot behind your place every hour when he makes his run down Main. Don't you worry, McCulloch, we'll make sure nothing happens." He turned back to me. "Now, Miss Malone, is there any detail *you* remember about the man you saw? Any little thing can help if we're going to find him."

"He was big, tall, and broad, like a man who works outdoors, not fat." I stared at the cluttered desk, trying to think of details. "He had on a thick jacket. It had a hood, I think, but it wasn't up so far that I couldn't see his face, even though it was mostly in shadow. He was just standing in the rain staring at us." I tried hard to remember details. "I think he had something in his hand. A stick maybe."

"Did he have a beard?"

I shook my head. "Longer hair, though. It hung down his face."

"Any glasses or scars or tattoos you could see?"

"No."

Watson looked at Mike. "Did you see the same man she described?"

"I didn't get a good look at his face," he said. "Only it wasn't a stick in his hand. It was a rifle."

Watson leaned closer. "Are you sure, McCulloch?"

"I'm sure. I wouldn't be here if I wasn't."

Chapter 7

We drove away from the sheriff's office in silence. I was shivering. I didn't know if it was from fear or from the cold that settled over my skin. I felt wet to the bone.

"You all right?" Mike asked.

"No," I answered. "I thought I left crime in Chicago. How often does this kind of thing happen around here?"

"Never to me," he answered. "But I used to hear my dad and grandfather tell stories. My dad had local labor union men storm the paper one time demanding he tell their side of a dispute in more detail. I was little, but I remember seeing him come home with a black eye. My grandfather fought off the KKK more than once after he got back from the First World War." Mike headed toward the interstate. "And my great-grandfather fought for his right to publish in courtrooms and saloons. He's the one who started the gun collection on the wall in my office. Thought it might warn off people looking to do more than argue. From 1882 until he turned the paper over to his son in the twenties, old Adam McCulloch wore a gun to work every morning."

I remembered hearing that McCulloch was the fourth generation, but I hadn't really given much thought of how more than a hundred years of history breathed into one paper. The entire history of these people could probably be found in the back issues.

Mike turned the heat higher. "Adam used to say he'd keep the press free even if he had 'to kill every son-a-bitch' to do it."

I laughed and felt the blood flowing in my body again. "I would have liked to meet him."

"I would have too," he admitted. "But I have all his papers in the basement. He was quite a man. He had only one employee, named Smithy. From his business log, he fired Smithy every Monday because the man came in 'hung over and worthless.' One entry read, *Smithy came to work sober today, but I fired him anyway, just for the hell of it.* He always hired him back by Wednesday."

"Sounds like a few bosses I've had," I volunteered.

We were silent for a mile, and then I asked, "Where are we headed?" It didn't much matter as long as we were moving away from the alley.

"There's a truck stop that serves a fair cup of coffee out on the interstate turnoff. You look like you could use a gallon or so to get warm." He glanced at me. "I don't know about you, but I'm in no hurry to go back to get your car."

"I agree." Tugging my shoes off, I stretched my feet near the warm air coming from the heater.

Five minutes later, we pulled between two trucks and climbed out. The rain had slowed, but we were both dripping by the time we got inside. We hung our wet coats on the racks by the door and found a table near the grill. I finger-combed through my hair, knowing it would curl up as it dried.

I tried to relax, to tell myself that I was being foolish for thinking we'd somehow dodged a bullet, but I wasn't that good at lying to myself. "Do you think Toad will find him?"

"I hope not," McCulloch answered. "Toad's not a boy like Sheriff Watson said. He's almost forty, and most folks in town think he shouldn't be allowed to carry a gun, much less drive around in the patrol car."

"Then why is he acting sheriff?"

McCulloch shrugged. "No one wanted to hurt Watson's feelings. As long as the old man is around, Toad will be fine, but I'd hate to think of him running into our guy in the back lot."

"I could never live in a small town. It doesn't make sense."

He stared directly at me. "And the big city does?"

"You've got a point."

After we ordered, I thought about how he talked and reasoned differently from anyone I'd ever heard. We couldn't have been that different in age. He'd hired a boy who could barely read and a woman who thought she ran the paper. And strangest of all, he carried scars on his hand that a plastic surgeon could have smoothed out. I might not know that much about weapons, but I'd bet that selling one of the antique guns in his office would have paid the bill.

I glanced at his right hand, but he'd already slid it beneath the table.

I made a few attempts at conversation, but the silence between us wasn't uncomfortable. I noticed that every time the door opened, he looked to see who came in. The man in the alley was not as forgotten as we pretended.

After a few minutes of arguing, he agreed to split the

check and we stepped outside to a cloudy night. The rain had turned to a soupy fog.

He walked close to me, matching my steps. "Your hair looks different," he commented, as if unaware he'd said the words aloud.

I pushed it back away from my face. "It's naturally curly. Every school picture I have looks like a little face hiding in a black bush."

He laughed. "My niece has curly red hair. She calls it 'corkie hair.' She swears when she's an adult she's going to shave it off and wear wigs."

"I know how she feels."

We drove back to my car. It couldn't have been much after ten, but the whole town seemed asleep. He'd offered to drive me home, but the last thing I wanted was to be left at the trailer without a way to escape.

When we turned into the alley, my senses went into overdrive. I could feel my heart hammering against my chest. A watery moon offered little light. I searched every corner for the man, knowing that if I saw even a shadow I'd start screaming.

McCulloch circled and pulled up so that my door would open within inches of my car. "See you tomorrow," he said, as if nothing had happened.

"Tomorrow," I echoed as I opened the Jeep door.

My Saturn looked even smaller than it usually did. I just stared at it.

Mike voiced my thoughts. "Something's wrong."

"I think it sank in the mud."

"Impossible," he said as he reached behind me and grabbed a flashlight.

He climbed out and circled the Jeep before I managed to stand. The beam of light from the flashlight illuminated the problem.

Both tires were flat on the driver's side.

Michael walked around my car. "All four have been slashed," he said when he returned.

"I guess there's no chance it was an accident?" I tried to be funny even though tears were threatening. I didn't have insurance, or AAA, or even one spare in the trunk.

"I'll drive you home." He waited until I climbed back into the Jeep before circling to the driver's side.

Neither of us said a word as we left town. We both knew who had slashed the tires.

"I live . . ."

"I know," he interrupted. "At Wilma Davis's place at the corner of the orchard. I run an old trail past the back of her place some mornings. Beautiful peach orchard out there in the summer."

"You're a runner?"

"Just for exercise. I like to run at dawn before the town wakes up."

I didn't bother asking him how he knew the old trailer belonged to Wilma. "You know my aunt?"

"Sure. She was Doc Harris's nurse when I was growing up. She even worked nights at the small emergency room before she retired. With only three doctors in town, her job was mostly deciding which one to wake up if trouble walked in."

He knew more about her than I did. "She's got a cat named Herbert," I said for no reason.

He turned off the main road. "You worried about the cat being out here all alone in the storm?"

"No," I answered. "I'm worried about me being out here all alone. I don't suppose you'd reconsider locking me in at the office for the night."

He stopped the Jeep, his lights sparkling off the silver of the wet trailer. "I could take you to the hotel, but it isn't rated more than half a star." He hesitated. "You could have my couch, but I live on the main drag."

"I understand," I said before he could say more.

I shouldn't have said anything. My problems weren't his. "I'll be all right here. Herbert and I will watch a movie."

He left the headlights shining as he walked me to the door. He didn't seem to like the idea of me staying here any better than I did. "Are you sure you—"

"I'll be fine." I unlocked the door and flipped on the lights.

Mike reached into his pocket and pulled out a pad of paper and a pen. "Call me at this number if anything seems strange. Anytime."

I watched him walk away, fighting the urge to pull out my cell phone and dial the number. I wanted to scream that the whole day had been strange. I was tired and cold and dreading the hours before dawn. I had no car to drive, and the stew at the bakery had just gone out of my budget.

He opened his Jeep door and turned back toward me. "I'll be home in ten minutes. Call me in fifteen. That way we'll both know everything is fine."

He got into the Jeep and backed up the dirt road to the pavement. His headlights flickered against the trailer like an old movie about to start.

Inside, I checked all the locks twice, then took a hot shower until the water turned cold. With my hair still wet, I curled up in one of Wilma's quilts and sat on the flowery couch between the pillows. I checked her Elvis clock with the swinging legs. More than fifteen minutes had passed. I dialed his number.

"Pepper," he answered. "You all right?"

"Yes, I know it's more than fifteen minutes, but I took a shower to get warm."

"I think I'll do the same." He sounded tired. After a pause, he said, "I'll pick you up at eight."

The thought that I didn't have transportation bothered me more than I wanted to admit.

Note to self: Buy two cars when you get rich.

"Did you fall asleep, Malone?" he asked.

"No. I was just planning my life."

"How's it working . . . the plan?"

"Not so well, just now, but if I take notes maybe I'll get it figured out one of these days." I couldn't believe I was telling him my thoughts. He probably wasn't a man who cared about people he just met. For all I knew about him, he didn't care about people he'd known for a lifetime, either.

"Well, make a note about me picking you up for work at eight, would you?"

"I'll be ready."

He hung up the phone.

"Good night," I said, wondering how this strange man had somehow become my friend.

Chapter 8

Mike flipped off the kitchen light and walked through the dark house to the stairs. On the second floor, he checked on Morgan and found her asleep atop her covers with teen magazines circling her. Lifting her legs enough to pull back the covers, he tucked her in.

"Dops," she whispered, sounding more asleep than awake. "Are you my guardian angel?"

"That's me, kid," he answered as he turned down her light and stood at the door for a moment, making sure she was asleep.

He could see his brother, Dave, in her features sometimes. The way she smiled bigger on one side of her mouth, the way she laughed like all the world was funny. Dave had wanted to run when he found out eighteen-year-old Anna was pregnant. Their father had made him marry Morgan's mother. Dave joined the army a few months after Morgan was born.

Mike couldn't remember his brother ever holding Morgan or asking about her when he called home. Morgan became a ghost at the McCulloch house. They all thought about her, but no one mentioned her. Anna only wanted monthly checks, and Dave seemed to want to forget he had a family.

Mike walked down a hall where history was recorded in framed front pages of the *Bailee Bugle*. The stock market crash, Pearl Harbor, D-Day, Kennedy shot, the *Challenger* exploding, and twenty more. Sometimes he felt like he lived more in a museum than in a house. Most people could go home and shut out the world; for him it was catalogued along every wall.

McCullochs might report the world news, but they'd keep their family secrets to themselves.

When Mike passed his housekeeper's door, May's light was on and he could hear her TV blaring away.

He climbed the narrow flight of stairs to his bedroom in the loft, stripped off his wet shirt, and placed the phone in the center of his bed.

Listening to the rain tap against his windows, he fought the urge to call Pepper back. It would feel good to talk to someone, even if all they talked about was the stranger in the alley tonight.

Mike had intercepted most of the threats coming into the paper the past six months. They'd started slowly, then twice a month and now almost every week. Audrey had answered only a few calls, but they'd upset her so much that she'd threatened to call the FBI. The caller hated the paper and wanted it closed.

He'd seen the stranger once before in the alley and thought him only a drifter. Men working the rigs to the south dropped into town most winters. The work was slow on the rigs, and they needed somewhere cheap to hole up until spring. The stranger had the make of a roustabout before.

But not tonight. The look in the man's face left no doubt that if they'd stayed five seconds longer, there would have been far more violence than a few slashed tires.

Until tonight Mike had never thought there was any real danger. But a few hours ago, on the back lot, fear had registered in his numb brain. Not for himself, but for Pepper. He'd thought the threats personal, between him and some crazy fool out there somewhere angry at the paper. Until now, he figured he'd taken enough precautions just by following all of Audrey's rules. The others left together. The doors were kept locked when he was alone. They all parked away from the street so that no one could drive by and toss anything at their cars.

Tonight, he realized he hadn't been careful at all.

Mike rolled onto his back as he pulled his journal from his satchel. For a while he wondered if he cared one way or the other. He hadn't felt alive for ten years. He'd sparked the chain of events the night of his brother's crash. It was his fault Dave drove drunk that night. His fault his brother left the bar in a rage.

The only thing that hadn't been his fault was the rain.

Rainy nights always brought the memories back as crystal clear as if it were yesterday. He'd been so sure he was right. Looking back, he realized right or wrong hadn't mattered.

Mike rubbed the scars across his right hand. Wilma Davis had been at the emergency room that rainy night. Despite all the craziness surrounding the wreck, she'd patched him up and told him to get the burns treated. Mike had refused.

He deserved the scars. He'd gotten them trying to pry Dave's car door open. He'd left the flesh twisted just as he'd left the lie about Dave in place.

Pulling the pen from the journal's folds, he wrote.

Journal Entry: Never get involved. Never care. Loss hurts more than loneliness.

The phone jerked him out of his nightly hell.

"Yes," he answered, guessing it was Pepper.

"Were you asleep?"

"No," he answered. "Is something wrong?"

"No." He could hear her breathing. "The lights are still on and Herbert is stretched out spread-eagle on the kitchen tile. He licked up a cup of milk, swore at me in cat talk, peed on the welcome mat, then fell asleep like a drunk."

"Is this some kind of obscene phone call?"

"No."

He thought he could hear her smiling.

"I was just wondering if we could talk for a while. I've some questions about work if you're not asleep."

He thought of telling her that he had a few hours of waiting before sleep would come, but he just said, "Ask away."

"Well." She seemed to be trying to think of a question, and he wondered if she might be frightened of the storm and just didn't want to admit it. She struck him as a tough city girl who wouldn't admit being afraid of anything, but then what little he knew of women was long past rusty.

"Well," she started again. "I was thinking I could write a few human interest stories about some of the people in town."

"Most of us know each other fairly well."

"I know, but I could kind of take it from the angle of 'what no one knows about their neighbors.' You know, like maybe someone can paint or speak another language and never mentioned it."

He leaned back against his pillow and smiled. It wasn't much of an idea, but it might prove interesting. "All right, we'll give it a try. Only no dirt, just good."

"Of course," she said too fast. "I thought I might start with my aunt Wilma. I know next to nothing about her. When I was little, my mother mentioned her family even less than she did the tooth fairy."

Mike closed his eyes, remembering the way Wilma had worried over him that night ten years ago. "She was a nurse in World War Two." She'd talked about her days in London while she'd wrapped his hand. Strange how he remembered every detail of that night.

"Really! I can't imagine her as the Florence Nightingale type. How'd you know?"

He gave the answer he always rattled off when asked how he knew facts. "I've spent my life reading the paper." He liked her excitement over finding out some little fact. A true reporter. "If I remember right, she told me once that she lived in France for a while after the war."

"Really!"

"I think she said she met Churchill when he visited a hospital she was working in."

"Really."

Mike grinned. "Is there an echo on this line?"

"I'm sorry. I had no idea. To me she's just a sour old woman whose only interest is bingo."

"I don't see her like that at all," he admitted.

"But why did she never marry, have a family?"

"You'll have to ask her."

"I will, Chief."

"Don't call me *Chief*."

"Then what do I call you?"

He thought about it a moment. "Call me *Mike* or *Michael* or *Mr. McCulloch* or *McCulloch*, but not *Chief*. That's what everyone called my dad."

"All right," she said. "I pick *Michael*. Did you learn the business from your father?"

"Sure. My brother and I worked for the paper every summer from the time we could type. My dad loved being the editor. He used to insist that all McCullochs bled ink. I don't think he missed a day of work in forty years. He died at his desk." Mike paused. "And I am not going to be one of your stories, Malone, so stop taking notes."

"I wasn't." She answered again too quickly for it to be the truth. "Your brother was Dave McCulloch. I saw an article about him framed on the back wall. He was a war hero."

"That's right, a bronze star for bravery."

After a pause, she added, "A war hero who comes back to die in a car wreck."

The line was silent for a moment, and then he said in a low voice that sounded exhausted, "It's late. Good night, Malone."

"Good night," she echoed.

As he put the receiver back in its cradle, he added, "Dave the war hero." Then he swore a low oath and added, "I hate the rain."

The phone rang again before he could move it to the nightstand.

"Yes?" he answered.

"One last thing," Pepper snapped. "When I make an obscene call, you'll know it."

"I'll look forward to it."

Chapter 9

Bailee, Texas
Population 15,009
Friday, March 21, 2008
8:00 A.M.

Rain still poured from a brooding sky when Michael picked me up the next morning. He talked brusquely about all that had to be done on Fridays. By the time we reached Main I'd taken a page of notes.

Without coffee, my brain was still asleep, but I couldn't help wondering where the man I'd talked to on the phone late last night had gone.

"I'll unlock the office," he said as he pulled into the only space left in front of the paper. "The others usually start their day at the bakery, if you want to join them for breakfast."

"You don't?" I asked, not surprised.

He shook his head. "I eat breakfast with my niece on Fridays. It's the last I see her until Sunday night when I pick her up from her grandparents'."

He climbed the steps to the *Bailee Bugle*. This man, this morning McCulloch, I would never call *Michael*. Not only did he need work on his conversation skills, his pants were too baggy, his faded green shirt needed ironing, and the jacket he wore matched nothing else. His sandy-brown hair was too long. I had to stare to even figure out that his eyes were blue. I should turn him over to one of those makeover reality shows.

Sloshing across the street, I decided I wasn't a morning person either, but I was cheery compared to McCulloch and definitely better at dressing myself. It occurred to me that *he* might have slashed my tires to get fifteen minutes work out of me in the car.

Opening the door to the bakery, I noticed that the noise level dropped to zero. For a moment I didn't want to step into the cave of silence, but everyone seemed to be breathing, so I gave it a shot.

They all looked normal, except for the fact that they were staring at me. The two lawyer types were still there. The round table of old farmers was probably on their tenth cup of coffee by now. Three women, who looked like they worked in one of the offices on Main, and the usual mismatch of folks at the counter.

"We heard!" Lorie rushed over and gave me a cinnamon-scented hug. "Toad came in an hour ago and told us all about it. Are you all right? It must have been so frightening. I can't even imagine." She patted my shoulder and directed me toward a table in the center of the place. Her brown eyes were filled with worry.

Some old man with egg in his beard grinned at me and said, "I went over and saw your car, honey. Real shame, all four tires slashed. It weren't just a hole poked, somebody put in the knife and tugged."

I didn't know if I should thank him for the observation or bop him in the head for not minding his own business.

"I'm fine," I said with a fake smile plastered on. "All I saw was a shadow of a man near the alley. When we got back an hour later the man was gone and someone had slashed my tires."

"We?" Lorie whispered, and the entire room tilted toward me, or at least that's how it felt.

I did my best to look pitiful. "Could I have a cup of coffee before I take the stand?"

She laughed. "Coffee, black. One egg scrambled and dry toast."

Thankful she had let me off the hook, I took a seat at the table with Audrey and Webster.

Worry clouded Audrey's watery-blue eyes. "I told you we should all leave together. I was afraid something like this would happen. When Toad told us, all I could think was *poor, poor Pepper*. You could have been killed out there in the dark, and none of us would have known it until morning." She looked like she might cry. "I was wrong about parking in back. We should all park in front from now on. It's safer even if we do get dings from pickups parking too close." She nodded to Webster as if he got a vote. "Starting today we all park in front."

Webster shrugged and picked up his coffee. "Whatever you say."

"It's all right. I'm all right." I wondered what she'd think if I told her about being shoved by a pair of thugs in Chicago because I wrote a family story the family didn't want told to the world. Or about the guy I dated, Donny Hatcher, who thought he wanted to marry me but when he talked it sounded more like *own me*. He was always saying things like *You're mine and I'll take care of you.*

Compared to that, maybe the guy in the alley didn't seem so bad.

Note to self: Keep everything in perspective.

After breakfast we marched over to the paper with Audrey in the lead. It had stopped raining, but she held her umbrella high like a foreign tour guide.

McCulloch had already made coffee and looked like he was hard at work. Friday was the day the paper went to print.

He wanted all the stories in by eleven at the latest, and then Orrie Cleveland would lay them out. The work used to take hours, but with his powerful computers he could do the job of three men in half the time. Saturday morning he'd take them over to a printing center fifty miles away. While he had lunch, they'd print.

At ten after eleven McCulloch answered the phone, then yelled for Audrey to take the call. She ran to her desk, then squealed with delight. We heard several repetitions of "Yes, I have that" before she hung up the phone.

"Well?" Webster said for all of us.

"The Franks had a boy. Ten pounds, eleven ounces." She ran to Orrie's door. "Stop the presses. We got to get it in this week."

I fought down a laugh. As far as I knew the only press we had was in the basement gathering dust.

Webster swiveled back to his desk. "Ten pounds. The kid will be eating solids next week."

I glanced into Michael's office to see if he'd reacted at all. He was busy writing something in the blue leather-bound journal.

Lack of sleep caught up to me about noon, even with the endless cups of coffee. Webster offered to buy me a sandwich if I showed him how to get on the Internet. He said he'd heard about chat rooms for seniors. So while Audrey and Bob Earl left for lunch, Webster called in an order, and then we explored the world of online chats on an old computer that served as a backup in case Audrey's went on the blink.

The woman had a backup for everything. I noticed a new coffeepot above the counter in case the present one failed. The wall in the ladies' bathroom was lined with enough toilet paper and tissues to last my lifetime. Even the supply cabinets were packed with everything anyone might think they needed. She was a woman lost in the details. The only parts of the office she didn't control were McCulloch's office and the back computer world.

Speaking of missing monsters, I hadn't seen the strange man in the back office go to lunch. Orrie Cleveland's domain glowed in the light of several computer screens, but he hadn't bothered to roll out and say hello.

I picked up one of the sandwiches and a cookie and marched into the back office.

He didn't look up.

"I brought you lunch; since you're having to rework to get the birth announcement in, I thought you might not have time to eat." He made me think of a prisoner kept in the dark for years. Pale skin, watery stare, puffy body.

He stared at me.

"I'm Pepper, remember," I offered.

"I know," he answered as he took the food. "Thanks."

Backtracking out of his office, I felt good about my effort. Friendly wasn't something I did often or well. I went back to Webster and the world of chat rooms.

McCulloch sat at his desk, eating lunch while he worked.

He had his back to the door, but I had the feeling he was listening. I thought I even heard him laugh when Webster started coming up with online names.

We settled on Fedora Cool, and by the time the others returned from lunch, old Web could swim the chat rooms alone. Back at my desk, every now and then I'd hear him chuckle, and I smiled knowing he was having fun.

By five I was so tired I was ready to leave with the others. Orrie and Michael didn't join the group when Audrey called for the mass evacuation.

Webster offered me a ride home in his Buick, which seemed almost as long as Wilma's trailer. As I followed the old man down the steps, I looked back at the windows and saw McCulloch still working at his desk. He didn't look up. I thought he looked lonely.

"Isn't he leaving?" I asked, worried about what might happen if he were alone. Then it dawned on me that Michael was always alone, and before me no one had seemed to notice or care. In a caring town he seemed a homegrown outsider.

Webster shook his head. "He never leaves with us. He thinks he has to stay and go over everything one more time, make it a little better. Everyone used to say his father was a great editor. I think he's just trying to live up to his heritage."

I set my laptop in Webster's backseat. "And does he?"

"He's good, but his heart isn't in it."

"Would you wait for me a moment?" I asked Webster. "I forgot something."

"Sure," he answered.

I ran back up the steps and into the office. McCulloch hadn't locked the door behind us when Audrey had yelled for him to do it.

He looked up when I stormed in.

"Would you mind calling me about ten?" I knew he wouldn't appreciate the fact that I might be worried about him, so I added, "After last night, I'd feel better if I had someone to check on me."

He shrugged and turned back to his desk.

I had no choice but to leave. I hate it when I have these brilliant ideas and they crumble as soon as they reach air. A teacher at boarding school used to tell me to take a long breath before I said anything. If I followed her advice I'd be a relatively quiet person.

I walked back to Webster's car mumbling what I would have said if McCulloch had responded like a normal person.

"You talking to yourself?" Webster asked when I climbed in.

"Yes," I answered with the long breath. "Do you mind?"

"No." He smiled. "I've found that folks who won't even talk to themselves aren't much worth talking to."

I smiled back. "How'd you get so smart, Webster?"

He winked. "Three wives. With Pearl I learned patience, with Beth I learned kindness, and with Alice I learned self-defense."

"Two out of three's not bad."

He turned his boat of a car north. "Pearl died our fourth year together. That's when I had to leave Bailee. I couldn't take walking the streets without her. Beth and I made it nine years before we parted as friends." He grinned. "And Alice found someone new to beat on, so she left me. I was fifty by then and decided marriage might not be for the likes of me."

"Me either."

He glanced over at me. "You should give it a chance, Pepper. When it's good, it's grand."

"And when it's bad," I added, "it's hell."

He agreed.

We rode in silence for a few minutes before he asked, "If you're in no hurry to get home, we could stop by the Shades. It's Friday night and that means a party. For ten bucks we could play bingo for two hours and graze off snacks the ladies from the church bring in."

I'd planned on opening a can of soup for supper, but being stuck in the trailer was depressing enough at night, I didn't want to think about how slowly the hours would pass if I got there before dark.

"Ten dollars?"

"They got sandwiches, chips, and those little pop-in-your-mouth tomatoes," he added.

I needed to save every dime I could.

"And cookies," he primed.

"A party?"

"A great party." He turned into the parking lot of the nursing home.

Five minutes later, while wearing a headband that read LET'S PARTY TONIGHT, I realized Webster had lied. I wondered which one of his wives he'd learned that from. I've seen more lively shindigs at the morgue.

I was forty years younger than anyone in the room, with the exception of a sweet teenage volunteer calling bingo through her braces. Three men at my long cafeteria table were already asleep in their wheelchairs, and the old lady next to me was so blind she couldn't see her card.

I ate my bologna sandwich to the tone of *B-13, do I have that? O-63, do I have that? I-23, do I have that?*

By the second game I was playing not only my card and the blind lady's, but also the three sleeping guys across from me. The dollar-store Mardi Gras decorations were falling off the walls, and I'd started humming to the rhythm of an oxygen machine a few rows behind me.

Webster, on the other hand, was having a grand old time talking to some of his friends from high school.

Finally, the teenager took a break to talk on her cell phone, and I had a chance to straighten.

"Having fun?" someone behind me asked.

I turned to face Aunt Wilma. Dressed in a black shawl and hunched over her walker, I thought she could easily try out for the part of the witch in Snow White. "A blast," I said, wiggling my head so the silver balls on my headband could bang against my forehead.

She looked at me as if ashamed to be in the same family tree. "Mind if I sit down next to you?"

"Of course not." I pulled out a chair. "Glad to see you getting around so well. You're making progress."

"Did you get your nursing degree when I wasn't looking?" she snapped. "This isn't progress. It's just another level of pain."

I thought of suggesting heavier drugs, but then I wasn't a doctor either. "How can I help?" I asked lamely.

"If you hurry, you could get me some punch and a sandwich before that girl starts calling numbers again. Last week she broke up with her boyfriend in the middle of a game, and we had to listen to thirty minutes of her crying into the phone before the game resumed."

"Why do you come, then?" I asked as I folded up her walker and put it between two of my sleeping dates.

"This is the big-money night. The grand prize is a hundred dollars."

I suddenly became a great deal more interested in bingo. "What's the second prize?"

She looked up at me with a frown. "You get to keep that hat."

I saw it then. The tiny twinkle in her eye. My aunt Wilma wasn't quite as dried up and cold as I thought. But she wasn't going to make it easy on me, either.

"Any chance of getting that sandwich before the mayo goes bad?" she mumbled.

I rushed over and picked out what looked like the best of the leftovers. When I brought it back, she nodded her thanks and we settled down to another game.

At the next cell phone break, she asked me about my car. I told her every detail, figuring she already knew most of it. She had me describe the man twice, then shook her head, saying she couldn't place him.

"You'll be needing a car to get around," she said.

"I'll manage," I countered, not wanting her to feel sorry for me.

"Suit yourself," she grumbled. "I was just going to offer to let you use mine. It'll be a while before I can drive."

"You have a car?"

"Of course I have a car. It's sitting out front of the hospital by the emergency door. That is, if someone hasn't stolen it by now." She frowned at me. "Truth is, I'd feel better if you used it than leaving it parked out there."

I took a breath and decided pride wouldn't get me back and forth to work. "I'd love to borrow your car. Thanks for offering."

She fished her keys out of her pocket and handed them to me. "It's a white Ford two-door."

"I'll take good care of it," I managed, overwhelmed by her generosity.

"Never mind that," she said. "Take good care of yourself. There's trouble blowing in the wind around this town. I've seen it before. Old-timers used to say this town was built between two rock hills and it will never be an easy place to live."

"I'll be careful."

"You better bc. Otherwise, who's going to come pick me up when I get out of this place?"

Chapter 10

Mike didn't leave his desk until long after dark. He was never in a hurry to go home on Friday nights. Morgan went with her grandparents, and May always drove over to her sister's place in Fort Worth to help with the weekend business at their bed-and-breakfast.

He turned off his office lights and walked out the front door, very much aware of his surroundings for once. Cars were parked on both sides of his Jeep. Probably people attending the movie half a block away. The streetlight to the left of Lorie's bakery was out. It might have been out for months, but tonight he noticed. Last night's problem with the stranger had sharpened his senses.

Across the street and down a little was a space between the antiques shop and a used bookstore. A man could easily hide there and watch the entire street. Shadows doubled over that spot, making it impossible to see from any angle.

Mike stared, but all he saw was blackness. He could almost feel someone looking back. Part of him wanted to yell, *Come and get me!* He wanted an end to this now. Months ago he'd started getting calls with no one speaking, but he knew someone was on the other end. Then a few threats were whispered. "The paper is no good." "The *Bugle* should stop publication before someone gets hurt." A month ago the petty vandalism started. Broken news boxes. A rock shattering one of the small windows on the front door. A dozen hang-up calls made within minutes after he left the paper.

Keeping his eyes on the black space, Mike made himself walk, not run, to his Jeep.

"Evening, Mike." Lorie's voice caused him to jump.

He looked over and saw the little baker five feet away. "Evening, Lorie. You're out late for your walk."

He'd seen her walk the block a hundred times. She was a creature of habit, like him. She closed the bakery, walked down Main and around the courthouse, then climbed the side stairs to her apartment above her shop.

"I had a few big orders to work on for tomorrow." She rolled her shoulders, fighting off fatigue. "A baker's work is never done, but look at all the dough I make."

He smiled at her joke.

"Got time to walk with me?" she asked easily, as if his answer didn't matter.

He tossed his briefcase into his Jeep. "I could use a little exercise. With the rain, I didn't get my run in this morning."

They'd become friends over the years. Polite friends who never asked personal questions. The wedding ring on her finger made it plain to everyone except Toad that she wasn't in the market for a man, and Mike had no place in his life for romance.

"I'd enjoy the company." She moved closer, and he smelled cinnamon.

They strolled along, talking about Bob Earl and how her business was going. He even kidded her about how many times Toad stopped by her place.

They circled past the courthouse and returned by way of the other side of the street. When they passed the bookstore, Mike moved a little closer to Lorie, knowing the dark corner was only a few feet away.

He paused for a second, glaring into the pitch-black passage between the buildings and listening for even the sound of a breath. Nothing.

"If you were in the market, Toad wouldn't be a bad catch," Mike said as they moved on down the street.

"I'm not looking. I've had one great love and I'd be greedy if I wanted more."

It was the most personal thing she'd ever said to him, and Mike knew if they were to become better friends he'd have to counter. "At least you've had one. I think I'm the kind to live alone." He laughed. "Asking a woman to share my life would be like offering her a seat on the *Titanic*."

Lorie laughed. "The paper is surviving."

"For now."

She must have sensed his worry. She changed the subject. "We need to get that streetlight fixed."

"Right." He caught up with her.

"You want turkey or ham on Monday? I know you take chicken usually, but I've got leftovers from that WMU luncheon I catered yesterday."

It took him a moment to place her question. "Turkey," he finally answered. She fixed his lunch and sent it over every day at eleven thirty. He'd made the standing order the week she'd opened her place, just as she'd bought an ad every week that listed her specials.

Shrugging, he admitted the truth. "We live a very dull life, don't we, Lorie?"

"Not dull. Orderly," she corrected. "I like order." She looked down at her hands. "I couldn't live in chaos. My heart isn't strong enough, I'm afraid."

For the first time he wanted to ask her a question that lay outside their polite friendship. He couldn't help but wonder about the sadness that seemed to surround her. Surely her one great love couldn't have caused such pain. He was closer to her than he was to most people in town. He knew her time schedule as well as he knew his own. She knew the way he liked his sandwiches—turkey with mayo, ham with mustard, and she never got it wrong. But he didn't know her well enough to ask about the pain he saw in her eyes when she stared down at her wedding band.

She should have been cherished instead; she seemed afloat, alone.

He stepped back onto safe ground. "Pepper has some ideas about your weekly ad. I heard her ask Orrie if he could do the work."

Lorie's smile returned. "Good. I'll want to see them." Then she giggled, making her seem younger than forty. "Did Orrie Cleveland actually talk to her?"

"The man can talk." Mike defended his employee. A few months after Mike took over the paper, he knew he'd have to have a genius to figure out the new computers and software. The only one he knew had been a few years older than him in school and still lived on his parents' farm. Mike discovered Orrie had two degrees from online colleges and would agree to handle all the layouts and computer problems on one condition: He didn't have to talk to anyone but Mike.

Now, after ten years of giving everyone else a stone ear, he'd decided to tolerate Pepper. Or, more accurately, she'd stormed through his barricades.

"I've heard him talk to her," he admitted to Lorie. "Pepper did about frighten him to death. Orrie finally told her the only way he'd talk to her was if she didn't step one toe into his office. So she stands at the doorway and yells at him."

"Poor Orrie." Lorie shook her head.

They'd reached the front of Lorie's store. His Jeep was parked directly across the street. He tipped an imaginary hat and said good night. She laughed and did a curtsy. By the time he reached his Jeep, she'd already climbed the stairs.

Mike glanced at his watch. Ten minutes until ten. He started the Jeep and threw it into gear. "Pepper," he mumbled as he headed for home. "Call Malone at ten."

He went in through the side door that May never remembered to lock and began turning on lights as he moved past rooms that had been decorated the same since he was a child. No matter how many years he owned this house, it would always be his parents' home.

In the kitchen he found a cold plate of fruit salad May had left for his supper. He passed over the water for once and grabbed a beer. The hall clock struck ten times when he settled into the chair in his office and flipped on the TV. Dinner with the nightly news team was a tradition.

He took the time to down a few bites and open his beer before he muted the TV and dialed Wilma Davis's number.

Pepper answered on the first ring. "Michael?"

"It's me. Everything all right, Malone?" Calling her by her last name would definitely keep things professional.

"Herbert is missing."

"Herbert?"

"Wilma's cat. He wasn't here when I got in, and I brought him a plate of scraps from the party."

Mike took a bite of salad. "Party?" he mumbled.

"Yeah, I was the life of a happening party earlier. In fact, I was pretty much the only one alive at the party. Don't tell me you've never been to the Shades for bingo."

"Nope, too wild for me."

He leaned back in his chair while she told him all about Friday nights at the nursing home.

"I saw a dog tonight with a seeing-eye person attached."

"Mr. Edison," he guessed.

"You've seen him?"

"Of course, everyone knows him and his old dog, Bull."

"They let Mr. Edison and Bull in a place where they serve food. Isn't that against some health code?"

"But the dog's blind, so it's an exception. If it works one way, it might as well work the other."

"But Bull ate several of the bingo balls."

When he didn't say anything, she asked, "So, what did you do exciting tonight?"

He hesitated, telling himself the question was casual conversation, not personal. "Nothing," he finally said, so fast it sounded forced.

Pepper's friendly manner chilled a little. "Wilma said I could use her car until I get mine fixed. She told me there's an old house a few hundred yards behind the trailer where I can park it."

He smiled. "I could come get you in the morning and take you to pick Wilma's car up."

"Don't bother. I'll walk."

He could feel her coolness coming through the line. She was being polite, businesslike, but she wasn't friendly or funny as she'd been a minute before. He knew this Pepper was safer, correct, but he missed the other.

Could it be possible that he'd forgotten how to just talk to a woman? Hell. Mike doubted he ever knew.

"I'll pick you up at ten," he said. "If Wilma's still driving that old piece of junk I saw her in a few months ago, you'll probably need a jump to get it started. I don't mind, honestly."

"All right. I'd appreciate it." She hung up.

He'd made it up to his loft when the phone rang again. The Caller ID read *Wilma Davis*. He grabbed the receiver and wondered if now would be as good a time as any to stop this. She was his employee, no more.

"Pepper," he began.

Before he could say anything else, she whispered, "I found Herbert on the porch. There's blood everywhere."

Mike dropped the phone and raced down both flights of stairs two at a time. He was in his Jeep before she could have hung up her phone. Driving eighty on the back road to her, he didn't think, he concentrated on getting to her as fast as possible.

About the time he turned onto the dirt road he noticed he'd picked up Toad as a tail. Mike didn't slow down. One fact kept him driving: Whoever killed the cat had put Herbert on the porch after she got home.

Which meant, if it was their alley man, *he* was out there now and she was alone.

Chapter 11

Bailee, Texas
Population 15,009
Minus one cat

I stood at the door until I saw two cars coming toward me, kicking up mud. One looked like a Jeep, the other a police car with lights silently flashing.

Stepping over Herbert's still body, I ran toward them.

Mike jumped from his Jeep and met me in the headlights. Without a word, he pulled me close. For a few seconds I clung to him, letting my own fear settle.

"It's just a cat," I said, more to myself than to him.

Neither of us believed me.

Over his shoulder I watched the patrol car pull in beside the Jeep, bumping its way off the dirt road and onto the rocky ground. A fat man seemed to tumble from the driver's door.

"That you, Mr. McCulloch?" Lights reflected off the large man's badge. "I thought that was your Jeep, but you was going so fast I figured someone stole it."

"It's me, Toad. Thanks for following." Mike pulled away from me. "I thought one of my employees might be in danger, but she appears to be fine."

Mike stared at me as if measuring for himself whether I was all right. When he seemed satisfied, he turned his attention to the acting sheriff.

I felt the slap of his words. That's all I was, just one of his employees, not even a friend. For a second I thought he'd worried about me, Pepper Malone, and not just as an employee. I thought I'd actually gotten close enough to someone that he cared.

Toad hitched his belt up and walked across the uneven ground like a man who'd never ventured off the sidewalk. "You figure she had a run-in with that guy from the alley. Am I right?"

"Right, Toad. Better get the sheriff on the radio. Tell him you think our alley man could have been at Wilma Davis's trailer. He left a dead cat on the porch as his calling card."

While Toad called in his report, I followed Michael over to the dead cat. I focused on my boss's back as he leaned over the animal. "This could have been an accident, Malone. Someone who hit him out on the road and knew he lived here."

I didn't answer.

"Did you do much crime reporting while you were at the *Sun*?"

I wanted to admit that for the past four years all I'd done was the crime beat, but then he'd start asking questions I didn't want to answer. "A little," I managed. "No cat murders."

Even under the sixty-watt bulb of the porch light, I could see that Michael didn't believe me. Somehow he was piecing the inconsistencies in my story together. It didn't take much to realize that a top reporter at the *Sun* doesn't just pack up and move to a small town in Texas.

"Mr. McCulloch!" Toad yelled. "My uncle says he's on his way and we're not supposed to touch anything." Toad sounded like he was quoting from a book. "We don't know if we're dealing with an accident or a crime scene."

"Don't worry." Michael backed away with his hands in the air. "Touching anything never crossed my mind."

I walked over and stood between the Jeep and the police car. Closing my eyes, I took several deep breaths and tried to get the smell of blood out of my nose. I know it doesn't make sense, but I swear, dead blood smells worse than live blood.

When I opened my eyes, the blackness of the night had closed in around me. I hated how dark it gets out here at night. In the city, no matter what the time, there were always lights and sounds. I'd never felt so alone. Here, town wasn't that far away, but tonight it might as well have been a hundred miles.

Michael leaned against the car a few inches away. He didn't touch me, but I could feel the warmth of his body. "It's only a cat," he echoed my words.

"Then why did you come?"

Before he answered, another car turned off the main road onto Wilma's dirt path. The sheriff climbed out carrying two flashlights.

I followed close behind Mike as we moved back to the tiny wooden porch. All three flashlight beams fell on poor Herbert. The blood looked black in the sharp light. We all stared as a thin trickle of blood dripped from one step to the other.

The sheriff took a step back and began searching the scene. After a few minutes, he said to himself, "It's no big crime to kill a cat. What's important here is why."

Toad followed his uncle around to the side of the trailer. Bare branches from the peach trees behind the trailer stretched out like bony fingers in the pale moonlight. I could see Toad swatting at them with his flashlight as his legs brushed against weeds almost to his knee. Watson was more seasoned. He moved without sound and left no trail.

"Mike," the sheriff yelled. "Toad and I are going to take a walk up to the old house and back. You mind staying with Miss Malone?"

"Will do," he answered as if simply following an order.

We stood in silence for a while, listening to every sound.

I was glad when Michael suggested we sit in his Jeep. We watched the flashlights bob like drunken fireflies in the dried weeds beside the trailer.

"Who lives in the old house?" I asked.

"No one since Wilma moved the trailer in. The trees in this area are old and have the best peaches you'll ever eat, but she's let them grow wild for years. Every woman who cans in town can tell you when they're ripe. Wilma usually puts up a sign that reads, 'Come and get um.'"

I didn't have the heart to tell him I'd never really liked peaches. Neither did Wilma, apparently, if she gave them away.

Toad walked by us and said he was going to bag the cat and take it, if I didn't mind. "I'll hose down the porch for you, Miss Malone, before I go."

"Thanks."

When the sheriff pulled away, I asked Michael if he'd mind taking me to get Aunt Wilma's car tonight.

"Are you sure you want to stay out here?"

I couldn't tell him I had nowhere else to go. I wasn't his problem. "If I have the phone and a car, I'll be safe enough."

We drove to the hospital in silence. I slipped my shoes off and tugged my knees to my chin. Part of me wanted to curl into a ball and forget about this night. No, more than that, I thought. If life had a Delete button, I'd be clicking away the past six months.

I'd delete all the way back to the night I passed Donny Hatcher on my way to the bathroom in Potter's Bar. If I had do-overs, I'd walk right by him no matter how sexy I thought he was with his tailored suit and perfect hair. Then he wouldn't have bought me that drink. And I wouldn't have gone home with him. There would have been no pillow talk, no story written, and I'd still have my job in Chicago.

I picked grass off the pair of old workout pants I had on and tried not to look as if I were studying Mike's scarred hand. Apparently, he had more to worry about tonight than hiding it from view. The scars weren't all that bad, not gross anyway, just scars. I'd be willing to bet ten dollars that if he winked at one of the rodeo queens at the sale barn, he would have a date by tomorrow night.

I frowned. I'd bet twenty he'd never even thought about asking one of them out or probably any other single girl in town.

I tried to look more presentable by palm-pressing a few wrinkles out of my shirt. Not for him, of course, but because I'd never been out in public like this since my early college days. The old cotton pants and a faded T-shirt I wore were my pajamas, but he didn't have to know. He wasn't the kind of man who noticed what women wore anyway.

When we got to the lot, the only car there was a little white Ford. That had to be Aunt Wilma's. The two pickups near the emergency sign didn't count. I couldn't see Wilma climbing into a Dodge Ram or a truck with EAT MY DUST on the back.

"It must be a slow night in the ER," Michael said, as if the silence between us was starting to bother him. "In a few hours, when Buckles and Boots closes, the local troublemakers will stop by for stitches before they go home. You want to stay around and count the teeth left on the parking lot?"

Michael looked so serious, I smiled. "No thanks, I've had enough excitement for one night."

He got out and followed me to Wilma's car. While I tried to start it, he leaned against the window telling me I was giving it either too much gas or not enough. Finally, aggravated, I climbed from the car and told him to give it a try.

To my total frustration the car started.

"There," he said proudly. "I'll follow you home just in case you have any trouble." He stepped out, leaving the car running.

"Thanks," I said, tight-lipped. If he'd thought to impress me, he'd missed totally.

"You're welcome," he said a bit too smugly.

I put my hand on his shirt to push him aside, but he didn't budge. Looking up at him, I asked, "Why didn't you call the sheriff instead of coming when I called?"

He stared at me for a long moment, and I had the oddest feeling he was about to kiss me. We were so close I could feel his breath on my cheek. His heart pounded beneath my palm and I knew I should pull my hand away, but I didn't. If he didn't like me touching him all he had to do was step away. *Or step closer,* I almost whispered.

His cell phone rang. Mike stepped back and answered it.

When he flipped the phone closed, he stared at me as if trying to find the right words.

"What?" I said.

He let out a long breath. "The cat wasn't Herbert."

"How does the sheriff know? There was so much blood."

Mike smiled. "Because Herbert sat watching Toad bag the dead cat."

I drove Wilma's car back to the trailer trying to figure out how a strange dead cat had ended up on my porch. Maybe Mike's guess was right. Maybe someone had hit it on the road and simply brought it to the nearest house. Herbert had probably fathered dozens of cats that looked like him. To tell the truth, once I saw the dead cat, all I saw was the blood. I hadn't looked at the markings that close.

Mike followed me back to Wilma's place and sure enough, there was Herbert waiting for me.

Chapter 12

Saturday, March 22, 2008

Saturday morning, after burning two fingers trying to cook a real breakfast on the oldest working stove in existence, I gave up and drove over to the Blessed Saints German Sausage Festival.

The entire basement hall was decorated in spring. Flowerpots that wouldn't go outside for another few weeks were lining the entrance and on every table. All the staff for the event had on tulip-print aprons. Huge bowls of sauerkraut, potato salad, and sausage sat out on the side tables, ready to serve. Everything around me reminded me that I wasn't in Chicago anymore.

I saw Michael long enough to wave at him, and then he blended into the crowd, almost an invisible man.

A few minutes later, I tried to remember what he'd been wearing. Tan pants, blue striped shirt that didn't match, hush puppy shoes only teachers wore. He looked like he'd gotten even less sleep than I had. If I were guessing, I'd say he hadn't even bothered to comb his hair, but in this windy country it was hard to tell. I thought of weaving my way through the cafeteria tables scattered about so I could talk to him, but knew if I got closer I still wouldn't know what to say to him. The man and I not only weren't in the same league, I'm not sure we were in the same atmosphere.

Mrs. Harsch, who ran the boarding school my ninth through eleventh years, would have said he looked intelligent. That's pretty much what she said about every young man she thought had money, but wasn't handsome. Mike could have been, if he'd just try a little.

He probably thought I was interested in him. I could have told him that men were nothing but distractions in my life. Interesting, but not essential. I'd never met one I couldn't walk away from at dawn. Or more accurately, I'd never found one who made me want to stay. I was no more attracted to him than I was to Orrie Cleveland.

A man had to have a bit of danger about him to interest me. Maybe that was it with Donny Hatcher. He was rich enough not to have to play by the same rules as everyone else. It also didn't hurt that he looked like he'd walked out of an ad. Powerful, handsome, and dangerous. Mrs. Harsch would never accuse him of just looking intelligent.

I glanced around the sausage festival and went to work doing what I'd always done, looking for a story. A real story. My first editor called it the "holy shit" story. Other papers call it the "Hey, Martha." It's that account a reporter stumbles across that is so good the guy at breakfast holds out his paper and says, "Hey, Martha, did you see this!"

I'd had more than one editor tell me I had a gift for just such a piece, but if I found it in this town, even I would be surprised.

When a German band began to play off-key, I sat down as far away as I could from them. If ever there was a fundraiser people would pay *not* to go to, this was it. Bad decorations, fatty food, and a three-piece band offering no peace.

An old couple already occupied the other side of the last table. They were one of those salt-and-pepper-shaker pairs. They'd lived together for so many years that they looked just alike, right down to the same haircuts. She was trying to clap to the music and he was eating off her plate. They absently brushed one another, and I wondered if either noticed.

The man smiled at me, said hello, then introduced his bride of fifty-seven years.

I told Clyde and Nadine Dunn who I was, and to my surprise they both started asking me questions. I fought the urge to yell, *Wait a minute, I'm the reporter here!*

He asked me if I'd gotten my tires changed out and then advised me on who to go to so that I wouldn't get cheated. Nadine wanted to know how I liked working at the paper and asked if my aunt Wilma was doing well with her recovery. She then took the time to explain, in detail, *her* hip replacement.

Finally, I got a question in. "How many people in town do you think are of German descent?"

The old man smiled. "We all are, just like we were all Irish last week for the St. Patrick's Day party, and when the Presbyterians have their picnic with the bagpipes, we'll all be Scottish."

Nadine giggled. "What he's trying to tell you is we're all pretty much mutts in this town. But we've got great peaches here. Some believe the hills protect us just the way it protects the crops."

"Do you believe that?" I asked.

The old woman's gaze met her husband's look, not mine, when she whispered, "No."

He laid his hand gently over hers, and I could almost smell a sadness that neither one would talk about. The hills hadn't protected them from a sorrow they'd shared.

The music started up again and we watched for a while before I asked about interesting stories the paper could publish. They told me about twin girls who each had twins and about the Maples, who had eighteen children.

"They were homeschooled," Nadine said. "Of course when you got eighteen kids you pretty much got a school."

About the time the old man started on how Henry Downs had to cut what was left of his arm out of a machine, I felt a tug on my shoulder.

"Sorry," Lorie Fuller whispered. "I hate to pull you away, Pepper, but we could really use the help in the kitchen."

I apologized to the Dunns and almost ran to join the baker. She looked younger in jeans, and the navy sweater she wore didn't make her seem near as chubby as the white smock she lived in at the bakery. I'd thought her to be forty, but now I guessed midthirties.

When we reached the kitchen she giggled. "I was watching your face. When I saw you starting to turn green, I knew Clyde had begun that arm-chopping story. He tells it to everyone who will listen. I had to save you from the details."

"Thanks. What can I do to help?" I've never given much thought to reincarnation, but Lorie Fuller seemed like a friend I'd known for more than one lifetime.

She handed me an apron and for the next two hours we worked, side by side. She filled me in on the people as they passed through the line for food. She had something good to say about almost everyone. The few she couldn't think of anything good, she'd just say, "Bless their hearts, they're trying."

Sometimes they were trying to keep a job, or trying to be a good mother, or trying to stay off the whiskey. Of the people I'd known, I could never be so kind. I could think of a few who were trying to act human.

When we finished the dishes, she invited me to her place for a drink.

We sat out on her tiny porch overlooking Main Street through ivy vines serving as curtains shielding us from the world.

I told her about finding the cat, and she looked even more worried about me than I'd been.

"Tell me the details," Lorie insisted.

I walked her through the facts, then tried to laugh when I said, "It probably wasn't the man from the alley. Michael said someone might have run over the cat and thought it belonged to Wilma."

She frowned. "I'd like to get my hands on whoever it was."

I fought to hold a laugh as the image of Lorie confronting the big man came to mind. He'd probably run away when she raised her wooden spoon. She might be healthy, but there wasn't a fighting bone in her body. I was surprised she even beat eggs.

I laughed. "You'd teach him a lesson like you did Border Biggs."

She nodded. "Border's not bad. He just likes to pester people. Bless his heart, he'll grow out of it one day and be sorry for all the trouble he's caused."

I doubted she was right. I could almost see him five years from now stealing cars to go joyriding.

Lorie turned mind reader as usual. "Pepper, he's not. You mark my words, he'll straighten up."

"Yeah, when he runs into a bigger thug." I smiled. "Bless his little heart."

She laughed at my mocking her and poured both of us another glass of wine.

Her little apartment was like Lorie: understated and charming. The mixture of quilts and crafts could have made it look old-fashioned, a granny house, but her sense of color and placement gave a country French cottage look to the tiny space.

Though some might think we were very different women, we had a great deal in common. Neither of us liked to talk about ourselves. We both lived through our work, and, near as I could tell, she had even less family than I did. No school shots of nieces on the refrigerator, no old portraits of grandparents, no sweet pictures of her in younger days with family, or college days with boyfriends.

I might be a head taller than her in flats, but from the moment we met we saw and accepted one another. It was like in grade school when you're assigned a seat and you never really question it—Lorie Fuller was like my assigned friend.

Finally, I asked her about the old couple, Clyde and Nadine.

Lorie took a long drink of wine before she answered, "They've outlived all their children. Parents should never have to do that."

I make my living reading people, and the words were out before I could stop them. "You know how they feel."

She opened her mouth as if to lie, then slowly nodded. "I lost a daughter at birth. You'd think because she never breathed, never lived, that I wouldn't feel the loss, but she lived inside me."

The silence was so thick I couldn't breathe. I had to say something. "I've never come close to having a child,"

I said. "I think I was born to be alone. The nesting gene must have been left out." I knew I was rambling, but somehow I thought my words would wash away the sorrow in her brown eyes if I kept talking. "You know those logic games where you have to decide who stays in the boat and who goes? I was the only one in my psychology class who tossed out everyone except me."

Lorie laughed. "Remind me never to get in the boat with you."

I shrugged. "Just remember to bring your own life jacket, because if we're down to one seat, you'll have to swim."

She raised her glass. "I like that kind of honesty. To dry-land friendships."

I clinked her glass, and we both drained our wine. I thought about it a moment, then rushed in. "What about your husband?" I'd almost said *the baby's father*, but with the ring, she had to have been married.

"We weren't right for each other. Different worlds. The only glue we had was the pregnancy. When that didn't work out, we went our separate ways."

"Oh." My next question would have been to ask why she still wore the ring, but she didn't give me time.

"I have to deliver a birthday cake before five," she said. "Want to come along?"

I agreed and we spent the next hour laughing at two-year-olds finger-painting with the icing from the cake. When she drove me back to my car, I knew we'd somehow become not just friends, but best friends. She didn't have to tell me not to mention to anyone about her losing a child. I had a feeling that Lorie knew and was friendly with many people, but let very few close. I was more the opposite. I wasn't friendly with anybody beyond hello, and I let even fewer near.

I'd learned long ago that friends drift in and out of my life. Lorie would be the first one in years that I'd miss when I moved on.

I made it back to the trailer just before dark. Toad's patrol car pulled up at the other end of the dirt road as I stepped out of my car. I don't know if he'd been following me or just happened to be making his rounds, but the sight of him gave me a sense of safety. I walked up the steps, unlocked the door, and flipped the porch light off and on. He blinked back and moved away.

Herbert was waiting for me when I stepped out of the car. He tried to trip me all the way to the porch and then refused to come in when I held the door open for him.

"Suit yourself," I said and stepped inside. "No leftover birthday cake for you."

I noticed the answering machine blinking but took the time to pull off my shoes before pushing the Play button.

The first two messages were hang-ups after a little heavy breathing. If it had been my machine I would have thought it was a hesitating dirty caller, but on Wilma's phone it was probably only one of her oxygen-dependent friends.

When I pushed the button the third time, Michael's voice snapped, "Malone, call me in the morning."

I frowned. Didn't the man know this was the weekend? Surely the job wasn't seven days a week. Or maybe he'd just called to remind me that what almost happened last night in the parking lot never happened.

Surely if he had anything important to say to me, he could have walked across the church basement and told me. Otherwise, whatever it was could wait until Monday.

Unless it was something about our alley man? I wouldn't mind getting the news that he'd been arrested. But for what? Last I heard, running in the alley wasn't a crime, and proving that he slashed my tires might not be easy.

As I undressed, I tried to find the missing puzzle piece. Maybe the sheriff wanted me to look at mug shots? Maybe Michael had thought of some detail he'd forgotten. Maybe something else had happened.

No. I marked that off my list. If anything had happened, he would have had me call him back tonight. It was only eight fifteen.

I shoved in an old tape of *Red River* and decided I'd have time to watch it twice before I could even think of sleep.

Michael McCulloch was going to drive me crazy, and it wasn't all that far a drive.

Chapter 13

Dallas FBI Central Office
10:15 P.M.

"Fuller here, how can I help you?"

"Heath?" Her voice was little more than a whisper, but it slammed against his senses like a tidal wave flooding dry land.

The line went silent while he shoved the exhaustion of the day aside. He forced his hard tone to soften and leaned forward as if she were just on the other side of his desk and not miles away. "Lorie?"

"I just called to ask you a favor." She had no idea how even her voice affected him; she never had.

"Name it." There'd been no hesitation. There never would be.

"Could you run a check on a description of someone?"

"Are you in danger, Lorie Girl? I could be there in an hour."

"No, but a friend of mine might be. Things have been

happening. Nothing bad, yet, but I'm worried. Will you do this for me, Heath? Just check, don't come."

"Give me the facts, and I'll do what I can." He shoved the half-empty glass of bourbon aside. He wouldn't need it to numb the loss of her tonight.

He could hear her fighting down tears as she gave him the details, a flimsy description of a man who could have been half the drifters in Texas. A stranger who might have a habit of killing animals. A man who walked in the shadows.

She paused as if giving him time to write everything down, and then she added, "How are you?"

"I'm fine," he lied. "How are you?"

"Fine." She returned the favor. "Call me if you find out anything."

The phone went dead before he could say more. For a long time Heath sat in the middle of his office and tried to remember to breathe.

She finally needed him. He'd waited five years. The hell of it was, he'd needed her every day.

Chapter 14

Bailee, Texas
Population 15,009
Sunday, March 23, 2008

The next morning I slept until almost noon in the cold shadowy world of Wilma's old trailer. After a breakfast chosen from my collection of small cereal boxes stolen at continental breakfast bars in crummy hotels, I dialed Michael.

He wasn't home. I tried the paper. Near as I could tell, the man was a workaholic with no life other than the *Bailee Bugle*. I wouldn't have been surprised if he'd been grown like a mushroom in the basement.

The answering machine picked up at the *Bugle*. I didn't leave a message.

"The alley man must have got him," I said to Herbert, more casually than I felt.

The cat refused to comment.

"The Chief is growing on me," I admitted.

When Herbert didn't answer, I added, "Maybe I haven't

reached the point where I am actually worried about him, but I'm considering it." For me, that marked the point when I would usually cut and run. Attachments were about as welcome in my life as Christmas tinsel in February.

It seemed to me that people like Michael McCulloch who drift through life are often labeled *Innocent Victim* in the morgue. Some of us are builders, or fighters, or lovers, or even actors in life. McCulloch was a watcher.

I curled up on the flowery couch with Herbert and flipped channels for a while, then finally decided to get dressed. The cat refused to watch anything, and I found I was of the same mind.

But dressing wasn't easy. Everything I owned was dirty and wrinkled. A few outfits had even reached the smell-bad stage at the bottom of the laundry bag. In the city I would simply drop them off on my way to work and pick them up on the way home. Here I would have to get acquainted with a washer that looked older than me.

After two loads of laundry, I tried Michael again.

No answer.

I called Lorie simply because I had no one else's number. If Wilma had a phone book around, it was well hidden.

Lorie answered on the first ring.

When I asked, she told me Michael always drove to Fort Worth on Sunday afternoon to pick up his niece, who lived with him. Her mother was killed in a car crash about ten years ago and the girl had been his ever since, except from Friday afternoon until Sunday. Then her mother's people watched over her.

I shivered and decided to jump on the dryer for warmth. "That's when his brother died too, right?"

"Right," she answered. "It's said the two McCullochs had a big fight at a bar over the county line late one night. Dave, Mike's older brother, reportedly ran for his car and

Anna, Morgan's mother, along with a posse of friends went with him."

I had nothing to do so I asked, "What about the crash?"

Lorie hesitated. "I don't know much. It was five years before I came to Bailee. Dave had had too much to drink to be driving. The curve at the train tracks is a short one. He hit the railroad gate. Folks say you could see the fire from town."

"Where was Mike?"

"Following. From what I heard, he was the only one who ran into the flames. He managed to get Anna out, but she was already dead. When he went back for his brother, the fire was too hot. He couldn't get the door open."

The reporter in me wondered if anyone had managed to get a picture. I opened the pantry door above me and bopped myself in the head for being so heartless.

Lorie continued, "Dave's death shook the town. What little remains were found were buried in the McCulloch plot." Lorie was silent for a moment, then added, "Mike probably did it for Morgan so she can visit her parents."

"Thanks for telling me."

"You needed to know," Lorie answered. "One other thing. Big brother Dave had just been released from the army. Big hero. They even printed his letters to his father in the paper every week while he was gone, just like the *Bugle* printed his grandfather's letters from World War One. Everyone says Dave planned to take over the *Bugle*. He'd been a hero all his life. First in football, then in the war. And, from what I hear, Mike lived in his shadow."

I could almost see the two brothers. "It's hard to compete with a ghost."

"When he died, Mike resigned from his teaching job and came home. Their father was ill before the crash. Folks say Dave's death killed him."

"So Michael never wanted to be editor?"

"Right. But he was the last McCulloch." Lorie paused, then added, "What is that noise?"

I confessed, "I'm doing laundry. The warmest place in this whole trailer is on top of the dryer."

She laughed.

"It's not funny," I pleaded. "I'm thinking of sleeping up here tonight. I thought Texas would be warmer than Chicago, but I swear I've been cold since I've been here."

"Don't worry, another few weeks and it'll warm up. By summer you'll be wishing for these cold days."

I wanted to scream that I wouldn't be here when summer came, but right now I wasn't sure. Things would blow over in Chicago; they had to. Donny Hatcher would get over me and move on to some other girlfriend his rich parents could hate. He probably already had. I wasn't sure I could ever get my job back. What my editor thought I'd done—getting close to someone just for a story—would not easily be forgotten. In the paper's eyes I'd acted unprofessionally. Something no reporter wants to happen. My boss had said more than once that if one of his reporters slept with a story, she'd better be wearing her press ID so the guy knew he might see whatever he said in print.

I thought of Lorie's story about the McCullochs long after I hung up the phone. I understood why Michael didn't get his hand fixed. It was like a tattoo reminding him of a failure. The wreck hadn't just taken Dave's life, it had taken Michael's future also.

Part of me wished that he'd fought for his life. I couldn't really understand how a newspaper could matter so much, not even one that had been in the family for a hundred years.

I tried to think of one thing I valued from my parents. I'd kept nothing. Mom had removed all of Dad's stuff after he died, and then she'd removed herself from my life. Some of the girls at school saved letters from their family, but it would have been hard to save one phone call a month reminding me to study.

The McCullochs had roots deep as hundred-year-old elm trees. Me, I was more like those tumbleweeds that snap with the first fall wind and blow away. I'd never understand a man like Michael, and he probably would never understand me.

By midafternoon I was so bored I started cleaning. I'd spent my life being able to pack up everything I valued in a car. Now I was surrounded by the belongings of a woman who hadn't tossed anything for fifty years. She must have had fifty plastic lids with no bottoms, a hundred folded bags, and about a million twists off bread. Maybe in some alternate universe this kind of stuff was used as exchange, but here it just cluttered up her kitchen drawers. By six o'clock I'd done all I could do and decided to go wild and drive over for a pizza.

The local pizza place also rented movies and sold used books. It was a long building that looked like it had been added on to one room at a time, and none of the rooms were the same size. Even the roof line changed every twenty feet like some kind of woodworking project.

I ordered a large pepperoni and a root beer, then watched a dozen local kids playing games in the back room.

When they called my order, I found a table in the corner of the middle room so I could watch people and catch the news on CNN at the same time.

Just as I bit into the first bite, someone's shadow blocked my view of the TV.

"Expecting company?" Michael McCulloch asked.

For a moment, I just chewed. "No," I said as I wiped pizza sauce off the corner of my mouth.

"Mind if I join you?"

I pulled the pizza pan closer to me.

He grinned. "I've already ordered my own meal, so I won't be stealing yours, Malone."

"Good." I relaxed. "Then you can sit down."

He probably thought I was kidding about my not sharing the pizza. Reluctantly, I offered him a piece, then frowned when he took the biggest one. It had been a long time since my box of stolen cereal and I was starving.

While he ate, I studied him. Today, he'd cleaned up more than usual. His trousers were pressed. His hair had been combed, and he'd shaved. He also seemed to be in a good mood, which was unusual.

About the time his pizza and drinks arrived, so did a thin girl with reddish-brown hair that curled wildly around her face. I guessed her to be twelve or thirteen, but she was still much more child than woman.

"Hi," she said. "I'm Morgan McCulloch." She propped her elbow on Michael's shoulder and leaned into him almost as if she were protective of him. "You're Pepper Malone, right? Dops says you are a real big-city reporter."

"Dops?" I glanced at Michael, loving the way he looked uncomfortable.

"That's what I call my uncle Mike," the girl said. "Neither of us remembers why."

I nodded as she sat down in the chair between us and stretched her arms forward as if building a wall. "What else does your uncle say about me?"

He suddenly became involved with separating pizza slices.

"He says you got long legs." She chewed, then added, "I'm going to be tall too before long. I don't remember my mother, but my granny and papa have pictures of her. She played volleyball in high school and was the tallest one on the team." She turned to Michael. "You remember her, don't you?"

Michael finally looked up and smiled. I guessed this was a question she'd asked many times before.

"I only met her a few times. I was away at college when your mom and dad married. Your dad said she was so beautiful that the first time he saw her he felt love hit him between the eyes like a hammer."

The girl smiled. "I like that story." She looked at me. "They died in a car accident. They were in each other's arms when they died."

I saw Michael's warning to ask no more questions.

Morgan downed two pieces as if in some kind of speed-eating contest, then jumped up. "Can I go play games?" she asked Mike. "Kami is over at the one I love to play. She'll let me play partners with her."

He nodded, and she was gone.

I looked across the table at him. "So you've been looking at my legs."

He choked on his pizza. After coughing and taking a drink, he said, "It's hard not to notice, but I assure you it was strictly in a professional way. I simply observed how fast you stormed your way across the main room to my office."

"Right." His lie was the worst I'd ever heard. "I did try to return your call, by the way, but I guess I missed you."

He seemed relieved to change the subject. "It was nothing important. I thought we might take a look at the back issues of the paper and see if there is any chance the alley man might be connected to a story. It's just a hunch."

"I wouldn't think there would be many cat serial killers in a town this size."

He grinned. "I know, but the *Bugle* gets several hang-ups within minutes after we all leave, and I think it may be more the paper he hates than me."

"Everyone gets hang-ups. I had two on the phone when I got in last night."

Mike leaned closer. "Does Wilma usually get that many?"

"I don't know. I'll ask her." I didn't like his train of thought. Could he be suggesting that whoever was bothering the paper might now be checking in on me? "You think it's all related—the slashed tires, the cat, the phone calls."

"I think someone hates the *Bailee Bugle*."

"Or," I had to add, "someone hates me." Donny Hatcher would never get his hands dirty pestering me, but he might pay someone to make my life even more miserable than it was. After all, I'd printed family stories he'd never wanted told.

The noise of the place circled round us. These past few days I'd thought all that happened had been because I worked at this new job. What if I'd brought the trouble with me? Before I got to town, there'd been only phone calls and vandalism.

My cell phone sounded, making me jump. No one ever called me. Even my mother couldn't remember my number.

It was Lorie, looking for Mike.

I met Mike's stare. "He's right here." I passed the phone, mouthing, *Lorie.*

Mike took the phone, listened for all of five seconds, and said, "I'm on my way."

He handed me back the phone. "Lorie found Webster Higgins hurt on the steps of the paper."

"What?"

Mike was up and heading toward Morgan before I could ask a single question. He spoke to her, then to one of the parents sitting near the games area. Then he was back.

"Morgan's going home with a friend. I'm headed to check on Webster. I'll let you know—"

"You won't have to. I'm going too." I shoved the leftover pizza in a box.

I swear the man growled at me when he noticed I followed him out, but he didn't try to argue. He also didn't say a word when I climbed into his Jeep. "Tell me the details," I asked before he growled again.

Michael started the Jeep and headed toward Main. "Webster's hurt. Someone hit him from behind while he was locking the door to the *Bugle*."

"What was he doing at the *Bugle* on Sunday?" I pulled a piece of pizza from the box. Crime and blood never stopped my hunger.

Mike frowned at me. "He was checking on his online chats."

We parked in front of the bakery and raced for the door. Only the lights near the counter were on. The place seemed graveyard quiet.

We found Lorie in the kitchen cleaning blood off Webster's forehead. The old guy complained every time she touched him, but Lorie kept working. In contrast to the rest of the bakery, the kitchen was immaculate.

A bright red break in the skin reflected through Webster's thinning hair. I took a step backward. No matter how many crime scenes I'd witnessed, the first sight of blood always got to me.

Deputy Toad stood near the counter that separated the kitchen from the café part. He was sampling what looked like warm cookies from cooling racks while waiting for instructions from his uncle.

Lorie looked up from her nursing. "Mike, I think he really needs to go have a few stitches."

"It's a clean break in the skin." Mike leaned closer.

"But he could get an infection. At his age any cut could be trouble."

"The thug didn't hit my ears," Webster complained. "I can hear you, Lorie, and I'm not going to the hospital. I've been hurt worse. I'll heal."

"What happened, Web?" Michael moved in front of the old man, still checking the cut now turning white hair red. "I want every detail."

Webster nodded, then swore under his breath. "Tell Toad to take notes. I'm not saying this twice."

Toad dropped the last bit of cookie and tugged out his notepad from his tight back pocket.

The old man straightened and began. "I dropped by the office to check my e-mail. I've been having a nice chat with a woman named Sexy Sag, and I didn't want her to think I'd forgotten her just because it was the weekend. She's a real sweetheart, used to work for the airlines. You wouldn't believe some things that happen on planes."

"Less detail about that," Mike interrupted. "More about how you got hurt."

Webster nodded, then swore with the pain. "Sorry, ladies," he said, looking from Lorie to me. "I don't usually cuss around the ladies."

"The details," Mike tried again.

Webster pressed the towel to his wound and started again. "I walked out on the steps, set down my briefcase, and turned to lock the door. The next thing I know, I was hit from behind. The first blow slammed into my head. The second I blocked with my arm. The third landed against my shoulder, knocking me down."

Lorie undid his shirt cuff and shoved the cotton fabric up. A bruise the size of a baseball blacked his wrinkled forearm. "It could be broken."

"It's not," Webster said. "Now stop worrying about me.

I'm tougher than I look. I only wish I'd been fast enough to get in a few blows myself. In my day I could take down a man armed with a club before he could get in a good swing."

"What did you see?" Mike asked.

"Not much. It was already getting dark and the tree limbs from that big elm make the light unsteady right there, but I think he was a big guy, bulky in an old coat with a hood pulled low over his face. When I got to my knees, he was already running into the night."

"Did you see a weapon?" Toad asked.

Webster shook his head. "I didn't see one, but he hit me with something more than a fist."

The old man leaned toward Michael and I heard him whisper so Toad couldn't hear, "I don't think he was trying to kill me. He had his chance for another swing while I was down, but he just ran."

I stared at Webster. There was more to him than I first thought. He might play the kind gentleman, but somewhere in his past he'd learned a few things about survival. He'd had the sense to take the measure of our alley man even when hurt.

Lorie checked the wound. "I think the blood's stopped, but you're going to have a knot on that hard head of yours."

"I'm fine." Webster rolled down his sleeve.

"Did he try to rob you?" Toad asked from half a room away. This might be a crime investigation, but he was still reluctant to leave the sweets.

"No," Webster said. "But I lost my hat and keys when I tumbled down the steps. I looked up and down the street and didn't see anyone but him, so I don't think there was a witness. Blood started running down my face, so I looked for help, thinking I might do something foolish like pass out in the street. Lorie's light was on."

I finally found some way I could help. "I'll go look for your keys and hat."

"Thanks, dear." He smiled at me as if just noticing I was there.

"I'll go with you." Mike hesitated. "If you think you'll be all right here, Webster?"

"I'm more mad than hurt."

Michael nodded toward me. "We'll grab the flashlight from my Jeep."

"Don't touch anything," Toad said as he opened the door for us. "I'll stand guard here until you get back."

I wouldn't have been surprised if he'd demanded we learn a secret knock to get in. I thought of telling him the crime had already happened, but if he wanted to guard the victim, who was I to argue?

As we went out the door of the bakery, I heard Webster ask Lorie, "Where's that pie you promised me if I sat still for your doctoring?"

A dusty kind of fog had settled over the street as Michael and I crossed. I'd heard the wind blowing all day and now an eerie stillness haunted the town, but the dirt still hung in the air as if refusing to give up space. No one was about. The movie theater was closed on Sunday and so were the few downtown restaurants. It wasn't the kind of night anyone would be out walking.

Even the thin sliver of a moon could have been called a mugger's moon tonight. I found myself walking close to Michael, matching his steps exactly.

"We've got another streetlight out," he said, more to himself than to me.

I clicked on the flashlight he'd handed me.

We found Webster's fedora at the bottom of the steps and his briefcase still beside the door. Whatever the mugger wanted, it wasn't these.

Michael checked. The *Bugle* door was locked. "The old guy carries a front door key on a brass ring. It used to hang just inside my office door. As far as I know he's never combined it with his other keys, so we're looking for one key on a thin ring."

I moved the flashlight beam along each step.

Nothing.

We retraced our path and searched again.

Nothing, but Web was right about one thing: The branches of the trees did blow back and forth between the streetlights and the porch, making the light seem to blink off and on.

I let my fingers run across the seat of the bench beneath the tree while Michael borrowed the light and walked back and forth along the walk.

"Well." Mike finally straightened. "Now we know what the mugger was after."

"The key," I whispered, feeling the darkness chill me more than the wind had all day.

Chapter 15

10:45 P.M.

By the time Mike drove Pepper back to the pizza place, Wilma's old Ford was the only one left in the parking lot. He pulled in beside the junkyard relic and turned off the Jeep's engine.

Leaning back, he said half to himself, "It's been one hell of a night."

Pepper didn't answer. They'd already explored every angle of tonight's trouble. She'd been right with him as he'd walked Main. Even now part of him couldn't accept the possibility that a stranger had the keys to his newspaper.

"You going home?" she asked, still staring straight ahead into the blinking red pizza sign.

"No," he answered. "I can't." The sheriff had said he and Toad would keep an eye on the place, but Mike knew he wouldn't sleep knowing that someone could slip past them and be in the *Bugle*. Not just someone, but a man who hated him or the paper, or maybe even both. A stranger who hated him enough to mug an old man for the key to the place.

"Webster offered to sleep in the office."

"I know." He shrugged. "But he's too old and hurt. Besides, it's my responsibility. I'll have the locks changed first thing tomorrow morning, but for tonight, I need to be there."

She finally looked at him. "You think you'd fare better if the alley man attacked you?"

"I wouldn't be the first McCulloch to fight for the *Bugle*. My great-grandfather faced gunfire in the streets a few times. My grandfather was nearly killed in a beating when he disagreed with the wrong people. It seems sometimes the fight comes as part of the job."

"And your father? Who did he fight?"

"He managed to keep all of his arguments between the pages of the paper, but I think he was threatened a few times. By his day, lawsuits were more the weapon of choice."

"I don't like the idea of you being there alone."

"Are you offering to stay with me?" He grinned, the weight on his shoulders lifted slightly.

"No." She laughed. "I was thinking someone more like Toad should."

"He'd be no help," Mike said.

"Neither would I. At least Toad has a gun."

"I've got an office full of guns. Maybe I should think about pulling a few of them down from the wall." Guns had never frightened him, but they'd never held any interest either. Years ago a dozen had been stolen; he'd hardly noticed.

Even in the dim light he noticed she was shivering. The night had chilled, but he guessed fear had more to do with her shaking than the temperature.

"I don't like this, Michael," she finally whispered. "It's like there's something evil out there coming for us and nothing we can do will stop it."

For a moment Pepper reminded him of his niece. Inside this grown-up woman was a little girl. He had a feeling Pepper let very few people see this side of her. Mike couldn't help but wonder how many times she'd gone home alone to her apartment, locked herself in, and let fear win.

He pulled her close and circled her with a hug. "Maybe the guy will just get tired and leave."

She stiffened against him. "Don't tell me you think I need cuddling? I don't need—"

"I know." He stopped her protest. "You don't need anyone, but maybe I do."

She hesitated a moment before melting against him. "Well, all right, but don't take this as anything personal, McCulloch."

"Don't worry," he said against her hair. "I expect you'll go back to yelling at me tomorrow."

For a hard-boiled, no-nonsense woman, she knew how to cuddle. Mike grinned, guessing he could use a little practice at the art himself. He couldn't remember the last time anyone near his age had hugged him. He'd forgotten just how good it could feel to be this close.

His hand absently brushed her hair off her shoulder. "I don't think our alley man is going away."

He felt her shiver again and, this time, knew it wasn't from the cold. Something else was frightening her. There were nightmares she didn't want to talk about, and he had a feeling they centered on why she'd left a great job to come here. A reporter like Pepper Malone doesn't just show up in a town the size of Bailee.

Fear flavored her next words. "There is a possibility that

the guy is after me, not you or the paper. I made an enemy in Chicago, and he or his family might just hate me enough to follow me to make my life hell."

Mike thought of asking questions, but now didn't seem the time. "I doubt you've made any more enemies than anyone else, but we're in this together, right?"

"Right." She didn't sound like she believed him.

"Whether it's my alley man or yours, if trouble is coming, it's going to have to deal with us all."

"Thanks for the offer, but I don't know that the others will feel the same."

"I do," he said. "You're one of us now, Pepper." His words surprised him, and he wasn't aware of how much he meant them until they were out. "You're not alone."

She raised her head, and he saw just how much his words meant to her. He didn't have to ask questions to know that Pepper was about as alone as any human gets.

They sat side by side in the darkness. He could feel her relaxing.

Brushing her arm, he asked, "You all right now?"

"I think so." She straightened. "I'll be fine."

When she pulled away, he thought of kissing her. Deep down he had the feeling she didn't need a lover, she needed a friend, and Mike wasn't sure he'd be any good at being either.

She turned so that she was facing him even though they were both in shadows. Before he could move, she leaned into him and kissed him on the mouth. The few brain cells he had that were still operating on logic told him this was not the time or the place or even the right person to be parking with, but the rest of his body reacted.

If she had any idea how starved he was for this kind of thing she'd jump out of the Jeep and run home.

Instead, she wrapped her arms around his neck and pressed her body against his. The kiss burned like wildfire in a drought across all reason.

A complicated woman and a simple man. He had no defense.

Maybe this was just part of the comfort she needed. Maybe he didn't care why. Maybe for once all he wanted to do was react.

Chapter 16

Monday, March 24, 2008

I got to work early the next morning thinking I might find Michael asleep at his desk, but Audrey and Webster were already there. The bookkeeper fretted over Webster's head wound, and Bob Earl asked questions about how much it hurt. The front desk was covered with doughnuts, fried pies, and cinnamon rolls, still in the warm pans they were baked in.

"Morning," I said when they didn't notice me. "What's all this?"

"It's Monday," Audrey answered. "And this is a wicked, wicked start. We've got a full day of work to do and people keep stopping by to bring Webster food and to find out the details of what happened to him last night. We'll be lucky if we even have time to turn on our computers today."

Webster shrugged. "I won't have to worry about getting

mugged again: The cholesterol in all this stuff will kill me." He winked at Pepper. "I e-mailed my two chat friends and they're both threatening to come down and nurse me while I'm injured."

I popped a mini roll in my mouth, checking out his theory on cholesterol. The day was warming up outside, but I'd been in a strange mood since I woke. My dreams had been of blood dripping. First the cat's on the step and then Webster's last night. I hated the sight of blood. "How are you this morning?" I asked as soon as I swallowed.

Moving closer, I examined the scab running an inch along the top of his head.

"I'm fine. Had one whopper of a headache last night, but it's better this morning. All I can think about is what I should have done. That fellow never should have been able to sneak up on me like that."

Picking another sweet, I mumbled, "I've been there. What-I-should-have-done was my favorite solitaire activity in college. Now I've moved on to the advanced version of what-if-I'd-taken-that-road. It's a far more useful waste of time."

Audrey and Bob Earl both looked at me with a stare that said neither of them understood a word I said, but I swear I heard Orrie Cleveland laughing in his cave.

The shock that I might have made the little man laugh drove me to eat another doughnut.

"I have no regrets," Audrey said, straightening like a statue.

Webster and I exchanged a glance, and I knew he was thinking the same thing I was: You have to do something to regret. I suddenly felt a hundred years older than Audrey.

I decided to stay on safe ground with my fellow employees. "How come you guys aren't across the street eating breakfast?"

Audrey scribbled up her face. "We don't want to be the center of attention. Besides, it's Monday and that's no time to be late to work."

"And . . . ?" I asked. This was the second time she'd told me the day. There had to be more to the sentence.

Webster offered up the rest. "On Mondays this stranger in a suit comes in to buy one paper."

Before I could add another *and*, Audrey said, "He's not from around here. He must drive a long ways just to get a paper. We can't get any facts out of him as to why, but every Monday before nine, he walks in. All dressed up and friendly but mysterious, real mysterious."

"I think he's a gangster." Bob Earl joined the conversation on his way to pick up a doughnut.

"Maybe, but if he is, he's more polished than they ever are in the movies." Webster shook his head. "One day I did think I saw a bulge just under his suit jacket. He could have been carrying a gun."

"Nonsense." Audrey pouted. "He's some kind of investor. My guess is he's thinking of building a huge housing project or a mall or something and he's reading the paper looking for the right time."

"He'll wait a long time around here," Webster said. "We thought it was real progress last year when the new eight-slot trailer park opened. They had it half full in less than a month."

I started to say, *Let me know when he comes in,* but I doubted I'd miss him. "I'll take a look at this Mr. Monday. I'm pretty good at guessing what people do. Maybe I can help."

They all agreed to give me a shot. When Mr. Monday

came in I was to sell him the paper while Audrey talked to him so I'd have time to look him over head to toe.

"Be sure and look at his shoes. I can tell you know about shoes, Pepper." She smiled. "I know quality when I see it, and you wear the best." She glanced down at my Christian Louboutin pumps. "I'll bet those cost a hundred dollars."

"I got them on sale," I said, hoping she didn't ask at what price.

Orrie Cleveland came out of his computer room, circled the food with a paper towel from the bathroom as his plate, and hurried back to his office without saying a word to anyone.

When he passed me, I broke the silence. "Morning, Orrie."

He didn't look at me, but I saw him nod slightly and figured we'd made a start in being friendly. At this rate we'd be wishing one another Merry Christmas in another nine months.

I poured myself a cup of coffee and walked into Michael's office.

If he heard me, he made no move. He just sat, staring out the window. His hair was out of order, his clothes were wrinkled, and a shadow covered his jaw. In other words, he looked pretty much normal.

"Morning. How are you, Chief?"

"It's Monday," he said without turning.

"So I've been told."

"By nine we'll be getting calls about mistakes in the paper. Every Monday, we have to rewrite something. Just once I'd like to get it right the first time."

"Wouldn't we all," I said, thinking about my entire life. Too bad you can't rewrite your life. I wouldn't have slept with Donny Hatcher without finding out who he was. In fact, as long as I'm rewriting, I wouldn't have slept with him at all. He made love like a major league ball player—moving from base to base as fast as possible. Loving for him was a short inning, but I had a feeling hating would last more than one season.

The phone rang. Michael picked it up, listened for a moment, then set it back in the cradle. "A hang-up. They've been coming in every fifteen minutes all night long."

"Any other problems last night?" I asked, realizing he couldn't have gotten any sleep.

"None," he answered, still not turning around. "The locksmith will be here as soon as he finishes breakfast."

I moved to the window so I could see Michael's face. Exhaustion painted shadows under his blue eyes. I took a drink of coffee and leaned against the sill. If he wanted to talk, he'd have to take it from here.

After a long silence, he said, "About last night. I don't want you to think I . . ."

"Tossed me out of your Jeep." I finished his sentence. We'd had one long, great kiss and then he'd almost pushed me out the door.

He smiled. "No." He didn't have to explain. I knew he had to get back and protect his paper. "What I meant to say was that I don't want you to think that I wanted what we started to end last night. Under other circumstances . . ."

"We started something?" I had to get his first sentence straight before I could move on to *other circumstances*.

All humor left his eyes. "You know we did."

I wanted to tell him that I'd kissed a lot of guys. Half the time it didn't mean anything but that I wanted to see how they kissed. But I couldn't joke about this. I'd felt it too. Nothing with Michael would be casual. He wasn't playing games. I'm not sure he'd even know how. And, suddenly, I didn't want to play a game with him. For once, if only in a small way, I wanted something to be real between me and a man.

I fought down a smile and tried to tell the truth. "I'm not a forever kind of person, Michael, so don't go believing there is more to me than meets the eye."

He grinned and raked his fingers through his hair. "I'm not a one-night-stand kind of guy, Malone, and I'll believe anything I choose."

"So we're opposites," I whispered. "We might as well face off and fight, because we'd never blend."

"Fair enough." He stood but didn't move close to me. "We fight. Winner take all."

This wasn't the kind of flirting talk I'd ever heard. He sounded as if he were challenging me not to care about him.

"Mr. McCulloch," Bob Earl yelled from the doorway. "Mr. Monday is getting out of his car."

I followed Michael to the main room. As always, he slipped his right hand into his pocket, out of sight.

"Remember, Pepper, you take the money," Audrey said as the others all took their places and tried to act busy.

A big man in his late fifties opened the door and stepped inside. He surveyed the office. My first impression was that here was a man who missed little.

"Morning." I smiled. "May I help you?"

He nodded a greeting. "You're new."

"I am. This is my third day. Would you like a paper?"

"I would." He handed me a dollar bill and pointed with his head toward all the food. "They giving you a party?"

"No." I wasn't sure how much of our business I should tell Mr. Monday.

Audrey had no such trouble. She stepped to the desk and began telling him every detail of what had happened last night.

I followed my role and studied the man. He asked just the right number of questions to keep Audrey talking without seeming overly interested in a crime. There was something about him that reminded me of a cop. Only cops don't usually wear hand-tailored suits. His shirt was far too starched to have been done by the little wife. No wedding band. No jewelry at all, as far as I could see.

When Audrey took a breath, I stepped in and handed him his change. "You might want to keep an eye out if you live around here."

"I don't," he said and smiled at me as if he knew my game. "I'm just passing through. But you might want to take care if you're planning to settle here. Unless, of course, you come from a place where muggings are common."

"I'll keep that in mind." I didn't plan on giving out any more information than he gave me, but Audrey wasn't playing by the same rules.

"Oh, she comes from Chicago. This kind of thing is probably nothing new to her. She was a big-time reporter at the *Sun*. Imagine that."

Mr. Monday looked at me, then at my desk. "Nice to meet you, Miss Malone." He tapped his rolled paper to his forehead and was gone before I could ask his name.

Audrey moved to the window. "Well, would you look at that. He's not getting back in that fancy car of his, he's walking across the street. I've never seen him do that before. He's heading into the bakery." She looked back at me. "What do you make of that?"

"Maybe he's hungry?"

I glanced over to see if Michael was laughing and noticed he'd already walked back into his office. Apparently he wasn't nearly as interested in Mr. Monday as the rest of the staff.

An hour later the place was noisier than a grade-school lunchroom. Two men were hammering on the massive front doors, not only installing a new lock but adding a deadbolt. I could hear Michael trying to calm down a woman because the paper had listed her wedding a week early. Webster chatted with a car dealer about his ad on the second line, and Audrey was complaining to Orrie about how he always cut her social page when a news story jumped the front page.

I'd been listing ideas for a human interest story, but the three-ring circus going on around me was far more interesting. All the sugar and caffeine we'd had seemed to have wound everyone up. Everyone except Bob Earl, who slept through all the racket at his desk.

The third line rang and I reached for it, but Audrey got there first. I watched as she lifted the phone to her ear. She wore big clip-on earrings like I hadn't seen in years. With each phone call, she worked both hands in an easy automatic gesture of pulling off the earring while she raised the phone.

"*Bailee Bugle*," she chirped. "How may I direct your call?"

Her face changed so suddenly, my first thought was that someone had flipped off the lights. But the lights were on bright. Only her expression had darkened.

"What did you say?" Her lip shook as she spoke.

I met her stare and saw panic as she lowered the phone without saying another word.

Darting to her, I held her shoulder, fearing that she might faint. "What is it?"

She stood so still it frightened me more than if she'd screamed.

"A man," she whispered. "A man just told me that someone at the *Bugle* is going to be sorry, real sorry, soon."

A chill went all the way to my toes. If I'd answered the phone I probably would have thought it was simply a crank call. But Audrey obviously believed every word, and her believing it made the threat seem so much more real.

Around one thirty I walked over to the café and took a seat in the back booth. The place was almost empty except for Border Biggs mopping up near the counter.

"Get a job?" I asked.

"Nope." He glared at me. "Not that it's any of your business."

I watched the kid work. Whatever he was trying to clean up seemed to not be cooperating.

Like a kid poking at an ant bed, I tried again. "Just like to mop, do you, Border?"

He looked up. "How do you know my name?"

"I asked." I must be making progress; he was looking at me. "I like your name. It's cool."

"I was born on the border out in the middle of nowhere." He waited, as if he thought I might say something he wouldn't like.

"That means you belong everywhere. You're lucky." If I thought we were getting on, I was wrong. He looked at me as if he were thinking of tossing the mop in my face.

Lorie ended our bonding. "Are you finished, Border?" She glanced over at me and added, "I'll be right there."

Border tossed the mop into the bucket. "I got it all off the floor," he mumbled to Lorie. "Now what?"

"Take the mop and bucket to the sink by the back door and rinse all the syrup off both of them with hot water."

Border grumbled.

Lorie raised her voice. "And next time you think about dripping syrup, remember how hard it is to clean up."

He grumbled again.

"Thank you, Border. See you tomorrow." She set two mugs down at my table and joined me.

"How'd you get him to clean up his mess?"

"I told him he couldn't eat here anymore if he didn't."
She smiled that sweet smile of hers. "We all do things
we regret from time to time. I just wish they could all be
cleaned up with soap and hot water."

Chapter 17

12:20 P.M.

Mike planned to stay in the office all day, but by mid-afternoon even the coffee couldn't keep him awake. He went home, crawled into bed, and slept for four hours straight. Morgan woke him for supper.

On Mondays the housekeeper had Bible study, so Mike had made a deal with Morgan years ago. He'd cook one week, and she had to cook the next. At first her meals had been peanut butter and jelly sandwiches, and his the next week would be bacon, lettuce, and tomato sandwiches. But slowly she'd learned to cook what May called the simple stuff. Lately, she'd been experimenting. His weeks were still BLTs on toast.

His niece questioned him about what was going on at the paper while they ate egg-and-sausage tacos. Morgan swore she invented them.

"What else happened, Dops? You got to tell me."

"Nothing."

"I'm not a kid. I'm almost thirteen."

"I know," he said, guessing she'd be bossing him around by this time next year.

The girl frowned. "Are you going up to sleep at the paper again tonight?"

"No," he said, unsure whether he meant it. "The new locks will work fine."

"I don't know why the sheriff can't find this mugger. Everybody in this town knows everybody. How could a stranger walk around? Maybe I should go into law enforcement. I could be sheriff in this town in ten years."

"Everyone doesn't know everyone, kid. It just seems that way." He tugged at the ribbon holding one of her pigtails. "And you can be anything you want to be."

"Well, if you go back up there tonight, I'm going with you. There'll be safety in numbers."

He finished off his taco. "If we start now, we might get your homework done in time to watch a movie before bedtime."

Morgan darted for her books while he cleaned the table. Monday night movies had been a ritual since she'd started school. He used to pick them up in Fort Worth on Sundays and pay the late charge every week. Now they ordered them by mail.

She did her homework while he wrote in his journal.

Journal Entry: If I could be anything, what would I be?

He started a list of things, then scratched them out and wrote,

*I'd like to just be me but sometimes that's
impossible.*

Morgan called him to check her homework. He closed
the journal, thinking that what he had was a collection of
started thoughts, never finished.

He moved into the kitchen and checked her work while
she popped the popcorn. By eight they were in the two old
recliners in the back room watching a movie.

More often than not lately, he slept most of the way
through the show, but tonight, he ignored the plot about a
poor, talented girl becoming a princess and thought of his
problems at work.

Part of him considered shutting down the paper for a
few weeks. But then, whoever was bothering them would
somehow have won. He still thought the threat today
was just that, a threat. But what if it were real and he did
nothing?

"Dops pause it for a minute while I run to the bathroom."

She jumped up without closing the recliner and darted
down the hallway.

Mike picked up the phone and dialed Pepper, telling himself he just wanted to make sure everything had
gone smoothly all afternoon. Webster didn't carry a cell
and was rarely home before ten. Audrey would have been
frightened if her phone rang this late. Pepper was the logical choice.

"Hello."

"Hello, Malone." He smiled at the sound of her voice.
"Just checking in."

"Hi, Chief. Nothing to report. After you left, the office
took a group nap then locked all the new locks."

"Good." He wanted her to stay on the line, but he couldn't think of anything else to say. "You all right?"

"I'm fine. I had dinner at the home with Aunt Wilma. The food wasn't bad. She thinks I should do a story on some of the old buildings in town."

"Not a bad idea."

"I was thinking of starting with the paper. Would you mind?"

"Not at all." He heard Morgan running down the hall. "I have to go. We'll talk about it later."

When his niece entered the room, he clicked Play and they settled in for the second half of the movie.

Mike couldn't have quoted a line from the film. All he thought about for the next hour was Pepper. It seemed he was always ending even their conversations in a hurry. But one day soon, they might have some uninterrupted time.

Chapter 18

Heath Fuller sat in the shadow of the courthouse and watched the main street of Bailee. It was the kind of small town he could see Lorie living in. With his job at the FBI, he'd never lived more than a few days in a city of less than a couple of hundred thousand. Dallas might be his base, but it didn't feel like his home. Nowhere was.

Trees lined the streets here. Park benches were placed by the sidewalks, and storefronts had no bars pulled down at closing. He could get used to it all, Heath thought.

He'd checked in with the local sheriff an hour ago and told him the FBI was looking into the threats at the newspaper. The old man had bought the cover whole, even promising to keep the investigation secret. Heath figured no one needed to know the real reason he was in town.

The newspaper threats were probably only a hoax, but if Lorie was worried he'd be near as long as she'd let him.

The bakery lights were still on. She worked too much. Hell, he worked too much. His shift ended at five and it was usually after ten before he left the office. He knew why he stayed so late. He had no reason to go home. Maybe it was the same for her.

The lights flickered and went dark. She stepped out the front door and locked up, then crossed her sweater over her chest for warmth like she always did.

He didn't like the fact that a mugging had happened right in front of her place.

She didn't turn toward the stairs heading up to her apartment tonight. She shoved her hands in her pockets and began to walk the street. He'd seen her take the walk before, the few times he'd driven over when he couldn't fight down the need to see her. She always circled the block and ended up back at her bakery.

But she shouldn't go for a stroll tonight. Not one night after a mugging. Not alone well after dark.

His Lorie Girl had never been reckless. In fact, she even checked the dates on milk before she drank. Yet tonight, here she was walking alone along the shadowy street, her head down, her shoulders slumped as if she were deep in thought.

He grabbed his jacket and got out of his car. His first instinct was to follow her, but he might frighten her, so he moved to the front of his Audi and waited for her to circle past.

Heath knew the second she saw him. She paused almost like she might turn and run, and then she walked slowly toward him.

"Hello, Heath," she said, as casually as if it had been only days since they'd seen each other and not almost two years. "I told you there was no need for you to come."

He didn't speak for a moment, wanting to take in

the sight of her before reality separated them. "I hadn't planned to, but I heard about the threat today at the paper, so I thought I'd drive over. I think you may be right. There may be cause to worry about your friends."

She nodded, then asked, "Walk with me?"

He draped his jacket over her shoulders. "You should—"

"No lectures." She didn't let him finish.

Motioning her to point the way, he stepped silently to her side.

He was surprised when she turned off her usual route and walked the street just beyond Main where there were fewer streetlights. Most of the houses were old and small, with wheelchair ramps along the porches. All but one of the homes looked dark inside. Heath noticed that the last house on the left had the glow of a TV in the front room.

He knew this town was as safe a place as any in Texas. He'd checked out every detail when she'd moved here. They'd talked only twice that first year, but he'd run background checks on everyone with whom she came in contact, from the movers to the plumber who fixed up her place. Then, he'd driven over now and then just to be close. Two years ago she'd caught him standing in the crowd acting like he was watching the Fourth of July parade. They'd talked, standing in the hot sun, like two strangers.

Now they were walking in the dark. Not much progress. "You pick this street because you don't want anyone to see us together, or because you know I can read your thoughts if I see your face?"

"A little of both." She laughed.

He liked the sound. He remembered her laughing a lot when they'd first met.

She stumbled over the uneven bricks in the road, almost falling.

"Take my arm," he said, guessing she'd never take his hand.

She slipped her hand around his forearm and he covered her fingers with his. "It's a little cold for a walk."

"I know, but it feels so good after being in the kitchen all day."

"You always work this late?"

"No. I've just got a luncheon to cook for tomorrow and I wanted to get all the salads and desserts finished tonight."

"What desserts did you make?"

She laughed again. "You don't care, Heath."

He smiled, wondering how many years it had been since they'd talked about nothing. "I might if one was chocolate. Nobody makes chocolate like you do, Lorie Girl."

"Don't call me that," she whispered. "I'm not your Lorie Girl anymore."

The easy time was over. "I know," he said, fighting down an oath. What they'd had was broken. Shattered into a million pieces he'd never be able to put back together, and it was all his fault.

They walked half the block in silence. He finally felt her fingers relax against his arm once more. They could have been any married couple out for a stroll.

"I knew you'd come, even when I told you not to," she finally said. "I'm glad you did. I'm worried about my friends. No matter what happened between us, you're the best agent in Dallas. If anyone can figure this out and help Mike and his people, you can."

"You care about Mike?" He didn't want the question to sound like he was jealous, but he worried that it might. He knew about Mike McCulloch. He seemed like a vanilla guy, no arrests, not even enough traffic tickets to bother counting. Mike was five years younger than Lorie, but hell, so was he and it hadn't stopped him from chasing after her.

"Of course, they're my friends." She bumped into his shoulder as she stepped around a puddle in the road. "I've only known Pepper a week, but she has this way about her that makes me want to know her better."

"Lost-puppy look," Heath guessed.

"Probably. She does seem down to her last friend. I don't think this was her first choice of places to come."

Heath knew all about Pepper Malone. He'd done his research after Frank reported in. She'd been a top reporter for the *Sun*. Considered one of their finest until a few weeks ago. She'd lost her job in Chicago over some story she'd written. The story was accurate, but apparently her methods of collecting the facts hadn't been. The agent who looked into it said she left town so fast he figured she was either hurried along or frightened. The family she'd written about had deep pockets and would have preferred to keep their family stories to themselves.

If Pepper Malone had brought trouble with her from Chicago, he'd have his hands full keeping them safe. The agent in Chicago said the family had shady beginnings, but as far as he knew they were aboveboard now. Still, if the family hated Pepper, they might send someone to make sure she changed professions.

He didn't voice his thoughts to Lorie. "Better watch those lost puppies. They sometimes come with ticks."

"Not this one."

"Tell me about her," he said, more to just hear Lorie talk than to find out about Pepper Malone.

They'd circled back to Main. When they passed his car, she was answering questions and didn't seem to notice that he planned to walk her all the way home.

Heath took in every detail around him in his mind, but his senses were centered where her hand rested on his arm.

When they reached her bakery, he said, "I'll find out all I can and get back to you. Don't worry."

"Thanks," she said, taking the first step up toward her apartment. "Good night, Heath."

He tried to act casual. "Those pies you made weren't chocolate, by any chance."

She was at eye level with him now. "Apple," she said. "Why?"

"Good," he answered as he stepped away. "Then I won't break in and steal one."

"Maybe next time." She laughed as she climbed the stairs.

He waited until she was in her apartment before he moved. "Maybe next time," he whispered.

Chapter 19

Bailee, Texas
Population 15,008
Friday, March 28, 2008

Friday morning Michael called a meeting of all the staff.
He even made Orrie roll out of his office long enough to
listen.

I was impressed. In the week and two days I'd been at
the paper, Michael McCulloch had gone from the resident
ghost to acting like a real editor. He might still look like
the absentminded professor, but he was making progress.
He'd even worn a brown tie, which went with nothing
else he wore, of course.

"I've got a few new policies to implement today," he
said. "One, I'm the only one who answers the phone during
business hours. I'll pass it along to one of you as soon as I
know who it is. After business hours, no one answers the
phone, period."

Bob Earl raised his hand. "What if you're not here or

have to go to the bathroom or something. Do we just let it ring?"

Michael frowned. "No. Web, you get it."

Webster nodded, accepting the task. He'd stayed at the office far more the past few days. I couldn't tell if he was afraid of missing something or if he found one of his chat women fascinating. Most afternoons I could hear him on the back computer mumbling as he typed out his part of the chats. He told me Sexy Sag was having some competition for most chatty from online babes called Curlers43 and Rolloverqueen.

"Now." Michael held up his pencil. "Does everyone get rule one?"

We all nodded.

For once Audrey didn't want any of the responsibility. Since she'd heard the threat, she hadn't picked up the phone. The main announcement in the office all week had been, "Audrey, it's for you." Since she got most of the calls, we were all starting to feel like her answering machine.

All week I'd received one call, from Peggy at the funeral home. She told me Andrew Jackson died. Before I could say *I know*, she added that he'd been the elementary school principal for thirty-four years.

"Policy two," Michael continued. "From now on, what happens in this office stays in this office."

I almost laughed. He was talking to a walking collection of colanders. Not one person in the room would make it past lunch without telling at least someone everything that happened all morning at the paper. I'd sat in the café and listened to Audrey and Webster visit with whoever walked in. It's a wonder anyone ever bought a paper. It was all on audio right before them.

"Policy three." Michael looked directly at me. "No one

leaves out the back door. In fact we're going to have desks in front of it, so even if someone picked the locks they couldn't get in. When we leave here after dark, we always leave at least two at a time and we leave out the front."

When I looked down at the paperwork on my desk, he added, "That means, Malone, no staying late reading back issues unless you talk me or Webster into staying with you."

I resented the fact that he thought I couldn't take care of myself. I didn't dare question him in front of the others, mainly because I knew they'd all be on his side, but if I wanted to stay late and check back issues in the basement that should be my concern.

"Does that mean you, too?" Bob Earl asked.

"Everyone. And if you come back after dark, bring someone with you or call Toad and have him drop by. Web, if you drop by to get online, make sure the sheriff's office knows you're in the building."

We all looked at him as if we were being punished. It had been three days and nothing else had happened. All of us, and most of the people in town, were beginning to think the trouble might be over. Maybe the "someone will be sorry" threat had only been someone's idea of a joke. Since Michael put Caller ID on the phones we hadn't had a single hang-up call.

He closed his notepad. "That's all the policies until I think of another one." He looked tired; we all did.

I stood and walked toward the basement stairs. "I'll be in the back looking for old stories about this building. Will the last one to leave please yell at me so I can run out with the other little pigs before the big bad wolf blows this place down."

Something in my nature made me resent a bully. I was

far madder about the slashed tires than a threat. I'd had about all I could take in the past month and was ready to throw open the windows and yell, *Come and get me. I'm ready for a fight.*

I didn't look back as I jogged down the steps. I could pretty well guess the expression on everyone's face.

I attacked my research, but an hour into reading old newspapers, it wasn't this building, but the McCullochs who had all my attention. I scratched out their names and important dates on a pad and smiled at the pattern. Adam McCulloch, the first. Benjamin, the second in line, a World War I veteran. Clark, Michael's father, a perfectionist. And Dave, the hero who died.

Lorie had been right. Dave was the chosen son. It was as simple as A, B, C, D. I pulled my laptop over and punched Dave's facts into a search.

While waiting, I couldn't help but wonder how it must have felt growing up with a brother one year older who everyone knew would take over the family business. No wonder Michael ran away to college and rarely came home.

"Want some lunch?" Mike yelled from the top of the stairs.

"No thanks," I yelled back. I'd already turned in all my assignments this week, so unless someone died, I was free to research.

Time didn't seem to exist in the basement. The more I read about the town, the more fascinated I became with the people. The town had been named after a rancher's wife everyone loved. Bailee and Carter McKoy had never lived in town, but their foundation had built a library when the few families here managed to construct the first school. Most of the reports were of everyday life. But now and then, one of these ordinary people did something extraordinary.

Wives and mothers took their husbands' jobs so the men could go to war. The women farmed and ran the grain elevators and drove trucks. And every week the paper highlighted one woman, just as they promised to send every Bailee man a free paper for as long as he was overseas.

The folks in town plowed up the grass on the courthouse lawn and planted victory gardens. When there weren't enough men to harvest the fruit, families pulled their children from school to help with the work.

In the Depression, they shipped canned peaches all over the state for the food lines in big cities. That same year one little store almost went bankrupt taking scrip, the substitute for cash when the school system was broke and had to pay teachers with promissory notes. One little store kept the county school system from crumbling.

During the flu epidemic two sisters, Grace and Lula Pickens, opened their family home to the sick. They were credited with saving a hundred lives even though they both died. Their courage made the front page of the paper for a week.

"Want some supper?" Michael shouted down again from the top.

I looked at my watch, not believing it could be after six.

He came halfway down so he could see me and I could see the pizza box in his hand.

"Yes." I jumped up and ran to the stairs. "For me?" I said, as politely as if he'd brought me flowers.

"No." He shrugged. "This is mine. You'll have to order your own."

If he'd reached into the box and taken a slice I would have had to kill him. Starvation had squelched all sanity.

He smiled and offered the box. "Pepperoni, right?"

"Thanks."

"Mind if I go get my pizza and join you?"

"Only if you bring root beer."

He took a few steps up the stairs and lifted down another pizza and a six-pack of root beer.

I ate the first slice in silence, then began to tell him some of the stories I'd found. If he knew them all, he didn't comment, he just let me ramble.

Finally, with half the pizza gone, I relaxed back in my chair. "These stories remind me why I love this job."

He opened another bottle and handed it to me. "Why *did* you go into journalism, Malone?"

"I don't know. I was good in English and I like watching people."

"Watching, but not getting involved."

He'd hit how I felt exactly. When you wear a press tag, you're in the middle of it all, but you're not part of it. The tragedy, the sadness, the crimes are all slices of life you're molding into a story.

"Why'd you get into the game?" I asked, already knowing his story.

"It's in my blood." He gave the pat answer I had a feeling he always gave, and I was a little hurt he didn't take the time to be honest with me. I knew this job wasn't his first choice. Even with his ugly tie gone, he still looked like a teacher.

He changed the subject and we drifted from politics to movies.

We talked until all the pizza and root beer were gone. It felt good just to talk to someone. I realized how little I'd done that in the past few years. With most people I was looking for a story. I couldn't name one friend I'd gone out with in the past year even for lunch. I was always too busy working. Donny Hatcher and I didn't talk much either, except that night he'd been drinking and decided to tell me about all the skeletons in the Hatcher family closet. When we broke up, I still had the stories and decided to use them. I never really thought about how everyone, including my boss, would think I had slept with the man to get the story. I also never considered how mad Donny would be.

I shrugged. Chicago seemed a long way away.

Finally, Mike stood. "You about ready to head home? We're the last two here. I can't leave until you leave. It's a rule."

"I'm ready." I picked up my sweater, saved the info on my laptop, and was ready. "I wouldn't want to break a rule, Chief. Besides, I've got a date for bingo." I shoved the empty box in the trash. "Thanks for the pizza."

"Anytime," he said as he headed toward the stairs.

I followed him all the way to the front door, picking up my purse by my desk. I even stood next to him when he locked up as if I were his bodyguard.

"Michael," I said, feeling awkward. "Would you call me at ten like you did last weekend? It'll be after dark before I get home and that place is a little spooky. I swear at night the peach tree branches behind the trailer look like they're waving for me to come over."

"Sure," he said. "I'd hate for the peach trees to get you."

I climbed into my car and backed out. When I looked forward, I saw him crossing the street to Lorie's bakery. She was also closing up. I thought of parking and saying hello, but I wanted to talk to Aunt Wilma and the only time was between bingo games.

As I drove over to the nursing home, I saw a huge old house with gingerbread trim. I'd never noticed the sign out front before reading simply THE LULA-GRACE HOME FOR VISITING NURSES.

I added a question to my list of things to ask Wilma, then smiled remembering the two sisters who'd died caring for the sick. That old house might be the perfect place to start my series on the buildings of Bailee.

My computer had turned up three David McCullochs who seemed to be about the same age as Michael's brother. Just for a lark I'd e-mailed each to see if any one was related to Mike.

A few minutes later when I made it to the bingo game, I found Wilma already there. Tonight's theme was "Over the Rainbow." Someone had painted a huge rainbow behind the girl calling bingo, and all the napkins and plates were multicolored. I was happy to report I didn't see a hat in the room.

Webster was there surrounded by ladies. His online chats seemed to be improving his conversation skills. Two of the trio of sleeping guys in wheelchairs were across from Wilma. One must have had another engagement. They had been awake for the snacks because one had cookie crumbs all over his chest. The other snored with a humming sound.

"About time you got here," Wilma yelled. "It's too late to buy in tonight, but you can play one of my cards. I told them you were coming." She pointed to our dates. "They stayed awake for a while waiting for you."

"I'm sorry."

"No matter." She shrugged. "We'll just tell them they saw you. Tomorrow they won't remember anyway." She passed me a card.

"Thanks." I'd called her last Sunday and told her about the dead cat on her porch and found her only worried about me. She said she was glad it wasn't Herbert, but she and one-eyed Herbert were like roommates sharing the trailer. He'd moved in uninvited, and most of the time she got the feeling he thought she should be the one to move out. If he'd been killed, she figured she had survivor's rights to the place.

I asked her if she wanted me to bring Herbert up for a visit and she said no, but if Herbert did ever die, she'd like one of those little yelpy dogs. She'd always wanted one, but Herbert wouldn't hear of it.

The girl with braces started calling numbers, and I began to play my borrowed card as well as the cards of the guys across from me.

Between games I asked her about some of the stories I'd read in the old papers, and she filled in details that hadn't been reported.

When the games were over, I walked her back to her room and discovered she'd cut out the articles I'd written in last week's paper and posted them on her wall. I had a feeling I'd embarrass her if I said anything about it, so I acted like I didn't notice.

When I walked to my car, I couldn't help but smile. Never once in my life had my mother put a paper of mine on the refrigerator door or even the grocery bulletin board in the laundry room. She'd said it would only look tacky. But Aunt Wilma had. I added her to my growing list of people I could learn to care about.

I was almost halfway to my car when I noticed Michael's Jeep, with him standing next to it. Even at his height, with long legs and wide shoulders, he had a lost-boy look about him.

"It's a little cold to be hanging out in the parking lot." I laughed. "Your chances of getting picked up might be better at a mall than a nursing home."

He didn't answer. He just watched me.

I stopped a foot away from him. "Is something wrong, Chief?"

He straightened. "Could you drop the *Chief* tonight? I was hoping we could just talk. If you've no objection, I'd just like to spend some time with you. Then I'll follow you home and leave my lights shining until you get past the peach monsters trying to pull you over the property line."

I wondered if the conversation over pizza earlier had been as rare for him as for me. I had a feeling it might have been. "Sure, if we can go somewhere warm, I'd enjoy spending time with you, too."

He moved around to the passenger side and opened the door. "How about someplace warm that serves ice cream?"

"Sounds great. I'm hungry."

"I can see where keeping you from starving could be a full-time job." He laughed easily.

"Would you rather I pretended to eat like a bird?"

"Never," he said. "I prefer you honest and direct." He winked at me. "And always hungry."

As we drove to the Dairy Queen I told him all about my night of bingo. I could almost feel him relaxing next to me, and I wondered what had wound him so tightly between the time we said good-bye two hours earlier and now. Then I remembered seeing him walking over to the bakery.

"How's Lorie?" I asked, doubting that she'd caused him any stress. She was one person who calmed everyone around her.

"She's fine, I guess. We walked the block tonight, but she looked tired. Neither of us could keep a conversation going." He pulled into the parking lot and cut the engine. "She's a gentle soul and I have a feeling all this with the paper is upsetting her more than she lets on. She probably has to listen to everyone talking about what might happen all day long."

"You care about her." In other places, other times, this would have been a question a woman asks a man that held a far different meaning. Now it wasn't even a question, just a fact.

"Of course. We're friends." He opened his door and added when we both stepped out, "I knew we would be the first day she opened the bakery and brought brownies to the office. Orrie won't talk to her, but every time she brings him brownies I notice her ad doubles and her bill is cut in half. If she crossed the street any more often with treats, I'd be losing money."

"How'd she end up renting Bob Earl a place?" I asked as we walked into the Dairy Queen and took a booth.

"About the time she was settling in, the kid had dropped out of school and was getting into trouble around town. He lived with his great-grandmother. I think he'd been left there years ago by a parent who didn't have time for him. I gave him a job delivering papers, which is only a one-day-a-week thing, but he shows up to work every day anyway. When the great-grandmother died, everyone worried about who would keep an eye on him. They were all afraid he'd go back to wandering the streets. Lorie heard about it and walked straight into my office without even taking the time to take off her apron. By nightfall we had him fixed up with a place in the back of her store and she promised to make sure he had breakfast and dinner."

"Poor kid."

Michael opened the menu. "I love ordering by picture," he said, then continued our conversation. "Bob Earl's not poor. He inherited his great-grandmother's house. He's not rich, but he could live comfortably for the rest of his life. Only when the banker told him he should move back into the big house, he cried for hours. He wanted to stay where he was in the back room of the bakery and work for me. So the banker set him up accounts at every place, even the movie theater. I pay him in cash and that seems enough to buy his Cokes and candy bars. If he needs more money, all he has to do is tell the banker."

I thought about the easy way Michael and Lorie had taken on responsibility for the kid. Neither of them realized what an incredible thing they'd done.

"What'll you have, Malone?" Michael asked.

"Your pockets deep enough to go for the works, a banana split with extra toppings?"

"Are we sharing it?"

"No way."

He closed his menu with his left hand. "I didn't think so."

While he stood and ordered our ice cream, I looked around. The place was almost deserted: a few travelers passing through and a father near the back with three little boys, all smearing ice cream on themselves.

"Two banana splits with the works," Michael said as he returned with two ice cream boats.

When he slid back into the booth, our knees bumped. We both acted like we didn't notice, but it took a minute of straightening to make room for four long legs beneath the small table.

As we ate our way through a mountain of ice cream, we talked of our college days. I was surprised at how much Michael had traveled. I guess I thought he'd always been around here. Finally, I asked, "You didn't come home from school in the summers?"

He shook his head. "My brother was a big football star

in high school. He even played college ball. When he came home the whole town almost had a parade. For me, I was pretty much unnoticed. I was only one year behind him, but I spent my life being invisible. Even the few times I did come home, people would either think I was him, then look disappointed when I wasn't, or they'd ask me all about how Dave was doing." He looked guilty. "I guess I was just selfish enough to want to be just me, not Dave's little brother. So I took classes and traveled in the summer."

"I took a road trip once." I played with the chocolate sauce on my ice cream. "I'd just finished my junior year and decided to drive across country to see my mother in San Francisco."

"Did you enjoy the drive?"

"I did, but when I got there she was gone. She'd moved to Washington with a man she called a 'dear friend.' Forgot to tell me."

"And . . ." He leaned forward.

"And I enjoyed the drive back."

He smiled. "For a minute there, Malone, I thought you were going to tell me something personal about your life." He reached across the table and wiped chocolate off the corner of my lip.

"I don't have a personal life. No family, no friends, no strings."

He bumped my leg with his knee. "Just you and your tapeworm, right?"

I glanced down and noticed I'd finished off my dessert and he hadn't eaten half of his. "Mind if I share yours? Mine seems to have evaporated." I smiled.

He moved his boat to the center of the table. I brushed my leg lightly against his as I leaned forward for a bite. We were talking about nothing really, but we were communicating beneath the table.

When we left the Dairy Queen I felt like I needed to walk off a few thousand calories, but the wind chilled me.

I must have shivered because he wrapped his arm around my shoulders and tugged me against him.

"Maybe we should have had coffee," he mumbled close to my ear as we moved to the car. "All that ice cream is freezing you from the inside out."

Neither of us said much on the way home. He talked about the wind that came off the quartz hills, and I complained about how dark it was here at night.

When we pulled in front of the nursing home, the parking lot lights were out. He stopped next to my car and left the Jeep's lights on as he climbed out.

I fumbled for my keys as he walked beside me. "I'll be fine from here," I said as I jingled the keys.

He didn't comment, just reached over and opened my car door.

"Is there something you forgot to say?" I hesitated, thinking he'd finally decided to tell me the reason he'd waited for me.

"No," he said. "There's something I forgot to do."

He brushed one hand down the sleeve of my coat until he gripped my fingers, and then he tugged me closer. "I forgot to do this."

I saw no reason to protest.

When his mouth came down on mine I had the oddest sense of coming home. He let go of my hand and pulled me against him. I wrapped my arms around his neck and kissed him back. It seemed the perfect sweet ending to an ice cream date.

When we finally came up for air, he whispered, "Any chance you'll come home with me?"

I laughed. "Shouldn't you buy me dinner first before you take me home?"

"I did," he answered.

I sighed as he kissed my neck. "It wouldn't be a good idea. You're my boss. It wouldn't work."

"I agree," he mumbled. "You're fired."

"I'm fired if I don't sleep with you?"

"No. You're fired if you do. Then we won't have a conflict."

I pushed away. "You're one hard man to resist, Michael McCulloch, but I need the job."

He grinned. "I had a feeling that would be your answer, but just once I had to try. It's been a long time since I've been attracted to someone. I don't really know how it's done. I know you won't believe it, but I was never much good at asking girls out or dating, even in college, and I've forgotten what little I knew since then."

I wanted to say that I was no good at it either. If I took a poll of my encounters with the opposite sex, I'd have far more in the regret column than in the good-time column. In fact, my boyfriends were kind of like one-eyed Herbert. They just moved in and then looked at me like I should be the one to leave when the time came.

I grinned at him, thinking he wasn't a move-in kind of guy. "You're right, Michael, I don't believe you. You've probably dated every single woman from sixteen to sixty."

"Liar," he said. "I swear sometimes I can tell you're getting a kick out of the pain I'm going through trying to act like I know what I'm doing."

"Okay, you could use a little practice but I find you cute as a bug."

He brushed my cheek with his and whispered close to my ear, "That's strange, Malone, because I find you sexy as hell."

He pulled away as if deciding he'd made a fool of himself . . . again.

"How about we start as friends?" I couldn't believe I was saying *friends*. How many times had I watched him this week and wondered what he'd be like in bed?

"Friends," he echoed.

"Good friends." I leaned in, letting my body press against his side as I kissed his cheek.

He groaned and stepped away. "Good night, Malone."

"Good night, Michael."

I drove back to the trailer thinking that a month ago I would have slept with him. But now, I knew him. Michael wasn't the kind of man to do things lightly. I realized with a shock that as much as I wanted him, I didn't want to hurt him even more, and in the end I hurt every guy I dated.

Twenty minutes later I'd changed into my pajamas and just curled up on the couch when the phone rang.

I picked it up, expecting Michael. "Hello, Chief."

I heard a long pause, then heavy breathing.

I slammed the phone down.

Three minutes later it rang again. The breathing started immediately. I almost threw the phone across the room.

For the next ten minutes I sat waiting for another call and planning all the things I would say to this guy.

I still jumped when it rang. "Now look, whoever you are—"

"Malone." Michael's voice broke through my rant. "Malone. What is it? What's wrong?"

It took me a few breaths to calm down enough to tell Michael about the calls.

"Do you need me to come over or call the sheriff?"

"No," I finally managed. "I'm all locked in safe. The only way he can get to me is by phone."

"We'll get a trace put on your phone tomorrow and

Caller ID so you'll know who's on the line before you pick up."

"Thanks."

"Anything else I can do, Malone?"

"Yeah, stay on the line until I fall asleep."

Chapter 20

Heath Fuller had watched Lorie circle the street with the newspaper editor the night before, but not tonight. She was working late in her bakery, and the *Bugle* looked closed up tight.

Part of him hated McCulloch because she stayed on Main in the light when she walked with her friend the editor. With him, she'd picked the dark.

He told himself he couldn't be jealous. He'd lost that right when he'd walked away from the hospital five years ago. Lorie had miscarried a baby he'd never really wanted. He'd tried to act like he was happy about the pregnancy, but she'd known. The doctor had told them before they married that she should never have children, but she'd been determined even though it might mean her life.

That night in the hospital the birth almost killed her.

Then, as if to show Lorie he could be reckless too, he'd

signed onto an undercover job he knew she'd hate him taking. He'd been angry when she'd begged him not to go. What had she wanted, him to stay around until she got pregnant again and killed herself having a child? When she'd threatened to divorce him if he left, he'd called her bluff.

They'd made a clean break that almost shattered them both. She needed peace and quiet to mourn, and he needed something to do to forget. They'd both found what they needed in work.

After the first assignment, he'd taken another and another. The second time he'd come home, their divorce was final. The third time he returned, she'd moved away. After that there was no reason for him to come home.

Heath watched her from a half block away, but it might as well have been a hundred miles. He knew he wouldn't be welcome if he just dropped by. She no longer needed him as her husband, or as a man. All she wanted was the shell of him she saw as an FBI agent. Maybe that was all that was left of him after five years of being without her.

He waited until she went inside her little apartment. Fifteen minutes later, he saw her bedroom light go out.

His wife, his life, was tucked into bed and he was still standing in the wind. If he could go back and relive one day, one hour in time it would be the hour his child died. He'd take all the pain of it, all Lorie's tears and sobbing. He'd stand the hurting and stay. He'd hold her through the hours that followed and the impossible decisions to be made. He'd let her cries echo in his ears. He'd feel all the heartache. He'd stay.

Because if he *had* stayed, he'd be with her tonight.

Slowly, he walked to his car and drove away, knowing he'd not contact her until he had something to report. She wanted the agent . . . not the man . . . not the husband who ran . . . not him.

When he passed the sheriff's office, Heath pulled to a stop. The old man had invited him in for coffee any time. Maybe tonight would be a good night to stop. On a slow night cops liked to talk, and Heath wanted to know everything about the town.

He found Watson at his desk doing paperwork. The place smelled of pipe tobacco and gun oil.

"Thought I'd take you up on that cup of coffee, Sheriff," Heath said as he tapped on the open door frame.

Watson's smile was genuine. "Wonderful. Agent Fuller, right?" The two men shook hands. "I could use a little company. My dispatcher called in with a sick kid so I'm running double duty tonight. Lucky nothing's going on." He pointed to a chair. "What brings the FBI to Bailee so late?"

"I was just driving through town. Thought I'd head up north for a weekend of fishing." Heath had learned working undercover that a small lie served him better than avoiding questions. Fishing was almost always a good one. Every man liked to talk fishing, but few knew enough about it to detect a lie from the truth.

"I took off the middle of last week." Watson blew the dust out of a cup and poured Heath some coffee. "Thought I'd drive up to Oklahoma for some bass fishing, but the weather didn't cooperate. I think all the fish must have gone south for spring break."

Heath accepted a cup. They talked fishing for a while, and then Watson shared his worries about Toad.

"He's a good boy," Watson said for the third time. "He wants to help people and I trust him to do what's right, but I'm not sure he can think on his feet."

Heath nodded. Every man in law enforcement thought about that one day, one time when everything went to hell.

Would he react fast enough? "Maybe he'll grow into the job. Some men do."

"Toad would make a good deputy." The sheriff lit his pipe. "He can follow orders and do all the basic duties. But I'm not sure he can be the kind of sheriff this town needs."

Heath admired the old man's honesty. In a bigger city, cops are more guarded with their opinions. He also noticed that the old man missed little. If Heath wasn't careful, he'd give too much away. Sheriff Watson had already probably noticed that he wasn't dressed for fishing.

Finally they got down to discussing the threats on the paper. The phone calls had stopped, but the vandalism hadn't. Someone had tried to pick the back lock Thursday night and almost gotten in. The sheriff also mentioned that all the newspaper boxes had been damaged. If McCulloch planned to sell the extra papers on Sunday, he'd have to stand on the street corner.

"Who knows about this?" Heath asked.

"No one except McCulloch. He seems to think whoever is doing this might get his kicks out of hearing others talk. His reasoning is, if we say nothing, maybe the guy will stop. He gave his staff orders not to talk about the problems, but I'll be surprised if that works."

Heath frowned. "You buy the theory that it's just someone who wants folks talking?"

Watson shook his head. "Nope."

"Me either."

Toad came in for coffee. He seemed happy to see Heath as he pulled up a chair in his uncle's office. The big man did look like a boy even though he had to be near middle-aged. He hadn't downed half the cup when a call came in.

Watson answered, made a few notes on a pad, then hung up the phone.

When he looked up, Heath knew something was wrong. He leaned forward and waited for the bad news.

"Someone's shot out the windows of the *Bugle*," Watson said as he stood, reaching for his coat. "Scared a bunch of folks coming out of the movie theater half to death."

"Was anyone hurt?" Toad asked, tossing his paper cup in the trash.

"Not that I know of, but we'd better get down there." Watson loaded his belt with an extra flashlight and a cell phone. With a press of a button, he switched the phones over. If another call came in, it would be picked up by his cell.

Toad was already heading for the door.

"You park down by the courthouse," Watson yelled after him. "The agent and I will block the street off at the light and move toward you. Keep an eye out for anyone who looks like trouble."

"I'm on it," Toad answered as he disappeared.

"Who made the call?" Heath asked a minute later as they hurried down the steps.

"Lorie Fuller."

The old sheriff's gaze met Heath's stare, and in a blink Heath knew Watson had figured out the truth. "You want to ride along on this call, Agent *Fuller*?"

They both knew Heath was free to do whatever he wanted.

"You bet. Thanks for inviting me." He wasn't sure whether he'd been invited or simply questioned, but either way, he was going.

They were in the patrol car racing toward Main when Heath spoke again. "You know, this is more personal than professional with me."

Watson nodded. "I figured that. You're here to protect her."

"Right."

"Did she call you?"

Heath knew that the answer mattered to the old man. "She did," he answered.

Watson didn't look at Heath when he asked, "You hurt her bad once, didn't you? I can see longtime sorrow in her big brown eyes sometimes."

"I added to it." Heath had given up trying to defend what he'd done. He'd left her alone to mourn their child. No amount of excuses mattered. "I'm here to help now. I won't hurt her again."

"Better not, son," the old man said. "Because if you do, you'll answer to me."

Heath was half the man's age, a foot taller, and in far better shape than the sheriff ever had been, but he had a feeling Watson meant every word.

"She's my wife," Heath admitted. "I'd die for her."

To his surprise, the old man smiled. "I've been married forty-three years and I can tell you, sometimes it's harder to live for a woman than to die for one."

Chapter 21

Mike could hear Pepper's even breathing through the phone line and knew she'd fallen asleep. He smiled, wishing that she were lying next to him. Logic told him he shouldn't get involved with her, but for the first time in years he found a woman fascinating. She was smart and quick-witted, beautiful in her very own way, and, best of all, she didn't put up with anything from him.

He grinned. Who was he kidding? A few kisses didn't mean she'd ever sleep with him. Women like her didn't get involved with men like him. He had so much baggage he needed a U-Haul, and she looked like the kind of woman who traveled light through life.

She wore clothes with designer names, and the best he could do was find a *Made in America* tag on most of the stuff he owned. But just for tonight, he liked the idea of listening to her sleep.

His cell phone sounded, shattering the calm. Mike pushed the house phone aside and answered it as soon as he noticed the sheriff's number. "McCulloch here, what is it, Sheriff?"

"We got trouble down at the paper!" Watson shouted. "Can you hear me, Mike? The wind is kicking up and messing with my signal."

"What . . ."

"You'd better come down here." The sheriff's voice crackled unevenly.

"I hear you. I'm on my way."

The cell went dead.

Mike shoved his foot into his shoe and lifted the other phone. He listened. No more slow breathing.

"Malone?" he whispered.

"I'm going too."

"No."

"I'm already dressed."

He knew that arguing with her would be a waste of breath. "Well, if you're coming, you might as well pick me up on your way."

She didn't answer.

He grabbed his coat and headed downstairs. With Morgan and May both gone for the weekend he didn't worry about making too much noise. He had a feeling Pepper wouldn't wait for him if he wasn't on the corner. Pausing, he took the time to lock the door, then shoved both his keys and his cell into his pocket and ran.

While he waited in the dark, he wished he'd asked the sheriff what kind of trouble. A tiny part of him wished the place would burn to the ground. He was tired of the day-to-day worries of running a paper. But most of him knew he loved the *Bugle*. It wasn't being the editor he cared about or the money the paper made, or even the building, but he loved what it meant to the people. He could never wish that away from them.

A Ford half a mile away turned onto Clifton and drove toward him at full speed. He swore Pepper didn't hit the brakes until she saw the whites of his eyes.

"Where'd you learn to drive, Malone?" he shouted as he climbed in.

She hit the gas. They shot down the street toward Main and the red blinking lights of the sheriff's car. Mike felt like he was in a 3-D movie with the police car flying toward him.

Amazingly, she managed to stop a foot before she hit the sheriff's car.

He climbed out thinking he'd walk home, but he wasn't too sure that would be safe with her on the road. Running, he caught up with her about the time she reached the sheriff and another man standing in the middle of the street.

"What's happened?" she asked before he could say anything.

The sheriff looked at both of them and grinned as if he'd just figured out a big secret where they were concerned.

Mike considered telling Watson that this time his instincts were wrong, but he had other problems. He waited for the old man to explain the trouble he'd called about.

"It's not as bad as we thought, Mike. Two windows were shot out, a third has a bullet hole in it, but the glass looks like it's holding. We're checking it out now. Give us a minute."

The lawman and his silent sidekick moved down the street a few feet until the sheriff noticed Mike and Pepper following. He stepped in front of them and held his hands up as if he could stop either one of them. "We'd like you folks to wait in the bakery with Lorie and Bob Earl until we check out the alley."

"Who's the *we*?" Mike looked at the stranger beside Watson.

The sheriff didn't give the man time to talk. "He's an FBI agent who just happened to be visiting me tonight." Watson glanced at the man. "You *are* armed, Heath? I'm not sure this kind of trouble will want to chat."

"I'm armed. If we're going to find any clues as to who did this, we need to get moving."

Watson nodded.

The agent frowned at Mike. "Tell everyone in the bakery to stay away from the windows until we report in."

Mike felt like telling the outsider to back off. This was his town, his paper, his friends. But now was not the time to argue, and this agent had a hardness about him that gave the impression he was looking for a fight.

"When you finish searching for who did this, I'm going into the *Bugle*." Mike met Heath's glare.

The agent nodded once and headed down the street to catch up to Watson.

The sheriff yelled back, "We'll come get you to open up as soon as we're sure the shooter isn't hanging around."

Mike and Pepper hurried toward the bakery. Within twenty feet he could see the front of the *Bugle* clearly. The huge window of his office had shattered, along with the main window where the words *Bailee Bugle* had been painted for all his lifetime.

Pepper took his hand. "We'll board it up," she said. "We can't leave it that way in this wind."

He closed his hand around her icy fingers. He couldn't stop staring. A hundred years of McCulloch blood boiled in his veins. Someone out in the night was trying to destroy the *Bugle*, and Mike knew he had to stop them.

Pepper pulled him into the bakery. When he bumped against her side, he realized he'd been holding her hand with his right hand.

He tried to pull away, but she wouldn't let go for a moment. He met her stare and could almost hear her saying, *The scars don't matter.*

He knew they did, of course. He'd seen men turn away when he offered his hand, as if the twisted skin might pass something contagious in a touch. Yet Pepper held tight.

"Mike!" Lorie shouted as she ran to him.

Pepper stepped aside, letting the baker hug him.

"Oh, Mike." Lorie looked like she'd been crying. "I can't believe someone did this. They shot out your window. The window you sit behind all day long."

Mike felt a bit of the anger melt away. "We'll find out who did this, don't worry." He moved farther into the bakery, away from the windows.

Bob Earl was sitting on one of the stools at the counter. Mike put his hand on the boy's shoulder. "It's all right, Bob Earl. We'll get new windows."

The boy nodded over and over. "I'll clean it up for you. Nobody should break the glass. I'll clean it up."

Mike and Lorie had noticed years ago that Bob Earl needed order in his life. He liked doing the same thing every week. He wanted to get up just after dawn and eat the same thing at breakfast every morning. He went to bed at dark, always at dark. Mike had the feeling the break in his routine was far more upsetting than the broken windows.

"Not tonight, Bob Earl. We'll clean it up in the morning," Mike said. "But thanks for the offer. I'm going to need your help putting a few boards over the space tonight."

Bob Earl smiled. "You got it, Chief."

Mike frowned at Pepper, but she only smiled.

Like a true reporter, she pulled out her notepad and began asking questions.

Lorie had heard the shots, three or four, and ran to her window. No, she didn't see a car, but she did hear someone scream. It sounded like it came from down near the movie theater. The glass held for a few seconds, then crumbled like melting icicles.

Bob Earl told pretty much the same story. He'd been standing closer to the windows, but he said it was too dark to see much. He thought he saw a car traveling fast down the street, but he couldn't be sure whether it happened just before or after the shots.

Lorie announced she had coffee ready.

They'd just settled around a table when the sheriff and the FBI agent came in.

Mike watched the hard agent. He did not look happy, but Watson appeared relieved.

"Well," the sheriff said, "we've searched all we can tonight and we think the shooter fired, not from a car, but from down by the used bookstore. He must have shot the windows out and then darted back to the alley. From there he could go any direction without anyone noticing him."

"Can I go over and see what damage was done?"

"I don't see any problem with you just looking."

Mike expected the agent to argue, but when he glanced at the man, the agent was staring at Lorie as she handed him a cup of coffee.

After they had all downed enough coffee to keep them warm, Bob Earl helped the sheriff unload boards while Mike and Heath hammered them up where the windows had been.

If Mike thought Pepper would stay warm inside with Lorie, he was mistaken. She stood out halfway in the deserted street, giving orders on how to do the job as if she'd worked construction all her life.

Mike thought of trying to make conversation with the agent, but he saw little point. The man would be gone tomorrow and they had nothing in common.

The paper with its back door barricaded and windows boarded up in front was starting to look like an abandoned building. Mike turned off the lights and checked the locks. He'd thought of going home for a sleeping bag, but he saw little point. No one was likely to pry the boards off tonight.

Toad promised to drive by twice as often as usual, but if he hadn't stopped the shooting, he probably wouldn't be able to stop the next wave of damage either.

The group stood around looking at the work they'd done, then slowly, without a word of good-bye, they went their separate ways.

The sheriff got into his car and turned off the blinking lights. Bob Earl walked into the bakery already so tired he looked half-asleep. Mike climbed into Pepper's car and braced himself for the ride home.

He didn't realize that he hadn't seen the agent go anywhere until they were almost to his house. The man seemed to disappear into the nowhere he came from. *Odd fellow*, Mike thought. The only time he'd looked human was when Lorie handed him coffee.

Pepper swung into his driveway like it was a pit stop at Indy.

"How'd you know this was my house?"

She smiled. "I'm a reporter, remember? I'm paid to know things."

He was too exhausted to argue. "Right."

When he didn't climb out, she asked, "What are you doing tomorrow?"

"Besides ordering new windows," he offered.

"Besides that."

"Nothing." Morgan wouldn't be back until Sunday. He didn't want to tell Pepper he usually spent his Saturdays reading and watching TV.

She smiled. "Want to go with me to a funeral?"

"Why not?" he answered.

Chapter 22

Heath Fuller walked the alleys one more time, moving slowly over every inch of ground. He'd found the shells from the first three shots in one place, but Lorie had said she heard "three or four" shots. It was his experience that when a witness said two numbers, the larger one was usually more accurate.

His movements were slow, soundless as the breeze. A clue could be as small as a gum wrapper, but the alley was layered in darkness, making it impossible to see beyond the thin beam of his flashlight. He had to keep the light low. If there was someone else in his path, he wanted to be the first to know.

Walking behind the bakery, he saw Bob Earl's light in the far corner window go out. The guy had had a rough night. Bob Earl wasn't the kind of person who dreamed or planned. He just sliced off one day at a time and lived it.

Heath circled. The bakery lights were off and Lorie's apartment was dark. He'd been watching; they hadn't come on since the sheriff and her friends left. Maybe she'd gone somewhere. Or maybe she'd been so tired that she'd just walked into her place and crawled into bed.

No. He smiled. Lorie was a creature of habit. She had this cute little routine she did at night. He used to call it "building her nest." Everything had to be in order: the clock set, fresh water on the night stand, robe at the bottom of the bed, night light in the bathroom shining.

Lorie wouldn't have left her place, either. Not this time of night. Not after what had happened.

He moved in the shadows until he reached the blackness under the stairs leading to her apartment. There he stood, listening.

"I know you're there." Her voice startled him. "You might as well come out."

Heath frowned and stepped around so she could at least make out his shadow. "How'd you know?"

"A feeling." Huddled in a blanket, she was sitting a few steps down from the landing.

"Mind if I join you?" He swung around the railing and sat on the fourth step. Close, but not so close he could touch her.

"It's cold," she said.

"Then why are you out here?"

"Waiting for you. I knew you were still around." She snuggled deeper into the blanket. "I wanted to know what you thought about all this. Knowing you, you've already got a profile of the shooter in your mind."

He climbed up a few steps and sat next to her feet. "I don't want to frighten you, Lorie, but I think you may be right about this being big trouble. Tonight wasn't a random shooting or some wild kids playing around. Those shots were meant for the newspaper office. The way they were aimed, I'd say someone hates the *Bugle* enough to destroy it and McCulloch as well."

She moved her blanket-wrapped feet to his lap. "I was afraid of that."

Heath laid his hand lightly over the blanket. He could feel her cold toes even through the wool. "Do you know anyone in town who might want Mike McCulloch dead?"

"No. People think he's a little aloof, but they see him as part of this town. I've never heard anyone say a bad thing about him."

"What about the paper?"

She laughed. "Everyone complains about the paper. Too many ads, not enough cartoons, too much about one story, not enough about another. The usual stuff. Folks also complain about the weather and the price of gas, but no one is shooting at the gas station."

"Good point." He could feel her toes warming beneath the blanket. He thought of telling her to wear socks, but the other hundred times he'd mentioned it hadn't worked. Plus, she'd only get mad about him lecturing her. He hadn't been aware he'd done that until she mentioned it the other night.

For a while, they just watched the night. Toad's patrol car circled Main slowly. A dog barked down at the far end of the street. Other than that, the place could have been a ghost town.

"Do you think we could reach a point where we could talk?" He finally whispered his thought. "Where I could be in the same room with you without your hand shaking?" He'd thought she would spill coffee on him earlier. "Maybe we can never be even friends, but I'd like it if you could learn not to hate me so much."

"I don't hate you." Her voice was dull, as if hating would have been too much effort after all these years.

He leaned back and rested his head on the railing. "I guess that's a start. I thought you did." She'd never said so, but she had a right to. He'd walked out of the hospital because he couldn't stand the sorrow in her eyes. He'd walked out, leaving her to deal with their stillborn child. She could never hate him as much as he hated himself.

"Heath, this isn't about us. It's about my friends. I'll tell you anything I can, but I need your promise that you'll be honest with me."

He closed his eyes. They were back to business. "All right. We'll start with the facts. Three shots or four? Think carefully, Lorie."

"Four. One pop that I thought might be a car backfiring and ten, maybe fifteen seconds later three together."

He patted her leg. "That'll help."

She leaned forward. "What do you think it means?"

Heath shrugged. "It could mean that he was nervous, not used to the gun. Maybe he fired the first round by accident. Or it could have been a signal. If that's the case, we're looking for two troublemakers. Or . . ."

"Or what?" she whispered.

"Or something got in his way just before he was ready to shoot the windows."

Chapter 23

Saturday, March 29, 2008
1:45 A.M.

I woke from a sound sleep and for a moment could not cata-logue the ringing sound in my mind. In my dream I'd been running to class, late as usual, and the bell kept sounding.

The phone. I fought my way out of my covers, tumbling off the couch in my hurry, and tossed Herbert halfway across the trailer because he'd been sleeping on top of my blanket.

Note to self: Give it up and sleep in Wilma's bed. The couch was a danger to my health, not to mention Herbert's.

I grabbed the princess phone, promising myself that if it was the breathing caller again I'd personally hunt him down and strangle him with the phone cord.

"Hello!" I yelled with Herbert still swearing at me in cat language from across the room.

"Pepper." Lorie sounded upset. "Can you do me a favor?"

"Now? What time is it?"

"Yes, please, and it's almost two." Her voice shook a little.

"Name it," I said, scrambling for my tennis shoes and feeling guilty for yelling at her. If she needed me, I'd be on my way.

"Heath found a wounded dog, and the town only has a vet who visits once a week. Could you—"

"Who's Heath?" I thumped my brain, trying to wake up. The Elvis clock on the wall wouldn't come into focus. All I could see were the legs swinging. I couldn't have been asleep long.

"Heath is the FBI agent," Lorie explained. "He thinks the guy who shot out the windows shot a dog."

I was still lost to my part in this picture. "What can I do?"

"Could you go get Wilma? I've already called her, and she said she'd meet you at the front door of the Shades in ten minutes. She's the only person I can think of who might know how to dig a bullet out. If I called one of the doctors they'd just tell me to put the pup to sleep. It's just a stray dog, but I can't . . ."

I could hear her crying.

"I'm on my way."

As I started the car, I hit speed dial on my cell and called Michael. I could have gone after Wilma alone, but I told him I needed help. I'm not sure why, but we were like Batman and Robin. Besides, if I was going to lose sleep, he might as well join me.

He didn't sound like he'd been asleep when he answered. I explained the mission, and all he said was, "I'll be waiting on the corner."

When I picked him up, he circled around to the driver's side and said, "Scoot over."

"I can drive," I mumbled as I moved.

"So can I, and there's a good chance I will get us there alive. Which is more than I can say after sampling your skills."

I thought of letting him have it, but I had asked for his help and he was losing sleep because of me and, knowing him, he'd get out of the car if he couldn't drive.

I settled for calling him a bully and trying to get my hair tied back in some kind of order before we reached the nursing home.

He drove toward the Shades. "Did you call your aunt and tell her she's about to be kidnapped?"

"Lorie did, but I'm not sure the staff will let her leave. A nursing home isn't like a hotel you can check in and out of at any time."

He grinned. "Let Wilma worry about that."

When we pulled up to the front door, Wilma and some guy in a wheelchair were waiting outside. She had on a ski jacket over her pink robe, and he was dressed in a long black coat, slippers, and a Fedora. I'd seen people dressed less conspicuously at the *Rocky Horror Picture Show* when I was a kid.

I walked up to them. "How'd you get past the nurses' station?"

"Don't ask," the old man said. "When you're in the slammer, all you got is time to think about how to get out."

I looked at him wondering whether he was an ex-con or just watched far too many of those prison life shows. "Well, thanks for breaking her out."

Wilma pulled to her feet and headed her walker toward the Ford. "He's going with us, Pep," she said without looking at me. "Grab that bag on the bench, child. There's no telling what I'll need and it's got a little of everything in it."

I picked up the bag. "He can't go—"

"Yes he can," she answered. "We've no time to argue. Give Mr. Gray a push."

Michael stood five feet away holding the door open for Wilma and grinning as if loving every minute of our pickup.

My old aunt looked back at me when she reached the door and handed over her walker to Michael. "It's the only way he'd help me escape; besides, Phil was an undertaker for fifty years. He'll know how to sew up the patient faster than me. He's had lots of practice and not one complaint."

Phil rolled out to the car. "I can stand and walk a few feet." He nodded at Mike. "Just put the chair in the back, Mikey. I'll let you know if I need it."

When I met Michael's glance, I had to smile. His blue eyes were dancing. He probably hadn't had so much fun in years. We settled the fugitives in the car and were at Lorie's bakery within minutes. Michael pulled the Ford all the way down the drive to where light shone at her back door, and then he started unloading.

We found the agent and Lorie in a small laundry room with the dog lying on a blanket on top of the washer and dryer.

Lorie introduced Heath to everyone. If possible, he seemed even less friendly than he had earlier.

Heath's big hand was holding a compress over the dog's shoulder, but blood was everywhere on the animal. I didn't see how he had enough to still be alive.

I just stood there and stared. I hated blood. The sight of it, the smell of it, the feel of it.

It was no surprise to me when Aunt Wilma took over. "Pepper, get Lorie out of here. She looks white as a ghost and you could be her twin. And you, young man"—she pointed her thumb at the agent—"can you stand the sight of blood?"

The agent nodded.

"Don't let him fool you," Lorie said from the doorway to the bakery. "He can't stand his own blood."

I pulled Lorie along, wondering how she'd known that about the agent. It didn't sound like something you'd tell a woman serving you doughnuts and coffee in the morning.

Wilma set her bag on the sink behind her and began rummaging for supplies. "Well, let me know if you're going to faint." She pointed a finger at Heath. "Because somebody your size will make a mighty big speed bump to have to step over. Otherwise, you stay and hold this dog. I don't want the patient biting me halfway through the operation."

She and Mr. Gray tugged off their coats and shuffled closer to Heath.

"Mikey, go get some clean, but old towels. I'll need soap and hot water."

Mike moved around her. "Don't I need to boil it?"

"No." She shoved her walker out of the way and braced one hand on the washer. Phil moved in slowly and did the same. They both put on plastic gloves. I wouldn't have been surprised if they'd reached for masks as well.

Wilma's hand rose holding a needle. As she lowered it, she whispered in a voice steady with caring, "This is only going to hurt a little, and then you won't feel a thing."

I glanced at the others and hoped this operation didn't take long or we'd have way too many speed bumps in the laundry room.

Heath slowly removed the compress.

"Let's get to work, Phil."

"I'm right beside you," he answered. "I say we do this fast and clean."

I stood at the door watching with Mike. Over my shoulder I could hear Lorie making coffee. She'd stopped crying when she'd found something to do.

The agent named Heath sat on the dryer and pulled the dog across his leg. The animal was a mutt, no breed, black with a brown spot right above his nose. He wasn't big, either, just thin and dirty like most half-wild dogs that run the alleys.

"Where'd you find him?" Mike asked Heath as the two senior citizens worked.

"About halfway between the back of the bookstore and here," he answered. "I'm guessing he saw the guy with the gun enter that long space between the used bookstore and that junky antiques shop. The shooter might have surprised the dog sleeping there. It would seem like a good place for an animal to bed down for the night. He shot the dog, then ran to the front of the space, where he had a good view of the windows. The time between shots couldn't have been more than a matter of seconds."

"Why kill the dog?" I asked.

"Because he didn't want the barking to attract attention." Heath's hand moved slowly over the fur. "I found him at the edge of the alley crawling in the weeds toward the bakery. Lorie says she gives him scraps. I guess he figured her place might be safe."

"Got it!" Wilma shouted.

When Heath held out his hand, she dropped the bloody bullet into his palm.

"Evidence," Phil announced. "Now, let's sew this puppy up."

Mike relaxed against the doorjamb, bumping his hip into mine.

When I didn't look up at him, he braced his hand on

my side of the doorway and asked, "Still mad at me about driving?"

I was about to say no, but before I spoke, I looked up at him and saw the laughter in his eyes. "Yes," I lied.

He didn't seem to mind. He moved his hand slowly between my hair and my neck and began to knead the tight muscles.

I jabbed him in the ribs. "Keep to your side of the doorway," I whispered.

"Or what?" he asked.

"Or I'll flatten you on the playground, Mikey."

He shrugged as though it might be worth a try, but before he could pester me any more, Phil asked for his wheelchair.

By the time Michael brought it in, the dog had been stitched up.

We all moved to the kitchen table usually covered with pies and cookies. Lorie served us coffee and banana bread. I was amazed how good it tasted at two thirty in the morning. It was almost worth waking up in the middle of the night to eat.

Wilma said she'd never doctored a dog, but if she were guessing, she'd say the animal had a good chance of making it. The bullet went into the muscle of his leg and struck a bone but didn't break it.

The agent stayed with the animal, but I had a feeling he heard every word we said in the kitchen.

Michael suggested letting the sheriff know, but all agreed that it could wait until morning. Watson had suffered a few rough days working late. He was probably already in bed and Toad was parked somewhere asleep.

Before we left, Wilma and Phil insisted on buying a box of cookies to serve as proof of their adventure. They talked all the way home. When I walked Aunt Wilma to the door, she hugged me. And I hugged her back.

"It's good to have family in town again," she whispered.

Until that moment I hadn't thought about her as family.

Chapter 24

The bakery
2:45 A.M.

Heath moved the dog to a pallet on the floor. He sat next to the mutt and patted him gently, not knowing if he was sleeping off the drugs the old nurse had given him or dying.

Lack of sleep settled over Heath. Leaning his head against the side of the washer, he fell sound asleep to the sound of Lorie cleaning up in the next room. In his dreams he was back in a world that seemed a million years ago. A time when they were still married. A time before he'd shattered their life all to hell.

He couldn't remember back before they were married. He'd walked in on a friend's birthday party one afternoon a dozen years ago. She'd brought the cake and had stayed to serve it. When he'd taken a slice, she'd looked up at him and he swore he felt married from that moment on. She had eyes that could look at him with just a smile or a twinkle in them and change his day. He lived for the sight of her, and he'd died when he'd seen sorrow he couldn't take away.

He didn't know how long he slept, but he awoke to the gentle touch of her fingers on his cheek.

"Heath," she whispered. "Wake up."

For a moment he didn't open his eyes because he knew when he did, she'd have moved away. He wanted one long breath of the smell of her near.

"Heath, it's nearly three. If you're going to drive back to Dallas, you'd better get started."

He looked up at her, letting the shock of her so close wash over him. "I'm not going home. I need to talk to the sheriff first thing tomorrow morning." *Besides*, he almost added, *no place is home without you.*

"Where are you going to sleep?"

"In my car." He yawned. "Or here. I was already doing a great job of practicing."

"You can't sleep in my laundry room."

He patted the dog one last time and stood. "I was afraid you'd say that."

She frowned at him. "You're a mess. Blood and mud all over you. Why don't you go up to my place and clean up? I don't suppose you have a change of clothes?"

"Nope."

"Well, strip here and I'll put them in to wash. This time of night no one will see a naked man climb up my stairs. You can sleep on my couch. I'll put your clothes in the dryer when I come down to start the doughnuts. By the time you wake up they'll be dry and waiting for you."

He grinned. "You always invite naked men to sleep over?" he asked as he pulled off his shirt.

"No, but this seems to be my night for taking in strays."

He pulled off his boots and pants. While she loaded the

washer, he stood in his underwear and washed off his boots at the laundry room sink.

When he turned around, she was staring at him.

"You've got a few more scars than you had five years ago."

He wished he could tell her about the ones inside. The deep cuts that would never heal. But he'd always hidden most of what he did from her, and that couldn't change now. "A few," he managed with a shrug, as if they weren't important.

She locked the back door and they walked around to the stairs. It was late and the whole town seemed asleep.

He stood just inside the door of her place while she turned on the lights. The apartment felt like her, smelled like her, looked like her. She'd always planted way too many pots in the house, always cluttered every shelf up with funny little knickknacks.

"The bathroom is that way." She pointed to the first of two doors off the small living area. "I'll make you some eggs while you shower."

He set his boots by the door and didn't dare say anything. Walking to the bathroom, he noticed a few things that had been in their home. Keepsakes from her grandmother, a quilt her mother made, a table he'd put together.

The bathroom was as cluttered as he'd expected it to be. Not a square inch of free space. The shower head was too short for him, but the water was hot. He took his time washing, then wrapped a towel around himself and stepped out of the steamy bathroom.

She'd set a plate of eggs and a glass of milk on the bar separating the kitchen area from the living room. She was busy cleaning up.

"I don't do much cooking up here. It's easier to eat at the

bakery. You're lucky, I only had eggs, milk, and wine in the fridge."

He realized he hadn't had a drink since she'd first called him. He hadn't even missed it. "This will be great," he said as he sat on the stool. "Your scrambled eggs are better than any meal a fancy restaurant could serve."

She looked over her shoulder and smiled.

He couldn't help wondering if she thought about the same thing he had. Heath wasn't modest when they were married: He'd walk around the house with little or nothing on. He swore Lorie dressed in the closet before she came out. One day, six months after they were married, she showed up to the breakfast table topless. "There." She pointed at his bare chest. "How would you like it if I came to meals without my shirt on?"

He grinned, saying he'd like it just fine. They were both two hours late for work that morning.

Heath ate his eggs, smiling at the memory.

She brought him in a quilt and a pillow. "Anything else you need?"

He finished off the rest of his milk so he didn't accidentally say something that would make her mad enough to kick him out. He wiped the corner of his mouth with the back of his hand and said, "No, thank you. I'll be fine."

She nodded as if not knowing what else to say and walked away.

An hour went by before he even bothered to try to sleep. His Lorie was only one door away.

When he awoke a little after dawn, his clothes were on the chair by the door with a note on top. It read simply, *Lock the door when you leave.*

Heath dressed and walked barefoot out on the balcony. The morning was cool and crisp but promised to be warmer than the past few days. Through the ivy leaves, he could see the newspaper directly across the street.

A plan crossed his mind. He shoved the note into his pocket and smiled. He'd lock the door, but it might be a while before he left. If she wanted her friends protected, there would be no better vantage point than her balcony.

When he walked into the bakery a few minutes later, Lorie barely glanced at him. She was in the middle of her busiest time.

Heath took a seat between the sheriff and Toad. After he'd downed half a cup of coffee, he filled Watson in on finding the dog.

When Lorie brought the lawmen their breakfast, Watson asked her as he poured ketchup over everything, "How's the mutt?"

Lorie glanced at Heath a second before she answered. "He licked up a little sweet milk an hour ago and went back to sleep."

Watson nodded. "Good, but not much of a witness. You want me to take him to the pound?"

"No," Lorie said quickly. "I think I'll keep him here."

"Not a bad idea. When he gets well, he might be a fair watchdog."

"That's what I was thinking."

Heath followed her to the back to check on the dog. The animal licked his hand but didn't try to get up.

"Thanks for letting me stay the night," Heath whispered as he knelt close to Lorie. "And thanks for washing my clothes."

She didn't look up at him as she adjusted the bandage around the dog. "To tell you the truth, I slept better than I have in a long time. I guess I felt safe knowing you were near."

He wanted to tell her about his plan, but now, with all

the racket from the bakery, didn't seem the time. He stood and offered his hand to help her up.

She didn't take it.

"I'll see you before I leave town."

"All right." She looked nervous. "You know where I'll be."

Chapter 25

Bailee, Texas
Population 15,007
Sunday, March 30, 2008

I followed Michael into the funeral home. Just beyond the lobby and the viewing rooms were the wide double doors of the chapel. Decorated with ceramic angels, the entrance reminded me of a crafter's idea of the Pearly Gates.

After reading about Raymond Hale in the old editions of the *Bugle*, I'd expected the place to be full. The old man who died had owned the grocery store that had taken the scrip teachers earned when the school ran out of money during the Depression. The school system gave out the promissory notes hoping they'd be able to buy them back sometime in the future. Many places in town accepted them, some at ten cents on the dollar.

But not Mr. Raymond Allen Hale. He took the scrip at full value from every teacher in the area. He'd saved a great many families from hunger and probably saved the schools, because even dedicated teachers couldn't afford to work for free.

I looked around as I signed the top of the guest page. There was no one to mourn a man who'd risked his business to do what he thought was right.

Two men, talking quietly, walked in and sat on the front row next to a plain pine coffin. I would guess them in their late fifties or early sixties and definitely from out of town. If I guessed their paper of choice, I'd say both would be *Wall Street Journal* readers.

A middle-aged woman sat by the organ thumbing through a pile of music sheets.

Michael and I walked to the third row and took a seat as the woman got up, walked to the organ, and began to play.

A young preacher stepped up and read from the Bible, then gave a prayer for peace in the world. His eulogy must have been one he'd learned in seminary. It sounded like a generic service where every now and then he filled in the deceased's name.

I found it interesting that the preacher always referred to him as Raymond Allen. I guess when you're born and when you die, there's some unwritten rule that everyone has to say both your names.

I looked at the printed program I'm sure was run off in the back somewhere. Raymond Allen Hale died a week before his ninety-eighth birthday. He'd been twenty when the Depression started. He couldn't have been much older when the schools ran out of money. A young man, a small store, fighting a battle no one remembered.

He was survived by two sons, six grandchildren, and eleven great-grandchildren.

I looked at the two men in front of us. They had to be his

sons. They both wore well-tailored black suits and looked as though they were comfortable in them.

When the music finally stopped, we stood to leave. Michael shook hands with both men. I had the feeling they didn't know who he was, so they must have moved away years ago.

I offered my hand. "Your father was a brave and great man."

Neither of them looked like they understood.

"He was just a grocer," one finally said. "He was a good father, managed to get us both through college, but he never did anything great, miss."

"Oh, but you are wrong." I ignored Michael tugging on my arm. I told them every detail from the article I'd read in the old papers. "Think of all the families who had food on the table because of him. And the children who had teachers because they didn't have to quit and look for jobs somewhere else. The schools didn't finish paying him back until the fifties, and even when they did, he wouldn't take a dime of interest."

I saw the surprise in their eyes. Both men thanked me.

"Your father was a great man," I repeated. "Who knows what this town would have been like today if he hadn't done what he did?"

One commented, "We were leaving after the service to get back to Austin tonight, but if you'd show us that paper we might stay."

The other nodded. "I think we need to make copies of that piece. I'd like my children to see it."

I said good-bye and followed Michael out. "I don't understand it. How could they not know? How come no one came to the funeral? The man had lots of grandkids and great-grandkids. That's a lot of families. Why didn't they come? Maybe he outlived all of his friends, but surely someone remembered him."

Michael linked my arm with his, and we walked over to where the funeral home had a nice little headstone garden arranged. "Look," he said when we stopped. "I've been to lots of these. Raymond Hale was in his late thirties before he had those two boys. Their children only knew him as an old man. They probably only saw him once a year, if that much. As for the great-grandkids, he's been in a nursing home all their lives."

I frowned at him. "You're trying to cheer me up, right?"

He pushed a few strands of my hair back over my shoulder. "I guess I'm not doing a very good job of it. It's just that Bailee is an old town. Most of the young people who leave for college never come back. They find jobs or marry someone from another place. They come home to see their folks for Christmas until they start families, and then it's a few days every other summer. By the time of the funeral, other commitments hold them to where they live."

He sat down beside me. "Tell me the truth: If Wilma had died and not just broken her hip, would you have come? You've got to be her closest relative: You'll inherit the manor."

"You're right. I probably wouldn't have been able to get away if someone had notified me of her passing." I made a face. "And some manor I'm up for. But you're wrong about one thing. Not everyone moves away. You didn't."

He looked at his hands. "I tried. I even thought I had at one point."

"But your brother died and there was no one to take over the paper."

He looked up, but the smile didn't reach his eyes. "Some people inherit the castle, some get the dragon."

"You could have sold it and gone back to teaching. You could have made a life wherever you wanted."

He shook his head. "I had a responsibility. I had Morgan."

I understood how he felt, but I didn't agree with what he'd done. If it had been me, I would have sold the paper and moved wherever I wanted to. Morgan would have come with me.

"Plus, the paper's made you rich."

"Of course." He raised an eyebrow as if trying to decide on something. Finally, he said, "I don't have to pick up Morgan this afternoon. May said she'd swing by and get her on her way home. So would you like to see something really different? I know a place if you're up for a hike."

"Something I haven't seen in Chicago?"

"I promise."

"All right." What else did I have to do? My other roads were bingo and cleaning the metal manor house.

We drove by his place so he could change. I was surprised when he invited me in. I wandered through the downstairs rooms looking at framed front-page covers while he changed into jeans. The house was huge and somehow sad, if houses can be sad. There were pictures of Mike and a young man who looked so much like him he had to be Mike's brother. They sat on either side of a mantel with a long space in between. No later photos. It was almost like both men's lives stopped.

In his office, I found a wall next to his desk covered with snapshots of Morgan. All ages, all seasons. The last one must have been taken a few months ago. She was smiling with her silver smile.

I noticed the leather book he always seemed to be writing in. It was open to a page that read simply:

*Journal Entry: I believe that love doesn't come
softly on the words of a song, but clicks across hardwood floors.*

I frowned. If he was writing lyrics, they were the worst
I'd ever heard.

I continued my tour, making it almost to the kitchen
when I saw him standing in the doorway watching me.

"Interesting," I said, noticing he carried a backpack.
"We're taking food."

He pulled the pack out of my reach. "Not until we get
there."

When he turned to lead me out the back door, I realized I'd finally seen clothing he looked good in. Jeans.
McCulloch looked great in old worn jeans.

Within minutes he stood in Wilma's tiny place while I
changed. I had no idea what he was doing, but I hoped he
wasn't as nosy as I'd been at his house.

When I walked out of the bathroom, he was looking at
the Elvis clock with the swinging legs as if it were a work
of art.

"Interesting." He echoed my words about his place.

"Fascinating really," I said. "If you stay around here
long enough you start talking to the King."

He turned and looked at me from my ponytail pulled
through my cap to my tennis shoes. "You look like a kid.
Are you sure you're legal?"

"You said a hike. Heels and suits wouldn't be right." I
winked. "I'm afraid you'll just have to trust me; I'm old
enough."

He held the door open. I followed him to the Jeep, feeling more relaxed than I had in weeks. We took the time to
take the top off and roll down the windows. It was a day

made to drive. I leaned back in my seat and enjoyed the view as we drove into the country. I could feel spring in the air. The winter gray of the land had its own beauty, but the view was gently changing. A few weeks ago it reminded me of line drawings done in bold black ink on cream paper; now color seeped through in soft shades of lime green and pale yellows.

The quartz hills grew closer, a cluster of rock jutting from the earth with only touches of scrub grass to soften the sharp edges. Farmers had cleared the land to the foot of the hills, making one edge of the field wiggly and uneven in sharp contrast to the other three sides.

"On the other side of the rocks is a great lake that a creek spills into. It's called Twisted Creek. I haven't been over lately, but last I heard it's becoming an artist community. Several big names from Austin and Dallas are buying lodges there to use as retreats. They're planning a showing in July."

"I'd like to see it."

He glanced at me and smiled, as if I'd just made a promise to stay. I knew the troubles with the paper were still in the back of our thoughts, but he seemed to want to escape, if only for an hour, as much as I did.

A few miles out of town, Michael turned onto a dirt road and kicked up the speed. We left a cloud of dust flying behind us.

I braced my feet on the dash and laughed.

He looked at me and smiled. "You like speed."

I nodded. "I guess I like life coming at me hard and fast. It's the only way to take it . . . big bites."

Another mile down the road we came to an old abandoned house that looked like it was made of mud and dug into the ground. Several old barns in different states of neglect circled around it.

Michael drove past the settlement and pulled to a stop at the base of the hill, where the weeds were as tall as the Jeep. I saw the road end and an overgrown path begin. If I hadn't been searching, I would have missed the trail between broken-down elms.

He grabbed the day pack from the back and said, "Ready, Malone? Let's see if those long legs of yours can keep up."

I figured now was not the time to tell him that I'd never hiked before, unless you count a few parks in the city. For me, roughing it had always been staying somewhere without a pool.

I matched his pace determined not to complain. The path zigzagged around tall pine trees and thorny little half-tree/half-bushes not much taller than me.

He seemed to think of himself as a guide. "This was probably an animal trail through the hills at one time. Then an Indian trail from one water source to another. Sometime around 1850 it became a crossing point for hunters. Horses could make it through here fine, but once wagons came along they had to go around. My great-grandfather bought that old dugout from a man who said it had been a trading post for a while before the town was settled."

I stopped to take a deep breath. "I think I'm more the sit-in-the-wagon kind of settler, and that little place could never hold enough to satisfy my shopping list." I took one more step. "How many people died out here trying to get from one watering hole to another?"

He laughed and took my hand. "It's not much farther. When I was a kid my mother used to bring me out here. Nobody lived down in that old dugout. I think my grandmother may have been born in it. My mom would come out here to pick wild plums and I'd roam these hills. After she died, Dave and I rode our bikes out here and pretended we were Lewis and Clark."

I kept up with his pace. If he noticed my left hand was in his right, he didn't comment. We'd gotten past the scars needing to be hidden. I had a feeling that was a rare thing for him.

He motioned me off the path onto a rocky trail that looked like it belonged to rabbits. "I found this spot one day and I've been coming here ever since."

"Do your mother's relatives still own the land?" I asked, more to slow him down than because I cared.

"They're all dead. I own it now, but I lease out the land to the farmer next door. Everyone calls it McGregor's place. He's farmed it for so long I'm guessing few in town even know my name's on the deed. I think he keeps some of his farm equipment and hunting supplies in the barns. The house probably belongs more to the snakes and skunks than anyone now."

He stepped up on a rock and offered his hand. "Come see my world, Malone."

When he pulled me up, I lost my breath at the view before me.

We stood on a ledge halfway up one of the hills, and before us I could see the whole valley. Bailee sat in the center of surrounding farms with roads coming from it like spider legs.

"It's beautiful," I whispered. The view could have been a painting, bigger than life.

"I always thought so. Down there I see all the problems, all the things that need fixing, but up here it looks so perfect. They say the first settlers heading north passed this land by. I kind of believe that one must have stepped out on this ledge and seen the valley and decided here is where he wanted to plant his life."

We sat on a rock a few feet from the edge and he pulled two bottles of Coors from his backpack. "If I'd had any brains I would have brought champagne and glasses. We could celebrate your first real look at Bailee."

I took the beer. "This is fine. Any chance you brought food?"

He laughed and pulled chips from the pack. "I couldn't forget. Feeding Malone could turn into a full-time job."

I ate a few chips and then offered to share. He shook his head and leaned back against the rock. The day was crisp and clear. A perfect day to view the world.

After I finished eating, I picked up a few rocks and tossed them off the cliff. "How far down do you think it is?"

"A few hundred feet, I guess," he said. "When my brother and I were kids, we used to call this ledge Lookout Point. We'd make up stories about how Indians could see a hundred miles from this spot."

"You still miss your brother?"

He shook his head. "Even though we were only a year apart, it always seemed like more. By the time we were in our teens we were no longer close. He was the popular one. I was the bookworm. He played football. I played chess. Once we were in college we'd try to go out together when we were both home, but it never worked. Dave always traveled with a pack. I never remember him ever being alone or going out with just me."

I could see his mood darkening so I asked, "How many dates have you brought up here?"

"None," he said with his hand raised as if swearing on a Bible. "You're the first."

"Oh, are we on a date?"

He looked like he was thinking about it, and then he nodded. "I think so. Though a funeral and a hike does seem a little strange."

I hugged my knees to my chin. "I got to be honest,

Michael, I'm lousy as a date. The last guy I went out with hates my guts, and I think his family probably wants to kill me."

Michael laughed. "You're kidding. You've got your problems, but surely the date wasn't that bad."

"I wish I were kidding."

He stared out at the town and asked, "You don't think this guy followed you from Chicago, do you?"

I saw his logic. "He could have. With all the things that are happening, several seemed to be targeted at me. I doubt it, but it's a possibility."

We were silent for a few minutes. He leaned back on the rock and finally said, "The last girl I went out with told me she'd rather die of leeches draining her blood than live in Bailee. We'd been together more than a year before I came home. Six months later when I went back to ask her to come here with me, she almost slammed the door in my face."

"I can see her point. When I drove into this place I thought this might just be the end of the world. When I met Wilma, I worried the town would turn me old and hard like her."

"You don't want to end up like her and Mr. Gray?" he asked. "Forgotten in some small-town nursing home?"

"Yeah, I guess, but the Shades isn't as depressing as I kid about." I'd been thinking about how, despite Wilma's complaining, the place took good care of its people.

Mike smiled. "I think Old Man Gray and your aunt had a great time patching up the dog."

I smiled back at him. "Between the two of them bossing us around Friday night I felt like I was still in grade school."

He winked. "You're not going to believe it, but they used to date."

"Now you *are* kidding." I almost slugged him in the arm, but with my luck he'd roll off the cliff, so I pulled my punch.

"No, really. Everyone in town knows about it. It's one of the legends of Bailee. When World War Two came, he went to fight and she signed up as a nurse. She came home to him, and he came home with a German bride."

"What happened?"

He shook his head. "It's all sixty-year-old gossip."

"But it's about my aunt."

He sat up and crossed his legs at the ankle. "All right, but don't tell Wilma I told you. My dad said that back in forty-five they came home, both twenty-two and healthy. Only Gray brought the wife with him and they set up housekeeping in an apartment above his dad's funeral parlor.

"Wilma got so furious, word is she stormed over to the funeral home and threatened to put Gray in the ground without buying one of his caskets. After the sheriff broke up the fight, they both lived right here and didn't speak to one another for sixty years. Then they end up in the same nursing home." He shrugged. "Judging from the way they were talking last night, I'd say they finally made up."

"I love this town," I said suddenly. "Here you can see the whole picture of life from the birth to the grave."

"I kind of like that about the place too. If you live here long enough you see families grow and change and die out. It's like watching a forest of trees. In the city you're lucky if you get to see a few seasons before a family moves or you relocate across town, where you no longer see anyone from the old neighborhood."

I sat close to him for warmth and we watched the sun dip low in the sky. I remembered something Wilma had told me the first time I asked about Michael. She'd said that like everyone else in this town, he had things he wished he could relive and do over. I didn't feel like I could ask about them. If I asked him one too many questions, he might do the same and I had scars I wasn't willing to show.

He told me about the first time he brought Morgan up here. She'd accidentally fallen in the sagebrush behind us and he panicked, thinking she'd tumbled off the cliff. When he found her giggling because she'd rolled all the way back to the path, she'd said, "Vanished. I vanished."

The sun was warm, the sagebrush just starting to turn a pale green but already smelling: The world seemed so quiet. I stretched out on the rock and watched the sky.

"I can see why you come here."

"I thought you would." He shifted until the back of his head rested on my middle. "With you here, it's perfect. I finally have a pillow."

I thought of shoving him off, but his eyes were closed and for the first time since I'd met him, he didn't look worried. I wondered when the man slept.

For a while we lay there sunning on the warm rocks, and then he rolled over and propped himself on one elbow. His kiss came soft and warm and tasting of the wind. When I didn't move, he raised his head and stared down at me.

Neither of us seemed to want to talk, or needed to.

He spread his hand over my abdomen where his head had rested and lowered his mouth over mine in another long, satisfying kiss. I wanted to touch him, but I had the feeling Michael needed to go slow and enjoy each moment to the fullest.

When I moved to roll closer, he pressed his hand against my middle, gently holding me in place. As I relaxed, his touch turned into a soft stroking along my side. A slow smile widened his mouth before he kissed me again.

When I moaned, he pulled away once more and pressed

his cheek against my ear. "Close your eyes, Pepper. Relax."

I thought of screaming that I'd had entire sexual encounters that took less time than this, but I decided to do as he suggested. I closed my eyes and relaxed as his hand moved lightly over me, molding over my hip, pressing just beneath my breasts, brushing along my arm.

His kiss came again gentle as a dream and I flowed into the warmth of it easily. I didn't open my eyes when he pulled away enough to unbutton the first button of my blouse so he could shove the collar away enough to taste my throat. His body shifted until he was pressed against my side, his arm across me, his breath against my cheek.

I didn't move as his breathing slowed, and I realized he'd fallen asleep. I did the same. My last thought was that this was the first time I could remember sleeping with a man, and it was sexy as hell.

An hour later he woke me with a quick kiss. We ran back down the trail hoping to get to the Jeep before dark. He kept my hand in his firm grip. We hadn't talked much after he kissed me, but something had changed between us. We'd gotten used to the nearness of each other. There would be no more awkward accidental bumping, no jumping back when our bodies brushed.

When we climbed into the Jeep, I said, "Thanks for the afternoon."

He didn't start the engine. "You're welcome. I don't know when I've enjoyed an afternoon more."

"You slept through most of it."

He winked at me without apology. "Yeah, that was great."

I didn't argue. In truth, it had been.

He took my hand in an easy way. "You want to come

over sometime? I'm grilling steaks and Morgan is in charge of the baked potatoes."

"How could I turn down that offer?"

I expected him to kiss me again, but he didn't. Somehow we were becoming friends. He wasn't a man who took relationships lightly. Me, I was more the kind to jump in and worry about how to get out of it in the morning.

When he backed the Jeep out of the brush and swung toward the road, I looked forward and we both saw the flames at the same time.

The dugout and one of the barns were on fire. The flames had just reached the windows of the barn, but smoke made a thin trail up all sides of the dugout roof.

Michael jumped out and tossed me his cell phone. "Call the sheriff and tell them where we are. I'll see what I can do."

It took me several seconds to find Michael's listings and locate Watson, but he picked up on the first ring. I told him where we were and he said he'd get the volunteer fire department headed that way and he'd be there as fast as he could.

"Are you and Mike okay?" he yelled over the line.

"Yes," I said trying to see Michael in the growing darkness.

"Stay where you are, Pepper. Unless the fire gets close to the Jeep, stay right there."

"All right." I hung up.

The fire was wild now, licking its way out through the roof of the barn and shattering the glass windows.

Who was I kidding? I couldn't sit still. I jumped out of the Jeep and ran toward the flames.

As soon as I felt the heat on my face, I slowed and began to circle. Spots on the ground around the barn fire were lit as bright as day while others, a foot away, were black.

"Michael!" I took careful steps, not sure of my footing on the uneven ground.

The barn door buckled and fell open, lighting the area around like a huge bonfire. I could see what looked like bales of hay blazing inside, and the skeletons of farm equipment seemed to wave and dance. I heard a sudden pop like cans of paint exploding, then an explosion that could have been a gas can. The side of the roof crumbled into the fire, cracking as it tumbled.

"Michael!" I stomped at small fires in the weeds.

The dugout fire was burning low like coals in a pit. All I could see beyond a few sparks was a huge pillar of gray smoke billowing into the night sky.

In the distance, blinking lights turned off the main road and headed straight toward me. Three vehicles and a truck.

I stumbled over a board. When I looked down, I saw Michael lying flat on the dirt.

Shoving pieces of wood off him, I rolled him over and heard him moan.

I leaned back and took a deep breath of the warm, smoky air. He was all right.

He sat up slow and easy.

"What happened?"

"I don't know. One of the boards must have flown out and hit you." I fought the urge to hit him for scaring me half to death. Beating up the wounded probably isn't in the Red Cross handbook.

We were still standing in front of the barn when help pulled up. The firefighters moved around us, but the sheriff stopped. "Why didn't you two stay in the Jeep? That's how folks get hurt, being nosy. A fire is an unpredictable demon."

"You're telling me." Michael rubbed the back of his head.

The agent from Friday night stood behind the sheriff. "Pepper." He looked directly at me as if testing to see if he had my name right. "What happened?"

I explained while we walked Michael to the Jeep.

"I'm all right," Mike said, rubbing ashes from his hair. "I just took a hit to the head."

Heath leaned in close and shone a light in Mike's eyes one at a time. Then, as if satisfied he had no brain damage, he clicked off the flashlight and asked, "What did you see?"

"Nothing, just one of the barns burning." Michael shoved the agent out of his face.

"No one walking away? No car leaving? No one inside?" Heath shouted, as if he thought Michael was lying.

"I didn't see anyone."

"How long has that barn been there?" Heath snapped, as if in a hurry to find answers.

"I don't know. Thirty, maybe forty years. The dugout's been there for more than a hundred years, I guess." Michael stared at Heath. "You think someone set this fire."

"It's a possibility. No lightning tonight. No hot machines put up after a day of work. No one around. Who owns the place?"

"I do," Michael said. "But whoever did this couldn't have seen m . . ."

Heath closed Michael's door with an angry slam. "I'll follow you home. We need to get out of this area." He looked at me still standing by the Jeep. "Now!"

I ran like a rabbit to my side and jumped in. I wasn't worried about someone out in the night getting me. Heath looked like he could easily snap me in half and toss me into the fire.

Michael frowned at the man, but didn't argue. "Pepper and I will be at my house if you need us. Call if you find anything."

The agent nodded and slapped the Jeep as if it were a horse and might move faster with a little help.

Michael flew away from the fire.

I braced my feet on the dash and whispered, "I hate that guy."

"He's just doing his job."

"What job? Terrorizing the general public?"

"No." Michael laughed at my anger. "Keeping us alive."

Chapter 26

The bakery
10:00 P.M.

Heath pulled his car into the alley behind the bakery and walked up the back path to the kitchen door. The lights were still on. He knew Lorie would be waiting for him to report in. He'd told her he'd stop by before he left town, so he knew she'd be up. He'd spent the night at her place, then gone back to Dallas to pack what he needed. When he'd headed back to town, he saw the smoke from the highway and had a feeling it would somehow be related to all the other trouble McCulloch was having.

The black dog met him at the door. He barely looked alive, but his tail was wagging. Heath knelt down to pet the animal. "How you doing, boy?" he whispered.

"He's doing great." Lorie's voice came from just inside the door.

She opened the screen and let them both in. "But *you* smell like a campfire."

"Sorry," he said. He'd gone back to the burn site after he'd seen Mike and Pepper to town. McCulloch didn't like or trust him, but Heath didn't care. His job wasn't to make friends.

"I heard the fire truck go by." Lorie led him to her kitchen, where she'd left a plate of sandwiches for him on her work table.

He stopped at the sink in the laundry room to wash up. When he dried his face, he noticed her still waiting. "It was just a barn out on some land McCulloch owns."

"Was anyone there?"

"Mike and Pepper were both there when it happened."

Lorie stormed halfway across the kitchen and stopped with her back to him.

"They're fine," he added, knowing that she was upset. "Don't worry."

When she turned around, he could see tears swimming in her eyes. "Do you think the fire was set? Could it be the same guy who shot out the windows Friday night and slashed Pepper's tires? Is someone trying to hurt them? Oh, God! Is someone trying to kill them?"

Heath had promised not to lie to her, but the truth would hurt. He wished she'd let him hold her when he answered, but he knew she wouldn't. "I think it's the same man who did the shooting. The same one they saw in the alley. I just talked to the sheriff and he said the fire was set, not an accident. One of the men reported that it looked like several small homemade bombs were set with timers. They were so poorly made that the firemen found two that didn't go off in another one of the storage buildings. But as far as who and why, I'll have to wait till morning to find any clues."

He watched her shoulders shake. "I can't stand it," she whispered. "I just can't stand it. Mike and Pepper could have been killed."

Lorie's heart was as big as Texas, but she couldn't take chaos. That's why he'd never told her when he was in danger, and when he did get hurt, he always made up some story about it being an accident.

He sat down on one of the stools at her work table. "I'll find him, Lorie, I swear. From the looks of things right now, I'd say the guy just wants to bother them, not hurt them."

Her head jerked unevenly in a nod. "How can I help? I have to do something."

Now was his chance, but he had to make sure he was doing what he was about to do for the right reasons. Hell and heaven were both only a coin toss away.

"I was thinking," he began, then bit into a sandwich and took his time chewing. "If you wouldn't mind the inconvenience, I'd like to set up surveillance on that balcony of yours. It would offer a perfect view of the paper and if something went down, I'd be close enough to do some good."

"Do it," she said simply.

"It'll mean me sleeping on your couch. I'd be in your way." He stood. "I want to watch over McCulloch's house tonight. In the morning will be soon enough to bring my equipment." He studied her. "Are you sure about this, Lorie?"

"I'm sure. If there is anything we can do to protect my friends, we have to do it."

Heath finished his sandwich, thinking that letting him into her life must look like the extreme sacrifice for her.

The mutt limped over and butted his nose against Heath's leg.

"You got to name this dog if he's going to stay around," he said, trying to think of anything to take the worry from her eyes.

"Bob Earl and I named him this morning. We're calling him Goggles."

"What kind of name is Goggles for a dog?"

She smiled. "As good a name as any, I guess."

He knelt and patted the dog. "See you tomorrow, Goggles. Take care of my girl until I get back."

If Lorie heard him, she didn't comment. When he looked up, she'd moved into the bakery, busy doing something, as always.

"I'll be back as soon as I can, Lorie Girl," he whispered and almost ran out the back door.

Chapter 27

"It's Monday morning and what will our Mr. Monday think of all this mess?" Audrey whined as she circled around her desk. "The back door is blocked, the windows are boarded, and the editor is wearing a gun."

She finally got Mike's attention. He'd hoped to strap the shoulder holster on without anyone noticing and then put on his sports jacket.

He didn't bother to turn around. He could hear Malone's high heels heading his way.

"What are you doing?" she snapped.

"Good morning to you too," he answered as he faced her. "I'm doing what my father and grandfather and great-grandfather did. I'm protecting the paper."

"Do you know anything about guns?" She folded her arms and leaned against the doorjamb.

He smiled. "Of course I do. I'm from Texas, remember.

Guns outnumber people in this state three to one." When she didn't smile, he added, "I've been cleaning these handguns since I was ten. My father made sure Dave and I knew how to use every one of them. Dave was a better shot with a rifle, but I did all right with a handgun. I'm not planning to shoot anyone, Malone. I just don't plan to sit by and let them shoot me."

"This is crazy."

She reminded him of a racehorse, ready to run but stuck in the gate. His office was too small for her to pace, and she didn't seem ready to leave.

"Then quit," he answered back. He'd thought about it and getting Pepper out of the line of fire might be a good idea. It seemed like every time there was trouble she'd been near enough to get hurt. If he could bully her into leaving, she'd be out of harm's way.

But he'd miss her like hell.

She took a step farther into the office and closed the door. "No," she said calmly. "You'll have to fire me and you won't fire me because you don't like conflict. Therefore, I'm staying."

He sat on his window ledge wishing he could look out in the street, but all he saw were boards. "Come here," he whispered and pointed with his head toward the door. "I'd rather no one overhear what I'm about to say."

She took a step toward him, and then another, until she was almost touching him. "I'm not leaving." She pouted. "I've already been run out of one town this month. If you think the alley man is trouble, wait till you see the fight you'll be in if you try to get rid of me."

"This has nothing to do with the office. It's not nine yet so we're not officially at work. There was something I couldn't do last night when I took you home. Morgan was too busy watching."

Before she could move, he circled one hand around her waist and pulled her onto his lap. He'd thought about kissing her all day, when he picked her up, while she'd played games with Morgan, when she'd helped May with the dishes, even when they were talking about the covers his dad had framed in the hallway. He thought about it, but he hadn't acted. "I'm going to kiss you, Malone. If you don't like the idea, you'd better speak up."

She lifted her arms and rested them on his shoulders. "It's about time." It took her a few seconds to calm from her rant. She took a deep breath and whispered, "I can think of nothing I'd like better."

He'd meant to kiss her hard and fast and then get on with the day, but she'd have none of it. She pressed her chest against his and taught him a few things about how hot a kiss can be.

When he came up for air, she pulled away. "We can't do this, you know."

"You're right. It's not proper."

"No. That's not it. You don't have a lock on your door and if I kiss you like that again I'm going to want some skin-against-skin action. How's it going to look when Audrey opens the door and sees us? We'd probably give her a heart attack."

He smiled. "Skin against skin?"

"Shut up," she said. "We can't get physical and I'm not quitting. This is not starting out to be a great day. Maybe we should just agree to stay as far away from each other as possible until after five."

"All right." He gave in. She was a born street scrapper and he was no match for her. "But tell me one thing, does loving ever come into this physical thing you do?"

She shoved her hair back. "It never has, and don't go

making this attraction we feel more than it is. I'm just passing through and you've got roots miles deep in this town."

She walked to the door. "Last night, after spending the evening with your family, I decided we were just going to be friends. I guess you set me straight on that point." She winked at him. "But what we have will be outside the office, and it'll be just for fun. I don't do strings."

He saw it then, the crack in her armor. The soft spot in this tough city girl. She kept it simple because she didn't want to be hurt. No one could get close. No one could matter to Pepper Malone. "Okay, we play by your rules, but you're going to miss me when you leave."

"Don't bet on it, Chief," she said with a confident smile as she opened the door.

"Oh, I plan to," he murmured as Bob Earl yelled, "Mr. Monday is here."

The day began. Mike sat down at his desk and listened to Audrey greet the total stranger who wandered in every Monday. She told him all about the trouble they'd had last week and how upset she was.

The gentleman in his fifties listened with kindness as always. Then he went around the room and asked everyone by name how they were doing. His friendliness had never seemed out of place, but today, Mike listened more carefully.

The phone rang with the first complaint of the day. Audrey had listed the bridesmaids' dresses as peach and they were mauve at the Smithy wedding.

Next the mother of the bride for the Donovan wedding called to say Audrey had mixed up the menus for the bride's luncheon and the bachelor party. Before Mike could apologize, she asked him what kind of idiot thinks they serve Coors at a luncheon.

Mike didn't comment that when he read over the article he'd thought beer was a good idea.

The third caller just called to complain about the paper in general. Mrs. Ima Smith always called to tell him the number of errors she'd found in the paper. On bad weeks, she'd circle them in red and mail them to him.

The fourth complaint was from the newly widowed Mrs. Flowers. Audrey had listed the casket as pine and it was oak. Mrs. Flowers had been widowed four times and apparently buried all her husbands in oak. She wanted the line amended so that no one in town would think she thought less of her last husband.

By the time he picked up the phone for the fifth time, Mike was starting to think a Coors sounded good for breakfast.

"*Bailee Bugle*," he said, sounding friendlier than he felt.

"How'd you like the fire?" a low voice whispered.

"What did you say?" Mike leaned forward, jotting down the number on the Caller ID.

"I said how'd you like the fire?" the voice repeated. "It won't be long until all signs of McCullochs disappear. Lucky break you were there to see it."

"Why don't you come over and say that to my face, you son of a—"

The phone went dead.

Mike leaned back slowly in his chair and pulled the Colt from its holster. He checked to see that it was fully loaded. He knew it was, but the action somehow calmed him.

The stranger wasn't after Pepper or anyone else.

Mike knew now that he was the target. Somehow the stranger had done his homework. He knew the land was Mike's, and few people in town knew that.

He grabbed his jacket and headed toward the door. "I'll

be back in a while," he said as he passed the others. "Web, you get the phone."

"I'm on it, Chief," Webster said.

Mike glanced at Pepper. He should have made her stop calling him *Chief.* Soon the whole office would be calling him that, but right now he had bigger problems to worry about.

He drove over to Sheriff Watson's office and stormed in past the dispatcher, who only worked nine to four, and a secretary who never seemed to work at all.

"Morning, ladies. I need to see the sheriff."

The secretary raised her nail file, but didn't try to stop him. The dispatcher sounded like she was talking to one of the daytime deputies. She waved him through.

Watson had someone in his office. Mike hesitated at the door.

The sheriff's guest twisted around.

Mike almost swore. The FBI agent from yesterday was back. Watson had called him *Heath.* Mike didn't know if that was his first or last name. The man was like bindweed; he showed up everywhere.

"What's happened, Mike?" the sheriff asked.

Mike glared at Heath, then decided the man would find out soon enough anyway. "I got another call. Our unknown guy asked me how I liked the fire."

Neither of the men looked surprised.

"You get the number?" Watson asked.

Mike handed him the note and the sheriff passed it off to Heath, who left the room without a word.

Sheriff Watson, in his usual Southern style, offered Mike coffee before settling back in his chair.

Mike took the chair Heath had left and tried to make his heart stop racing. He wanted to yell that he was too young to have someone trying to kill him, but he said, "I don't understand. If the guy wants me dead, why doesn't he come after me? Why all the games? I'm not that hard to find. He could have shot me any day through the window. Why'd he wait until we were all gone and just shoot the window?"

Watson steepled his fingers. "He's playing with you, Mike. He doesn't want to just murder you; he may not want to kill you at all. He wants to destroy you. This isn't the hot kind of hate that boils over in a bar fight; this is the kind of hate that's festered. Somehow, sometime you or the paper did something that destroyed his life. First he damaged the paper, then your land, and now he's threatening your life."

Mike agreed. "I thought of that. I'll get everyone reading old papers."

Watson leaned forward. "We've had several murder trials over the years. Maybe your father's help in an investigation sent a man to jail and he swore when he got out he'd destroy the *Bugle* and the McCullochs. Or who knows, maybe it was a lesser crime but the convictions cost this guy his job and his wife. Men locked up tend to blame everybody and anybody but themselves for their trouble."

Mike shook his head.

The sheriff tried again. "Think back, Mike. It's time to be honest. Any kid who hated you in high school? Any man you stole a girl from or had an affair with his wife?"

Mike almost laughed. "I hardly had a date in high school. I never stole a girl from anyone. That was more along my brother's line, and I swear I've never had an affair with anyone's wife."

"I believe you, son." Watson rubbed his face. "When this is all over we should talk. You're young, Mike. When we get through worrying about you getting killed, you oughta think about living just a little."

Heath stepped back into the office. Mike swore the agent's frown was tattooed on.

He looked from Mike to the sheriff. "We traced the number to a pay phone at the gas station out by the interstate. I'll check it out."

Mike stood. "I'm going with you."

Heath opened his mouth to object, but Mike didn't give him time. "I didn't get a very good look at the man that night in the alley, but I remember his build. I'll know him if I see him again."

Heath stopped Mike with a hand on his shoulder. "About that weapon you're carrying . . ."

"I'm wearing it."

Heath nodded. "I was going to say that you might want to wear a jacket and not a sports coat. The bulge shows less. I got one in the car you can borrow."

"What's this mess to you?" Mike asked.

"A friend asked me to help."

Mike looked at Watson, but the sheriff's head was down studying a paper on his desk. It wasn't like the sheriff to call in outside help, but maybe he had. Watson was getting older.

Mike followed the agent out. The sheriff's need for help was just another thing he'd have to deal with later; right now they had to get to the gas station. He guessed it was about a million-to-one chance that the caller would still be there hanging around the phone, but someone who had seen him might remember a detail. The make of his car. The direction he walked away. Anything.

When Mike climbed into Heath's car, he asked, "You live in this thing?" Clothes and electronic equipment were scattered everywhere.

He'd meant it as a joke, but the agent didn't smile. He simply said, "Sometimes."

On the way out to the gas station, Heath asked Mike to tell him everything he could remember, from the first hang-ups to today.

Heath talked him through every detail. How old would he guess the voice was? Any accent? Any hint of education level? Any background noise?

Mike was frustrated at how little he remembered.

When he finished the agent's interrogation, Mike asked, "You got a profile of this nut? I hear that's what you guys do best."

"Yep," Heath said as he pulled in at the station.

"Want to let me in on it?"

"Sure." Heath parked a few spaces down from the phone. "He hates you and wants you dead."

"Thanks." Mike shrugged. "I needed that expert evaluation."

Chapter 28

I figured I was wearing off the varnish on the wood flooring, but I kept pacing, trying to think to the rhythm of my heels tapping.

Mike called in about an hour after he left and told Webster he wanted someone to keep checking old newspapers.

Since I was the only one interested, they all agreed I should take the assignment. Audrey had to run the office. Webster had to answer the phone, and who knows what Orrie was doing in his office. No one had seen him all morning, but his door was open and the glow of screens told us he must be in there.

As Webster, Audrey, and Bob Earl left for lunch, one of the girls who worked for Lorie brought over Mike's sandwich. I took it down to the basement with me, deciding I didn't have the energy to go over to the bakery and listen to everyone talk about all that had happened. I'd been there. I didn't need a rerun.

The old guy with food in his beard would probably tell me one more time that he'd checked on my car and the tires were still flat. Then the round table of white heads near the back would tell me their theories, which pretty much blamed the trouble on everything except global warming.

I kicked my heels off and went to work. Within minutes I was lost in the stories. A hundred years ago Bailee had experienced a very active women's rights movement. Mary Margaret Tyler appeared to be the president of the local chapter. The paper published one of her speeches in its entirety. That could have made a few men mad, but they were all dead by now.

Then I got interested in a murder trial in the forties. Two ranchers, side by side, started feuding over a strip of land between the two homesteads. The argument went from barroom fights to a dawn shootout. One was charged with shooting the other, but there wasn't enough evidence to convict him. I found a follow-up story dated five years later saying that both ranches were sold. One councilman suggested that both families had spent themselves into bankruptcy in court battles. They would have been better off to split the land down the middle and forget about it.

Interesting story, but probably not related to Michael. I wrote down the names and dates anyway.

I flipped back through old issues, studying even editorials around the time of the feud. None by a McCulloch. This was a murder, but I couldn't see where anyone could blame the paper. Most of the reporting was directly from the sheriff or the court. Once the ranches were sold, I found no records of either family name in Bailee.

In the eighties there had been a drug bust at the local lumberyard. Several men ended up being fired. Two drew jail time. One was quoted as saying everyone, including the paper, was lying. I jotted down his name.

About a year after Mike took over the paper, one of the art teachers at the high school was fired for posting pictures of himself on the Internet. He claimed they were art, but the judge sided with the school board. One man's art was another man's pornography. The teacher's only statement was to send the entire town to hell. I doubted he was our alley man, but I added his name.

The others upstairs came back, sounding like mice above me, but I didn't stop reading. I'd reached the letters from Mike's brother. Long beautiful letters from a man fighting in an undeclared war a dozen years ago. He ended each letter with, "Tell Morgan her daddy loves her."

The letters made even me, a hard journalist, want to cry. I wondered if Michael had read them. If he had, did they draw him closer to his brother?

I'd seen the way Michael loved Morgan, but as near as I could tell he wasn't close to anyone else in town. A man who doesn't get close doesn't tend to make friends or enemies.

I moved through the first weeks Michael had taken over the paper. I could see his hand in the articles about his brother's crash and again, less than a month later, he'd written about losing his father. From then on, the personal journalism stopped. It was as if he'd turned his back on feelings and simply reported.

The *Bugle* was a classic case study of a quality small publication, but I couldn't find the heart in it. That was the difference between Michael's *Bugle* and his father's and grandfather's.

I laid down the paper and stretched, wondering what time it was. I hadn't heard the mice upstairs in a while.

When I glanced toward the stairs, I saw Michael sitting about halfway down staring at me.

"How long have you been there?" I asked.

"A while. The others have gone home. Lorie invited me and you to dinner. Leftovers from the chamber lunch. Want to go?"

"Sure, I'm—"

"Starving," we both said at once.

I picked up my shoes and followed him upstairs. "You find out anything today?" I asked as I braced my hand on his shoulder while I put on the heels.

"Nope. You?"

I handed him the names I'd jotted down but shook my head. "All I truly learned was that you're a good editor. I swear, reading the weekly is like reading the story of a town." I told him about some of the stories I'd come across, then asked him if Morgan knew that Dave talked of her in his letters home.

"I don't think so," Mike answered. "Dave left a few weeks after she was born. He and Anna hadn't really gotten along since their wedding. I think my dad made him stay until Morgan was born. Dave joined the army because he didn't want to be tied down with a wife and baby. As far as I know, he didn't see Morgan more than a few times during her first three years of life. My dad was the one who paid the bills and saw that Anna and she had all they needed."

"Really." The brother Michael seemed to remember didn't fit with the picture of the man I'd read about in the paper. "So your brother lied about loving the kid?"

Mike held the door open for me. "My brother lied about

a lot of things, but it doesn't matter anymore. Let Morgan believe the best about him. It's all she's got of her parents."

"But you're still mad at him."

Mike took a long breath. "No. I'm not mad. I just wish things had been different, that's all. Morgan deserved to have parents, and all she's got is an uncle and a set of graves to visit." He shook his head. "The undertaker said I should just have had what we found cremated, but I wanted Morgan to at least have a place to go visit them, and she does. Now and then I notice her riding her bike out to their graves."

"She probably wishes she could ask them questions."

"*I* wish she could too." He smiled. "She asked me about the facts of life the other night, and I didn't know what to tell her."

I brushed against him as I passed through the door. "How about I explain it to you, Chief?"

His grin finally reached his eyes. "I'm a slow learner, I'm afraid."

"That's all right. Maybe we'll have all night."

"Stop tempting me or I might take the sheriff's advice."

I locked my arm in his. "What did the sheriff suggest?"

"That I start living a little."

"Let me know when you're ready, Mikey."

We walked across the street to the bakery in a comfortable silence. I didn't know if we were just flirting, or planning. It didn't matter; even with all the trouble, I could never remember being attracted to a man on so many levels. I liked his mind and his slim body and his hesitant touch. Even his out-of-order hair and wrinkled clothes were starting to grow on me.

The sign on the door of the bakery read CLOSED, but several people were inside. He held the door and I purposely/accidentally brushed against him when I passed.

"Sorry," I whispered, loving the way his whole body seemed to tighten.

"No you're not, Malone, not one bit."

When we walked toward the kitchen I heard Webster say, "It doesn't make sense that a stranger can run around town and no one sees him. What are we dealing with, a ghost? Maybe we should post lookouts. He's got to be here somewhere."

The sheriff shook his head. "We've got lots of drifters in town. I've been having my deputies questioning them all day. This time of year they're staying out by the interstate, knowing there'll be work soon in the orchards."

"I think our alley man wants to destroy the free press," Audrey chimed in. "And for one I'll fight to the death for our rights."

One white-haired man from the morning round table mumbled that she should burn her bra in protest, but several others voted him down.

Michael looked over at Lorie. She shrugged. "I invited one person, who invited one person, and so on and so on. Now I've got more people eating leftovers than folks who ate on the original meal. Like my mother always said, it's time to add water to the gravy."

I counted twenty people. Even the two lawyer types were there.

Everyone seemed to be talking at once about what needed to be done, and Sheriff Watson was in the middle acting as referee. I noticed the FBI agent sitting near the windows, taking no part in the discussion.

To my surprise, Michael slipped him the paper with the names I'd jotted down of possible people who had reason to hate the press. The agent didn't unfold it but just shoved it into a pocket.

By the time Lorie and I served the meal, the sheriff had

managed to get everyone organized. I filled my plate and looked for an empty seat not in the middle of everything. I finally found one across from the agent.

"Why are you sitting with me?" he said in his usual Attila the Hun kind of friendly way.

"It was either next to you or the guy with the beard. He has enough food in that hair to make a kid's meal."

To my surprise the agent looked at me as if he were trying to figure out if I was joking. This guy must be great fun at a party.

"What's your name, besides Agent?" I asked, then shoved the first bite of rebaked spaghetti in my mouth.

"Heath," he said watching me closely. "Heath Fuller."

"Oh," I managed after the next bite. "Any kin to Lorie?"

"Only by marriage," he answered.

It crossed my mind that he might have meant *his* marriage, but I blew that idea off. Lorie would come nearer marrying an alien or Sasquatch than she would Mister Personality here. Maybe he was a cousin.

I tried another line of conversation. "How many bad guys have you killed?"

He frowned at me like I was starting to bother him. "Enough. How many have you slept with?"

"Enough, trust me." I should have been surprised that he'd checked my past, but I wasn't. It was his job. In fact, I thought more of him for being thorough.

To my shock, Heath Fuller smiled. "What does McCulloch do, starve you to death across the street?"

"Yes," I answered. "Would you arrest him for me? It's unbearable over there. No doughnuts this morning. No candy machine. I think it's reporter abuse and needs to be dealt with."

"Not my specialty," he said, "but if you starve to death, I'll look into it."

"Thanks," I mumbled. "That's comforting."

He stood. "I'm going to get some dessert." As an after-thought, he added, "You want any?"

"Anything but chocolate," I said. "Thanks."

He was back before I had time to even think about missing him with two slices of chocolate pie.

"I said—"

"I know," he stopped me. "These are mine. I couldn't decide what to bring you, so I figured you could get your own."

I watched him eat both pieces. "I don't think I like you much, Agent Fuller. You're a hard man who doesn't bother ever being kind, I'd guess. You could be nice to me. It wouldn't hurt you."

He looked up as if he'd forgotten I was across from him. "What are we, in the schoolyard?"

"No. I just thought you should know."

To my surprise, his lip twitched into almost a smile. "All right, Miss Malone. I don't like you either. You're a user, an anything-for-a-story kind of reporter. I know you're staying around hoping for a big story, but what I can't figure out is why you came here in the first place. Aren't there other holes reporters like you crawl into?"

"I'm not staying here for a story." For once in my logical brain I hadn't thought of all that was happening with Michael as a story. I thought about denying that I was a do-anything-for-a-story kind of reporter, but he probably got that one right. Except I hadn't slept with Donny Hatcher for a story; the story was just a by-product that happened after he left.

I looked at the cold man across from me and decided to be honest. "I'm here because I have nowhere else to go. When I left Chicago I didn't have any money to find another hole to crawl into. I came here because this is as close to home as anywhere for me."

"I understand," he said.

He stood suddenly and moved away, but for a second I'd seen something in his eyes. A bone-deep kind of sadness that surprised me.

Maybe he did understand.

Chapter 29

9:40 P.M.

Mike parked several yards from the trailer and walked Pepper to her door, wishing he could find some way to step away from all his problems long enough to get to know her. She could be hard and professional one minute and melting in his arms the next.

The night was crisp, almost cold with a moon that looked too big to be real. He found himself wanting it to be just a dull ordinary night like the thousands he'd had here in Bailee. Nothing happening. Nothing to worry about.

The only difference would be Pepper. He'd be "seeing her," as the old ladies would say, and they'd be getting to know each other's likes and dislikes. After a few months of dating, they'd begin a slow foreplay that might take weeks, then he'd ask her to Dallas or somewhere for the week-end, and she'd go. After that, they'd move from "seeing" to "being with" each other. Before long the *if you guys get married* questions would turn into *when you get married* questions.

Mike smiled at Pepper as they walked onto the porch. With all this trouble there'd been no time for what might have been.

"What did you and the agent talk about?" he asked, making conversation before his thoughts got too lost in places where he had no time to go.

"Oh, you know, murder, sex, and food," she answered. "Did you know his last name is Fuller?"

"No. Is he related to Lorie?" Michael took her cold fingers and tucked them in his arm.

"Only by marriage, he said." She moved closer to him.

"I'll ask him." Mike slid his arm around her waist, liking the way she fit against him.

"It would only be a waste of time. Lorie would never give a guy like that a second look."

"He said he'd be watching me." Mike laughed. "And then he said the strangest thing. He told me I should put a candy machine in the office."

"Strange," Pepper murmured, then changed the subject. "I think he may have a sugar problem. I saw the man eat four slices of pie tonight."

She might be saying one thing, but her body against him was definitely saying something else. For a few breaths he simply enjoyed the nearness of her. He'd always thought of himself as an intellectual, a bookworm in high school, a college student who kept almost a four-point GPA while carrying a full load. A grad student who couldn't wait to get out and teach. Yet with Pepper something in him responded on almost an animal level. He wanted to touch her, to protect her and feel her near.

"Did you spend all afternoon with the sheriff and Heath?"

He forced his thoughts back, knowing they'd return as soon as he tried to sleep. "I mostly answered questions. If I'm the target, then it makes sense that if we can find a reason we can find the caller. Heath thinks it's a local, someone who knows his way around town and who knows how not to be noticed. Watson disagrees. He swears that if we had someone like that around, he would know it. We drove back out to where the barn burned. In one of the sheds we discovered a spot where someone had spent the night. Judging from the empty cans of food, he'd been there a while. It might have been our man, or it might have been a drifter thinking he'd be safe camped there."

"Did they collect evidence?" She slipped her hand inside his jacket as if only looking for warmth, but he felt the bolt of her touch across his chest.

"Sure." Mike couldn't help tugging her closer, reacting to the feel of her hand resting over his heart. "But until the guy kills me, it's not a priority case. It seems that calling someone and saying you wish him dead won't make it on the Most Wanted posters."

"What about shooting the windows out?" Her fingers tickled down to his belt and then slid up, pressing his shirt against him.

He took a deep breath, trying to remember that they were talking. "Until we have a weapon, it'd be hard to prove. The agent says the guy probably tossed the rifle five minutes after he fired it."

"This is giving me a headache." She pulled her hand away and rubbed her forehead. "Nothing can be done until something else happens."

With a swift tug, he pulled her into the shadows. His hands moved beneath her hair and cupped the back of her head. "We only have a few minutes, but I have to touch you before I go." He felt her cool cheek with his mouth, tasting more than kissing. "In this craziness, thinking of you is all that clears my mind." He pressed his face into her hair and took a deep breath. Her body moved against his.

Whispering into her ear, he said his thoughts. "Closer."

She brushed her cheek against his chin as her body shifted, fitting into his.

"Can't you come in for a few minutes?"

"If you knew how much I want to."

"All we have to do is walk up three steps."

He forced his body not to move. If he took one step, he'd forget all about what had to be done. "No, I can't. Toad's out by the road waiting for me to come back. I've had a tail all day. If I stayed here, half the town would know it by morning." His lips moved over hers, enjoying the feel. "This is a hell of a time to be attracted to a woman. Why didn't you come along a year ago?"

"Please come in," she pleaded. "Maybe Toad's asleep out there."

He laughed against her throat as he pulled her hair back and kissed the warm skin of her neck. She tasted so good.

"I've never had to wait for what I want," she whispered. "I don't like the idea of waiting now. I want you, Michael."

He felt her melting in his arms, and he knew the time of flirting was over for them both. If he stepped away now, he might drown what was between them. If he didn't, he could ruin what might come in the future. He wanted more of Pepper Malone than a one-night stand, even if she said that was all she was willing to give. He wanted the dates and the flirting and the weekend of sneaking away and the *if we marry* time turning into *when we marry*. He wanted it all with Pepper. Thousands of one-night stands strung together during a lifetime.

He pulled away. "I've got to get home."

She groaned.

"But I'll call you at ten. We've got to be careful what we say; I gave permission for my phones to be tapped." His hand slowly moved from her waist to cup her breast.

When she let out a sigh, he tightened his grip, knowing his touch was fully welcomed. "No matter what we talk about on the phone, you'll know what I'll be thinking. It'll be of touching you."

She smiled and he couldn't help but wonder what she was thinking. He'd been doing the advancing tonight, and he didn't know how comfortable she was with that. She seemed a woman who played always by her rules. So he stilled, a breath away from her lips, and let her take the lead. He didn't have to wait long. Her whole body pressed against him, but to his surprise, her kiss was hesitant.

Maybe she wasn't as sure of herself as he thought she was?

When he finally straightened, he whispered against her hair, "You're a hard woman to turn away from, Malone."

She tugged at his shirt.

He laughed. "But I'm going to. I have to." He turned her toward the steps. "Good night."

She didn't say a word as she walked up the steps.

He stood on the ground watching until she unlocked the door and turned on the lights. Then he melted into the night, not wanting to see the disappointment in her face. He already felt the loss of her through his whole body.

He made it to his Jeep before he looked back.

She was already inside.

Mike stared up at the stars and felt the cold with her not against him. He'd heard someone say once that the right woman at the wrong time is the wrong woman. He didn't know if Pepper Malone would be the right woman, but she was definitely falling into his life at the wrong time.

Chapter 30

Heath Fuller stood in the open sliding glass door between the patio and the living area of Lorie's apartment. He felt like a giant invading a munchkin home. If he moved too fast through the cluttered space he might kill a hundred knickknacks in one blow.

The only light was the dim one over the stove, but it gave enough of a glow for him to see his way around her jumbled place. He heard her coming up the stairs and into the apartment, but he stayed with one foot inside and one out.

He was in two worlds, hers and his. He'd set up all his equipment so that he could see and hear beyond the ivy hiding her little balcony from the street. Outside had become his, but inside there was no place for him on her soil. Maybe there never would be again.

"Heath?" she called. "Is it all right to turn on the lights?"

He moved into her world. Her shadow stood just inside the door, which didn't have enough locks on it to keep anyone out. "You can turn on any but this living area. It'd light up too much of the porch."

She moved across the room to the sliding glass door. "How can you see anything out here?" she asked as she leaned past him.

"I'm used to working in the dark." She was so close he could smell the warm cinnamon scent of baked apples. "You make any more chocolate pie tonight?"

"No, just apple," she answered, trying to see through the telescope lens he'd set up. "I was surprised how popular the chocolate was tonight at the meeting."

He moved behind her and reached around to tilt the scope down for her to be able to see. "I'll try to stay out of your way as much as possible," he said. Every cell in his body was very much aware of how close he was to her. If he took a deep breath, he might touch her.

"Do you think we did any good tonight getting together to brainstorm?" She seemed unaware of him so near.

"No." He moved aside so she could walk back into her living room.

"I was afraid that would be what you'd say, but making everyone aware of what's going on might help. It couldn't hurt. I just wanted to try, to feel like I was doing something to help." She slipped out of her shoes and tucked her feet beneath her as she sat on the couch. "Maybe someone will see something out of order if we're all watching."

He took the chair opposite. "It's more likely that someone will get in the way if trouble comes riding in. People get killed trying to help when they should just stand back and let the professionals do their jobs."

"Who tonight would you want to have around? Besides the sheriff, if this trouble does come."

He shrugged. "McCulloch's pretty levelheaded. He doesn't like it that I'm here, but he knows it's for his own good. Maybe Webster Higgins would be a man to stand with me if I needed someone."

"Why Webster?" She tugged her stocking foot out from under her and began rubbing it.

"He's been around enough criminals to know how to handle himself."

"That sweet old man?" She laughed. "I doubt he's even been around a person who says *damn*."

Heath smiled, realizing the folks here didn't know where Webster had been all those years he was gone. Like everyone else in town, he'd looked up Webster Higgins. Thirty-two years with the prison system down in Huntsville, but Lorie didn't need to know. If Webster didn't want to tell, Heath would keep his secret.

Neither seemed to know what to say next. They just sat in the shadows. Finally she broke the silence. "Heath, can we just talk? Not about us, but about what's happening. I know you're probably still mad at me, but I've missed talking to you and I need to know that my friends are going to be all right."

"I was never mad at you," he said, surprised she'd even think he was. "And I've missed our talks too." He leaned forward. "If you want to know what's going on, I'll tell you."

"The good and the bad?" she asked. "I don't want you just telling me what you think I need to know. I want to hear it all."

He hesitated. The Lorie he knew five years ago would have never wanted to know both. He used to call her *Sunshine* because she saw only good and ignored the rest.

"You're not the same woman I knew five years ago. Then, you wouldn't have asked."

"And I'm guessing you've changed also. I always thought you were so strong, but now it's like you've hardened to rock. Pepper says you can probably rot fruit with your stare. Is the Heath I knew still in there somewhere?"

He shook his head. "You want the honest answer, I don't know." He made a mental note to tell Pepper how much he didn't like her again.

"Then we start on safe ground," Lorie announced, as if they'd made a pact. "Tell me about the threats."

Heath told her all he knew about each threat. The calls, the vandalism, the fire. To his surprise, she asked questions, pulling out more than the bare facts.

"I don't like Mike having to wear a gun," she said.

"I wear a gun," he pointed out.

She stood. "I never liked that either." As she walked to the kitchen, she asked, "Want some hot chocolate?"

"Sure," he said.

While she got it ready, he watched her, wondering why she'd never told him that she didn't like him armed. He could have left his weapon in the safe at the office. It had never occurred to him in the six years they'd been married to ask her if the weapons around the house bothered her.

When she came back, she handed him a cup and sat down. "I don't even know where you live now, but I'm guessing you knew I was here."

"I did." He almost added that he knew the day the bakery opened and the time she took a vacation to New England and the week she closed last year because she had the flu. If he told her just how much he knew of her life, she'd probably have him arrested as a stalker.

But he never would have bothered her. Not if she hadn't called. He didn't figure he had the right.

"Well, where do you live?" She laughed, as if they were playing a game. "Are you with someone?"

He stood and moved to the open window. Her question should have been easy enough, but he couldn't remember the last time he'd just talked to anyone. It wasn't something he did.

"When I left, I took an assignment in India, then another in D.C. By the time I settled back in Dallas I'd pared down my personal belongings to a couple of bags I could check. Right now I'm living at one of those hotels that rents by the month."

She wiggled her other foot and began massaging it. "How can you cook in those places? I've seen them. One pot, one wooden spoon, four forks."

"I don't cook." He smiled, thinking she was the only person he knew who would worry about cooking first.

"Knowing you, I'd say you only eat one meal a day."

"You guessed it."

"That's not good for you, Heath."

He sat down on the other end of the couch and motioned for her to stretch her feet toward him.

When she did, he hoped she couldn't see his surprise in the shadows.

He began to rub the bottoms of her feet. She sighed and leaned back with her eyes closed.

He smiled, knowing he hadn't lost his touch in doing one thing. "Did anyone ever tell you that maybe you shouldn't stand on your feet all day?"

"Shut up and rub. That feels so good."

He laughed. When she relaxed, he added, "Webster Higgins left Bailee after his wife died. He went down in south Texas to Huntsville and for more than thirty years he worked as a guard on death row. He saw more than his share of bad guys."

She opened one eye. "Really, that dear old man?"

"Maybe he'd had all of being tough he could take. Maybe when he retired, he bought a cane and a fedora and decided he'd be a gentle soul for the rest of his days. I don't think he wants anyone to know his secret, but I'm telling you because if I'm not around he'd be someone to turn to in a crisis."

"I'll remember that. If you retired, what would you do?"

"I'll have my twenty years with the Bureau in another five years. Maybe I'll quit and become a librarian."

She smiled. "Somehow I doubt it."

He doubted it also. Since their marriage had broken up he'd made no plans for the future. Part of him figured if he took enough of the assignments no one else wanted, at some point he wouldn't come home. He'd never spent a dime of the hazardous-duty pay. Her name was still listed as beneficiary.

"Maybe I'll buy a boat," he said, tickling the arch of her foot.

Now she laughed. "I really doubt that. Besides, have you ever seen how small some of those galleys are? It would be like cooking in a closet."

They settled into silence once more, but it wasn't uncomfortable as it had been before. He realized they'd set some ground rules tonight. Rules that might even allow them to be friends.

His hand gentled to a caress and he knew she'd fallen asleep. When a car honked below, she stirred and then stretched, pulling her feet away.

"Lorie," he said, "why'd you think I'd be mad at you?"

She made a show of picking up her shoes. "Because I got pregnant and we'd agreed I wouldn't."

"I was never mad about that, only worried."

"It was a long time ago, Heath. Let's forget that now." She crossed to her bedroom before he could ask more.

An hour later she'd taken her shower and gone to bed, but he was still wide awake. He was in hell, he decided. Being this close to her and not holding her was far worse than just missing her. She didn't have to worry about one meal a day being bad for his health; he was killing himself. Even now, just thinking about her so near made his temperature rise and his heart pound.

Moving out into the cool air of the balcony, Heath watched the street. He could do this job. He was good at his job. He could handle it no matter how dangerous, but how was he going to walk away from Lorie when it was over?

Chapter 31

"Morgan!" Mike yelled when he stepped into the kitchen and she wasn't there already eating. "Morgan, get down here. You're going to be late."

He heard her rapid thundering down the stairs, and then a moment later she rounded the corner, knocking her backpack against the framed front page announcing man's first step on the moon.

Mike waited, knowing she'd appear in one, two, three seconds. He took one look at her and frowned. "No lipstick. We've talked about that rule."

"But, Dops—"

"No *buts*." He pulled out her chair. "Eat. Maybe it'll be gone by the time you finish breakfast."

"But Pepper wears lipstick and you don't complain. Sunday night I even saw you staring at her when she put it on."

"Pepper is twice your age." He almost added that it never occurred to him to complain. "When you're thirty, you can wear lipstick."

His niece frowned. "When can I start dating?"

"Thirty-four or -five."

She made a face. "I'll bet Audrey Leland's parents said the same thing to her, and look what happened. She's an old maid working for the paper."

He smiled and took a seat. "Don't worry. That won't be you. You'll be the old maid running the paper."

The housekeeper clanked dishes on the other side of the kitchen.

"Morning, May," Morgan said to the old woman, who didn't seem to even know they were in the room.

"Morning, May," Morgan raised her voice. "I only want toast."

"She'll have the full breakfast," Mike corrected just as loudly.

He glanced at his niece and smiled. "She didn't hear a word."

Morgan put both elbows on the table and rested her chin. "She's deaf, Dops. Completely deaf. Haven't you even noticed? Probably all that swing music she listened to when she was young."

They both looked to see if May turned. The housekeeper kept cooking.

Mike winked at Morgan. May seemed a little less with them each year, but when he'd suggested she might want to retire, she'd informed him she'd let him know when she was ready. Now, she did breakfast and a simple supper a few nights a week. On the nights she forgot to cook, Morgan would call in something and Mike would pick it up on the way home.

When May finally turned around to face them, a plate in each hand, she smiled as if surprised to find them both at the table. "Good morning," she said as she set the plates down and pulled up her chair.

Mike looked right at May so she knew he was talking. "I need a favor," he said to her.

She nodded without asking what the favor would be.

"I need you to take Morgan to your sister's place in Fort Worth for a few days."

"What!" Morgan yelled. "That's crazy, Dops. I can't go. I've got school and band practice and piano lessons and lots of other stuff. I can't just take off to a crummy bed-and-breakfast run by people older than May."

Mike had thought it out. The one thing he couldn't afford to lose was Morgan. He'd take his chances with the crazy guy. If he burned all the barns, it didn't matter. If he burned the paper, they could rebuild. But Morgan had to be kept safe. If the alley man was really coming after him, Mike couldn't take the chance of Morgan being in the way.

"You have to go, kid." He couldn't back down on this one. "What kind of a guardian angel would I be if I let you get hurt?"

Morgan laughed. "Oh, I get it. This is an April Fool's joke. Very funny."

"This is not a joke. You're going."

She collapsed on the table like a broken doll. "I was afraid of that, but I was just hoping against all hope."

He had to smile. She sounded like an actress. When you're thirteen all the world is a great drama. "You're going," he leaned over and whispered. "So eat your break-fast."

She straightened back to a teenager. "It's because of the

nut pestering the paper, isn't it? Everyone at school is talking about it." She leaned over and locked her arm around Mike's. "Don't you see, Dops, if this guy is after the paper, he's after the McCullochs. That's just you and me. We got to stand together."

Mike was proud of her, but he couldn't risk it. "You got to go. I'd never forgive myself if something happened to you."

"I feel the same way," she said. "That's why I got to stay." She made a choking sound. "I'd die if I have to stay in that old house May's relatives live in. It's where doilies go to die. All May's sister and brother-in-law do is sit around and talk about what hurts. We got to think of something else."

Mike hated arguing with her, so he took the way out she offered. "I have to know you're safe. If you can come up with a place where you'd be just as safe, then you can stay there, but only if you follow all the rules."

She leaned over and kissed him, leaving the remainder of her lipstick on his cheek. "Thanks, Dops. I'll think of somewhere. Give me one day. If I don't come up with a plan you can ship me off to the old folks' home with the dust bunnies."

He grinned, deciding he'd better be ready to pay for law school in a few years. She was a natural. "One day, and I want you calling me the minute you get home from school."

He watched her finish her breakfast and thought about how much he loved her. Ten years ago it had taken him three days to find where Morgan's mother, Anna, had left her before going out drinking with his brother. With Anna and Dave gone, no one seemed to know where the baby had been dropped off. Mike remembered driving to the tenth lead and thinking that once he found his brother's kid he'd find someone to raise her. He was twenty-five and had all the responsibility he could handle.

Then he'd walked into the filthy shack with beer bottles and trash everywhere. She'd looked so tiny and so very dirty. Morgan didn't look like she'd had a bath or her hair combed.

She'd looked up at him with her huge blue eyes and he'd knelt down so he wouldn't frighten her. A moment later she was up and in his arms, holding onto his neck for dear life.

He walked out of the house with only the clothes on her back. He didn't know or care about anything but her. The woman who'd been watching her followed them all the way to the car demanding to be paid for babysitting, yelling that the kid had been nothing but trouble.

He'd taken Morgan home and found May cleaning up from the company after the funerals. They'd bathed Morgan, dressed her in one of his T-shirts, and gone shopping. She might have been three, but she already had her opinion of what she wanted. Blue dots, no turtlenecks, and anything pink. From the first night he often wondered if he'd saved her that day, or if she'd saved him.

Mike drove her to school and waited until she was inside the building before he pulled away. This time he might have to be the adult and make the decisions, even if she did think she got half the vote.

He crossed the three intersections to Main and parked in front of the *Bugle* as usual, then pulled the Colt and shoulder holster from his briefcase. He knew if he put it on before Morgan was at school, she'd be worried. She'd probably drive him nuts, text-messaging every ten minutes to see if he was still alive.

When he walked up the steps, he took the time to look

around. Maybe he was being paranoid, but he could feel someone watching.

Pepper was the only one already at work. They'd talked about her starting a series on the history of the buildings in town. She thought it would be educational and fascinating. He thought it might get everyone's mind off his worries. Her ideas were fresh blood to the paper, and deep down he knew the *Bugle* would be better for having her around even for a short time.

"Morning, Chief." She glanced up from her laptop. "You've got lipstick on your cheek."

He smiled. "Jealous?"

"Never of a woman who wears pink lipstick."

He rubbed it off. "How do I tell Morgan she's too young to start wearing makeup?"

Pepper didn't stop typing. "Do I look like Dear Abby?"

"Oh, sorry. I was just hoping for a little advice."

She stopped, making a great show of having been interrupted. "All right, since you asked. No daughter in the history of the world has waited as long as her parents would like before she started wearing makeup or shaving her legs."

"She's not—"

Pepper put her hand up to stop him. "Probably, and don't make a big deal about it or you'll scar her for life. Lesson over. We've got a paper to get out."

Mike rubbed at his cheek one last time. "That's what I love about you, Malone, so nurturing, so interested in others." He walked toward his office. "Get me a cup of coffee, would you?"

"Get it yourself," she yelled back.

"Malone, have I fired you yet today?"

"Not yet, but it's early."

He poured his own coffee and grinned as he walked into his office. Today the new glass for the windows would come and he'd be able to look out.

And, it occurred to him, whoever's out there would be able to look in.

Chapter 32

Bailee, Texas
Population 15,005

I concentrated on the writing all day so that I didn't have to think what might happen. Working at the *Bugle* was like waiting for the avalanche on spring's first sunny day.

It was only Tuesday and we'd had two deaths reported. One from the nursing home, an old guy who didn't survive his fourth heart attack.

Note to self: Go check on Aunt Wilma.

The other death had been ruled an accident, but Audrey said everyone knew Mrs. Morley hadn't been the same since her husband died. Rumor was, she drank and drove late at night until she ran out of gas. The sheriff had found her more than once on some back road, sleeping in her car. This time, he couldn't wake her up.

Audrey talked to everyone who came in, first about poor Mrs. Morley and then about all the trouble we'd had at the paper. By noon, I stopped listening. Her voice became background noise.

Webster escaped about eleven and didn't return. I couldn't blame him. For a man who'd lost his first wife it must have been hard to hear Audrey say over and over, "They say a person can't die from grief, but I don't believe it."

Webster must have truly loved his wife. He kept her picture on his desk. Maybe his love had remained the same just as she had, never growing old, never fading.

Men arrived to put new windows in. They banged around for an hour, making it hard for anyone to concentrate. The five of them passing through the office made it seem more like a train station. When they finally left, we had sunshine in Michael's office, boards still on the main windows, and headaches.

I was lost in work when I heard Audrey say, "May I help you, mister?"

I glanced up to see a perfectly tailored suit over broad shoulders. I'd only known one man who looked like that from the back. Donny Hatcher.

"Yes." He didn't turn around. "I wonder if I could have a word with Miss Pepper Malone about a personal matter?"

Audrey briefly looked like she might say no or remind him that this was business hours and I'd have to clock out first. Instead, she tilted her head toward me.

I stood, testing to see if my legs would hold my weight. Donny Hatcher had been so mad at me the last time I saw him he'd threatened to murder me, bury me under the rubble of the *Chicago Sun* building, and then dig me up again and murder me a second time.

"Donny," I managed, biting off the need to say, *May I help you*? Somehow I figured it would be a crime to help, something like assisting in your own killing.

He frowned at me. "Is there somewhere we can talk?"

I looked around. Audrey and Bob Earl were openly listening to our conversation, showing no sign of going back to work. Orrie had rolled from his cave and also watched. He huffed like a pit bull on wheels, ready to pounce. None of them knew Donny, but he was a stranger and they could smell trouble.

Only Michael remained in his office, unaware of what was going on just beyond his door.

"Sure," I said and walked out the front door, knowing Donny would follow.

We drifted over to the bench by the elm. I sat down and waited. Whatever he had to say, he'd come a long way to say it. Since he had his family plane, he'd probably flown to somewhere near Fort Worth then rented a car.

He stood next to me as if waiting for a photo shoot. I'd never noticed how his perfection bothered me. Next time I picked a boyfriend by how attractive he was, I'd just blow up a model in one of those ads for men's clothing. I'd still have the view and probably the same depth in conversation.

"How are you, Pep?" He didn't look at me.

"I'm fine," I said, thinking maybe now might be a good time to tell him I hated the nickname he called me.

"It took me a while to find you." He glanced at me, then looked back at the street. "You're a hard woman to track down."

I thought of yelling that he was the reason I left. He got me fired. He sent two of his men to help me pack. They left the impression that Donny wouldn't be needing a forwarding address.

He seemed to be waiting for something, so I said, "So why take the trouble?"

He looked at me then, and I was surprised at the sadness in his eyes. Maybe I'd hurt him. Maybe he just hadn't gotten things the way he wanted for once, but the pain in his gaze was the first honest emotion I'd ever seen in him.

I broke. "All right. I'm sorry."

"I forgive you, Pep." He smiled as if giving me a gift.

"I was mad at you, but I used the story about your family because it was a good story, interesting, a part of the city's history. We both know I didn't sleep with you to get it, but thanks for making everyone, including my boss, think I did."

"You're welcome," he said, as if not quite following the conversation. "You didn't need that job anyway."

I just sat still, realizing it had been like that all the time we were seeing each other. Only before, he'd stop my rambling by kissing me and the next thing I knew we were in bed. It occurred to me that I'd done the same thing to him. I'd stopped his lovemaking by pretending satisfaction.

I might have embarrassed him with the story, but he'd gotten me fired. He'd ruined my career. If anyone should be saying they're sorry, it should be him.

The old man who always hung out at the bakery walked across the street. I could see pieces of blueberry doughnut in his beard even before he crossed the center strip. He walked right up to the bench and sat down on the other end.

"Morning, Miss Malone."

"Morning, Howard." I hoped I'd gotten his name right.

Donny ignored him. "Of all the women I've slept with"—Donny leaned closer—"you're the one I can't forget."

I had no idea if he thought he was apologizing or asking me to come back, but Howard snickered. When I glared in his direction, he pretended that watching cars was his only interest.

"What are you saying, Donny?"

"I'm saying I want you back. I'm willing to forgive and forget."

I felt like a dog being picked up at the pound. My owner was here for me, but I'd tasted freedom and no longer wanted to go back.

Two court reporters walked by on their way to lunch. They both stopped under the tree and didn't even bother to pretend to have a conversation. I started to tell them this wasn't a bus stop, but why bother. Howard would probably tell them everything over pie.

Donny's ten-second patience timer ran out. "Make up your mind, Pepper. I didn't drive out to this godforsaken place to be kept waiting."

One of the court reporters wiggled her eyebrows at me.

Sweat was bubbling on Donny's perfect forehead. He played his last card as if figuring I was holding out for a better deal. "I could probably talk to the right people and get your job back."

This time I didn't keep him waiting. "Thanks for the offer, Donny, but I think I'll pass."

Howard looked the other way as if I'd think he wasn't listening.

Donny straightened. "Are you sure? We had some great times."

"Yeah, I'm sure." All I remembered was average times. "I've got a great job here."

He looked at the old brick building behind me, then back at me. For a moment I thought he might say he needed me, or maybe even thought he might be falling in love, but that would have been too much to hope for.

I wouldn't have believed him anyway.

He pulled his keys from his pocket. "One day you'll be sorry, Pep."

I fought to keep from screaming that I doubted it. "Maybe," I managed with a wave.

His eyes hardened as he pushed all emotion aside and returned to the vacant stare of perfection. If some people are deep water, some shallow, Donny Hatcher would be a thin drop splattering on hot sidewalk. I saw nothing in him I wanted or needed.

What bothered me most was I didn't know whether he'd changed, or I had.

I watched him go.

"Clothes don't take the measure of a man," Howard said as he dusted crumbs off his shirt.

"He's right," one of the court reporters said. I noticed that both them watched until Donny's car was out of sight.

"You think I did the right thing then?" I asked Howard.

He nodded, pleased to be asked. "You did good, girl. You did good."

They left me alone on the bench. It took a while before I smiled. My life was no better off than it had been an hour ago; Donny Hatcher still wasn't in it, and I still had a nothing job in a nowhere town. But under the elm my life had changed. The big difference—my choice. I stood and went back to work.

Audrey and I walked out together at five. Michael and Orrie were still in the office, but I was ready to call it a day. I felt like I'd been reporting from a war zone. After stopping at the grocery for a six-pack of root beer, I drove over to talk to Wilma. For some reason she was the one person who seemed to have a handle on the mood of this town.

I found her in her room talking to Mr. Gray. They were laughing about something when I walked in.

"What's so funny?" I asked as I pulled out the bottles.

"Nothing," Mr. Gray said. "Just an old joke. I hope that root beer is for us and you're not just bringing it for show-and-tell."

I sat on the corner of Wilma's bed and handed them each one. "No. I brought it for happy hour."

Mr. Gray looked at his drink and frowned. I didn't have to ask; I knew he was wishing for something a little stronger.

"It's been a hell of a day around here. Carted old man Johnson off." He shrugged. "When I was working, we used to call this place The Factory, because we got so much business from here."

"Mrs. Morley died today, too," I said, starting to feel like a local.

Aunt Wilma sighed. "She was a tortured soul, that one. When her husband was alive, he could never do anything right. After he died, she didn't have anyone to pick on but herself."

Mr. Gray took a long drink. "Yep, we're all dying like flies in this town."

"At the paper we're trying to stay alive," I said, changing the subject. "But there appears to be someone in town with a different goal in mind."

"I've been thinking." Mr. Gray leaned forward. "The guy you call the alley man might be a local or maybe he moved away, but he came back. Not some nut just driving in to pick on the paper, but a real native son."

It made sense. I'd thought about the logic of it. A local could move about town during the day and put on old clothes at night. With the hood, folks wouldn't get a good look at him. Even if he'd been gone for years, the area around Main hadn't changed all that much.

Mr. Gray continued, "When I ran the funeral home I knew where every vacant house in town was. What if your alley man is hiding away in one? He knows the folks in town well enough to move around without anyone noticing. There are dozens of places around here where no one even drops by on a regular basis. Houses that went back to the bank for taxes, businesses that closed."

"I'll see if Toad has checked them out."

They talked on about all the people who'd lived and died in town. I never realized that people in small towns know a great many more folks than people in the city. Their lifetimes flow in generations buckling over one another.

When the chimes rang for dinner, Wilma used Mr. Gray's chair as her walker and they made their way to the dining room.

I kissed them both good-bye and left as they entered the cafeteria.

Once in my car I noticed it was a little after six and I had nowhere to go. I decided to circle by the bakery and see if Lorie wanted to join me for dinner. When I parked I glanced across the street. Michael was still at his desk. It was almost like he was daring someone to come and get him.

I thought of crossing to talk to him, but he'd had next to nothing to say to me all day. Part of me knew he was concentrating on work and the threat, but another part of me wished he'd be just a little of the man who'd held me in the dark last night. That Michael warmed my blood in a way few men ever had. The only problem was, that man seemed locked inside a self-made dungeon of responsibilities.

I watched him for a moment, wishing I was the kind of woman to break him out, but I'd never been anyone's hero and my pattern of not caring had become a habit.

Chapter 33

The bakery
6:45 P.M.

Lorie was in the back cleaning up when I walked in. I smiled at the bells above her door. In the busy times I didn't notice them, but now at the end of the day with no one in the place they clanked in welcome.

She turned to greet me. I thought she looked tired, but her smile was as gentle as ever.

"I won't take no for an answer. We're going for a drink," I said, bracing myself for an argument.

She tugged off her apron. "Sounds like a great idea. I haven't had a drink out since I don't know when. Maybe it'll help me sleep."

"Do you need to go up and change?"

She glanced upstairs. "No. I think, if you'll have me, I'll just go as I am."

We climbed into Wilma's old Ford and drove twenty

miles to a motel down the interstate that had a small bar inside an empty restaurant.

After I woke the bartender and ordered, we took a place near the back. "We could have walked into this place nude and no one would have noticed."

Lorie giggled. "This bar has a reputation as *the* place to come if you don't want to be seen. The old guys at the round table started talking about it one morning. They didn't realize I was listening. One said that if he ever saw someone in here with another woman, he'd never tell. Another said, 'As long as it's not my wife I don't care who anyone is with; it's nobody's business.'"

I laughed. "Sounds like there might be a story here."

The Willie Nelson look-alike bartender brought out drinks to the table.

I thought about asking how many years it had been since he'd seen another customer, but the reporter in me decided to make it more interesting. "You have a lot of fights in here?"

He shook his head. "Not for years, but there were a few times this place needed a referee."

"Anybody I might know?" I learned a long time ago that most people love to tell the secrets they know.

"Two cowhands from the Bar H got in a fight a while back, but I convinced them to take it outside after they scattered a few teeth." The bartender didn't seem in any hurry to leave. "A couple of salesmen from Dallas got in an argument once and decided to throw their drinks at each other. I've seen girl fights with more action."

This could go on all night, so I narrowed the questions. "What about folks from Bailee?"

He shook his head, then seemed to remember something. "Ten or twelve years ago we had a McCulloch in here. He was seeing a woman, claimed it was a one-night fling, but the husband still objected. They broke up half the furniture."

"Which McCulloch?" Lorie asked.

"A young guy. I remember him telling his girlfriend's husband that his father ran the newspaper in Bailee. He was bragging like he was some kind of big shot."

"Do you remember his first name?" I asked.

Lorie whispered, "It doesn't sound like Mike."

The bartender shook his head. "I don't remember, but I think the husband's name was Young. Striker Young. I saw it on his check when he paid for the damages, and I remember thinking that was a strange name."

I asked the man another five questions, but he could add no more details to his story. When we ordered another round, he brought us nachos on the house. In this part of the world, chips and cheese passed for a meal.

When we climbed back into the Ford, Lorie voiced my thoughts. "Do you think this Striker Young could be the alley man?"

I didn't want to get my hopes up. From what Michael had told me, his brother was wild. There might be stories in every bar for a hundred miles about him. But a thread of a possibility lingered in my thoughts. What if this Striker Young didn't know the name of the McCulloch that night? What if he thought it had been Michael? Maybe all these years later he decided to end the argument that had started over his wife.

It was a long shot. Too long, I thought, but at this point all leads had to be followed.

By the time we drove back to Bailee, Lorie and I had a plan. I'd find Michael and tell him what we'd heard, and she'd find the FBI agent and give him the name.

My mission had to be the easiest. When I let Lorie out, I saw Michael still in his office. With night moving in I could see him plainly, a pencil stuck behind one ear, his shirtsleeves rolled up, his hair in even less order than it had been this morning.

Once in a while the man looked downright adorable, like one of those puppies in a box at the mall that you have to take home.

I waved at him as I walked across the street and wasn't surprised to find the front door unlocked. I whispered a hello to Morgan playing on what we now all called "Webster's computer" in the main office.

She touched her finger to her lips, telling me she planned to surprise Michael. He couldn't have seen her from his office door.

I touched my lips as well, agreeing to play along.

Walking around the front counter, I tried to think of a reason why I'd dropped by. I couldn't tell Michael about the bar fight with Morgan within hearing distance. It wouldn't be right. The kid needed to believe the best of Dave McCulloch, since that's all she had of him.

"Evening, Chief," I said, standing at Michael's door. "Any chance you're free for dinner?"

His smile looked tired. "As a matter of fact—"

The lights blinked and went out. Using more instinct than logic, I flipped the light switch. Nothing. The only light filtered in through the window, making us no more than shadows.

Michael stood and moved to my side in the doorway. He was so still I could hear my heart pounding.

"It must be a blown fuse," I guessed—or hoped.

"Maybe," he whispered. "It's not unusual for one to blow. I usually just call it a night and check the box in the morning. Without light, that basement is black as hell."

"So we leave and get something to eat?"

He didn't relax. "Give me a minute, Pepper. This doesn't feel right."

I'd felt it too. That hair-standing-up feeling you get when you can't see anyone but you know you're being watched.

"Stay here." Michael reached for the handle of the Colt at his shoulder. "I'll go have a look."

I stopped his hand. "Morgan."

"She's spending the night at a friend's place." He tried to move my hand away. "We don't have to worry about her."

"No," I said. "She's in the main office."

He stopped trying to push my hand away and for a few seconds didn't make a move, and then in a voice calmer than I would have been able to manage, he said, "Morgan? Are you all right?"

"I'm scared, Dops. I can't see anything." Her voice shook with fear. The main room still had no windows. It would be a cave now. "I'm at the back desk. Will you come get me?"

He grabbed my arm and pushed me forward. "Head toward the door. I'll get her."

I nodded as if he could see me and began feeling my way to the front door. My fingers kept brushing the frames along the wall. The rattling made a haunting echo in the big room sliced with thin lines of moonlight breaking through the boards covering the windows.

"Hold your hands out, Morgan, so I'll know when I'm close," Michael said. "Don't worry. It's just a power failure."

He must have bumped into something because I heard a thump, then a muffled oath.

"I'm sorry." Morgan sounded like she was about to cry. "I changed my mind about staying with Kami. I wanted to be here with you."

I heard a squeal and then Michael's calming voice saying, "Got you, kid."

When I opened the door, the pale light flashed on them, and both McCullochs walked hand in hand to the door. Tears streamed down the girl's face, but she smiled knowing that she was safe.

"It's all right," Michael whispered to her. "When you step out"—he looked at both of us—"I want you to see how fast you can make it to the bakery. Don't take even a second to look back. Just run as fast as you can."

Morgan nodded.

Michael passed her hand to mine. "Go!" he commanded.

I took off as fast as I could with the kid right beside me. We hit the bakery door, found it locked, and sprinted up the stairs.

"Lorie!" Morgan yelled as she climbed. "Lorie."

The door opened and the kid darted toward the light. I heard her squeal and I bolted up the last steps two at a time.

Just inside the door I saw Heath Fuller, his hands on Morgan's shoulders as if he'd stopped her from running straight into the wall of his chest.

"What are you doing here?" I would have pulled Morgan away, but Heath shoved her toward Lorie, who closed her arms around the panicked child.

"Take her," he said without answering my question.

"My uncle told us to see how fast we could make it here." Morgan's words came out like hiccups.

"Get out of my way," the agent roared as he pushed me aside. "And stay here with Lorie."

I turned to yell at him when I realized Michael wasn't behind us.

I watched, trying to make sense out of it all as Heath

ran across the street like a warrior running into battle. He wore black and had what looked like a tool belt around his waist. No matter how much I disliked the agent, the back of my mind registered two facts. One, he was going to help Michael and two, Michael could be in real trouble.

"What happened?" Lorie asked as she smoothed Morgan's hair back from her face.

"The lights went out and scared me to death," Morgan said. "Dops made us leave. He's going down to change the fuse, I think."

Lorie looked over the child's head, and silently we agreed not to say more. "He probably didn't want you bumping into anything. He'll be all right. He knows his way around that place even in the dark, and if I know Heath, he'll have a flashlight with him."

"Then why did he tell us to run?" Morgan's mind was piecing the facts together.

I took the question. "This time of night could be dangerous crossing Main."

Morgan calmed. "It was exciting." She giggled with nervous energy. "It was like I was in a real-life horror flick and the monsters were coming."

Lorie kissed her forehead. "Everything's all right now, but if you want to use my phone in the bedroom you can call your friends and tell them all about it."

Morgan glanced at the door. "I left my backpack back at the office."

"Michael will bring it as soon as he gets the lights back on," I hoped.

When Morgan moved to the bedroom, I whispered to Lorie, "Michael thinks someone is in the basement."

Lorie nodded. "So did Heath. The minute he saw the lights go out he grabbed his stuff."

I didn't like the idea that Michael had stayed or that

someone might be in the basement, but if one person had to be over there with Michael, Heath would be the one I'd pick.

I raised an eyebrow. "You didn't have much trouble finding the agent."

Lorie laughed and pointed to her balcony. "He's set up a stakeout out there."

I thought of a few questions I'd like to ask, but they would wait until later. Finding the agent in her apartment was shocking enough for a start.

Chapter 34

Bailee Bugle
8:45 P.M.

Heath opened the front door to the *Bugle* office and slid inside the black main office.

"Mike," he whispered, knowing it was risky to make a sound but not wanting the editor to accidentally shoot him. Nervous civilians were always an unpredictable variable.

No answer.

He held his flashlight at arm's length, flipped it on, and scanned the room.

Nothing but the desks and chairs he'd seen before when Mike walked him through the place.

Moving silently, he crossed the room, letting the light duck into any area that looked large enough to hold someone hiding.

Nothing.

He crossed to Mike's office, but it was empty. Pale light

from the new window made the room seem hollow, without depth, like an old faded photograph.

The computer room was locked. The double doors to the basement stood open. He clicked off his flashlight. Crouching, he looked into a black hole.

"Mike," he said again. "It's Heath."

"Don't come down here." Mike's voice sounded alarmed but rational. "I'm not alone. I can hear someone breathing."

"Do you want a light?" Heath knew that a light would make the danger plain to Mike; unfortunately, it would also offer the intruder a clear shot if he had a weapon.

"Not yet." Mike's voice sounded like it was coming from the opposite corner of the basement. If so, the intruder stood between the two of them.

Heath listened. He heard movement from beneath the stairs and guessed it wasn't Mike. The outsider couldn't know the layout of the space the way Mike did. He wouldn't be as comfortable with all the cluttered storage and winding trails between file cabinets and old machinery. The editor had the advantage. Heath only hoped he used it wisely.

"You are trapped down here," Mike said in a clear voice. "Look, whoever you are, it's time to give yourself up so no one will get hurt. So far all you've done is break into my place. I won't press charges for that if you'll just leave."

Someone shifted in the blackness. Then Mike's voice came again from farther back. "How about I step out of the way and you can leave through the same vent you opened to get in here."

Nothing moved in the silence that followed.

Then Heath swore he heard a gun cock. "Mike, raise your hands and tell whoever's down there to do the same." Heath slipped down the first few steps, keeping low, his

Glock in one hand, the flashlight in the other. This was what he was good at, reacting in a crisis. It was what he'd been born to do. He'd known it for as long as he could remember. If anything happened, he'd blink the light on and take his shot.

Logic told him this could be no more than a bum looking for a place to sleep, or a kid on drugs planning to grab whatever he could sell. But Heath had been around enough to know the odds were the stranger in the basement was their alley man.

He was moving closer, growing braver. There was no doubt in Heath's mind that the man meant harm, real harm. The tricks and pranks were no longer enough. He wanted to destroy someone's world, and Mike McCulloch was his target.

"Look." Mike tried reasoning with the ghost. "I don't know why you hate me or the paper so much, but all this can only be bad news for you. You were lucky you didn't break your neck falling in from that old vent. I'm surprised you found it; the thing's been boarded up for years."

"Shut up," a low voice whispered.

"Just tell me what you want." Mike tried again. "Maybe I can make whatever wrong the paper did right again."

Heath moved a few steps lower.

"All right," the whisper came again. "I want you to disappear. That'd make everything right."

Heath braced on one knee, knowing there would be no reasoning with a madman. If his eyes could adjust enough to see a shadow, he'd throw himself toward it.

"I was hoping we could come up with another compromise." Mike said.

The ghost laughed, a heavy smoker's cough.

Heath took another step.

The cell phone on his belt bumped against the stair railing, making a low *thump* that echoed.

An instant blinked before Heath saw what looked like a baseball bat coming toward him. A half second later he heard it crack as pain lasered up his leg.

He raised his weapon to fire as his right leg gave way, sending him tumbling down the rest of the stairs.

He hit the concrete floor hard, but didn't move. If he couldn't see anything, the intruder couldn't see him.

"Heath?" Mike yelled.

"Don't come any closer," Heath warned, knowing he was giving his location away. "Stay where you are, Mike."

Wind rushed past his cheek and he knew the ghost had swung the bat again. He started to twist away, but the bat came again, hitting him hard at the temple. As stars exploded behind his eyes, someone brushed past his good leg, then thundered up the steps.

"Heath," Mike shouted. "Are you all right?"

Heath didn't answer as he shoved his pain to the back of his mind and tried to move his leg. He spread his hands out across the floor searching for the flashlight as he forced his mind to reason. The madman must have dropped into the basement before dark and planned to leave before he needed light. Or, he came down thinking he'd stay here until dawn. Just before sunrise he could see well enough to collect everything of value and slip away.

The guy hadn't planned on anyone joining him.

Another possibility worried across Heath's thoughts. If this trespasser was a drug addict, about the time his need kicked in, his rational thought would vanish.

When the stranger flipped off the lights, he must have thought Mike would just lock up and go home.

Or, whoever was in the basement had wanted to face

Mike alone in the darkness. Maybe he'd planned to rob the place after he killed the editor.

Heath fumbled for his flashlight.

Mike knelt by his side. "Are you all right?"

The sound of a police siren drifted down the stairs as Heath gripped Mike's arm to silence him.

They heard boots stomping across the floor above. Heath found his flashlight and clicked it on. "I'm fine," he said, shoving the blood off his forehead with the back of his hand.

For a moment the siren seemed eerie in the still shadows. Then a racket exploded from above. The ghost was doing as much damage as possible before he left.

He flashed his light toward the stairs. "Go after him, Mike. Lead with your Colt. He's not armed or he'd have used it on me." Heath prayed he was right about the guy running as soon as he saw someone coming after him.

Mike took the light and started up the stairs.

"I'll be right behind you." Heath swore as he pulled himself up and followed.

Mike hesitated, then ran up the stairs.

Heath followed more slowly, dripping blood on every step. By the time he reached the front door, Mike was back at his side.

"He's gone." Mike passed the flashlight back to Heath.

"Good," Heath answered as blood dripped over his left eye.

"Not good," Mike answered. "He smashed the gun case in my office and took several of the old weapons."

"Do any of them still fire?"

"They all do." Mike didn't say more; he didn't need to.

They moved across the threshold. "One of the boards on the far corner of the window is loose. He could have slipped out into the bushes without anyone seeing him."

The sheriff's car pulled up. A moment later, Toad followed with sirens blasting. Suddenly the street was full of people.

Watson met them at the entrance. He didn't say a word. He just waited and listened.

Heath turned his flashlight to the loose board at the end of what had been the main windows. "It looks like the intruder planned his entrance and exit, but I'm not sure he had a plan once he got inside. Maybe he didn't think he'd encounter Mike in the basement." Heath shrugged toward the editor. "Maybe he planned to climb the stairs and shoot you in the back while you worked, but why not use the rifle and shoot you any time today?"

"I don't think he had murder in mind. The bat was his only weapon. I'm guessing he thought throwing the switch would send me home for the night."

"I agree." The sheriff finally spoke.

Heath kept thinking aloud. "He wanted something. Any chance you recognized the voice?"

Mike shook his head. "It sounded familiar, like he was from West Texas, but nothing more. When I first went down, I heard him cough the way people who chain-smoke do."

"I heard that too in his voice."

The sheriff walked with them down the steps. Heath leaned against the building and pulled a bandanna from his supply belt. He'd always told Lorie it was for luck, but the luck would be that it would slow bleeding when needed. He needed it now just above his eye, where the stranger had split the skin with his blow.

Watson questioned Mike without noticing Heath leaning against the building. They were all used to the agent stepping into the shadows by now.

Heath stood still as long as he could, then took a deep

breath and straightened. "McCulloch, I need you to do me a favor."

Mike stopped in midsentence and turned toward the agent. "Name it," he said.

"Put your arm around me and walk me to your Jeep like we're best friends. I don't want Lorie seeing the blood, and I sure don't want to pass out with her watching."

Mike nodded once, put his arm around the bloody shoulder, and talked to Heath all the way to his Jeep like they were telling secrets.

"I'm driving you to the emergency room," Mike said.

"I can make it," Heath answered, leaning heavily on Mike.

"Like hell you can."

Chapter 35

After an hour, Mike left the agent at the hospital in good hands and drove back to pick up Pepper and Morgan. All the way he thought of what he should have done. What he should have said. He'd let the alley man slip away.

When he got to Lorie's place, the street was empty and all quiet as if nothing had happened. He walked up to her apartment, realizing he'd never climbed her stairs. Lorie Fuller lived a quiet life, the kind he'd lived for ten years. Yet because of him, her world had been turned upside down. First her relative the agent shows up, then talks her into setting up surveillance on her balcony. Mike didn't even want to think how much Heath had disturbed her routine. When this was all over, maybe they'd go back to their simple walks along Main and laugh about all the excitement they'd once endured.

He tapped on the door, and Lorie called for him to come on in.

He found Pepper pacing and Morgan beating Lorie at checkers. The stray dog was lying at Morgan's feet, chewing on one of her shoestrings.

"What happened?" they all asked at once.

Mike plowed his hand through his hair and tried to make his voice calm. "Not much. Someone was in the basement, just as I thought. I don't know what he wanted, but he did some damage to my gun case. He left before we could catch him."

Lorie stood. "Where's Heath?"

Mike touched her arm. "He's going to be all right, Lorie. He took a hit with a baseball bat on the leg and tumbled down the stairs." Mike hesitated before finishing. "The intruder also clipped him in the head."

Lorie began to shake. "No," she whispered. "No."

Mike knew it was time to tell all the details. Lorie might be content with just a summary, but he guessed Pepper wouldn't. She came storming toward him as if she planned to demand the truth.

Mike didn't give her time to ask; he just started talking. "The second blow hit just above his left eye, but it didn't break bone, just skin. His leg is just bruised, no broken bones. The doc was patching him up when I left." Mike smiled. "Heath was cussing a blue streak. Dr. Patterson is used to delivering babies, and he kept telling Heath to breathe. Evidently, the swearing was nothing new to the doc."

Lorie turned so white he feared she might faint. She melted back in her chair.

Mike put his arm around her and knelt beside her. "Heath told me to tell you he's fine," Mike lied. The agent hadn't said a word about telling Lorie anything. "The sheriff's going to bring him back here as soon as he's all patched up, but I came ahead to get Morgan."

His niece spoke up for the first time. "Me?"

"I've asked Toad to take us back to the house. He'll stand guard while you pack your pajamas. The intruder made it plain he was after something tonight. Since we don't know what, we need to get you somewhere safe and away from me." He frowned at her. "And this time no sneaking off to surprise me. I want you where you're supposed to be every minute until this is all over."

"No," Morgan squealed. "I'm not going anywhere. I'm not! I can't leave. I want to be with you, Dops. I got to stay with you. Who's going to take care of you if I leave?"

Mike tugged on her ribboned braid almost as if he were sorry he had to be the parent. "Don't worry. I've had an hour in the emergency room to think about this. You're not leaving town, but I promise you'll be safe. I've already called and made the arrangements."

"It better not be that old hotel," she said, giving in. "I don't want to stay with a roach family."

"It's not. I promise." He hugged her. "I don't know how I'd handle it if I let something happen to you, kid."

She hugged his waist tight. "Ditto," she whispered as she cried.

He turned back to Lorie. "Will you be all right here?"

The baker looked like she might cry. She sat so still in her chair he wasn't sure she heard him. "Lorie?" He touched her shoulder.

"I don't think so. I think I need to go check on Heath."

"I'll drive you," Pepper volunteered.

While Lorie changed clothes and Morgan put away the game, Mike pulled Pepper aside. "If I asked you to go and stay with Morgan tonight, would you, Malone? Just for one night. Not because I'm your boss, but just as a friend."

She opened her mouth to give one of her quick answers, then hesitated. "Are you sure you know a place in this town where she'd be safe? If someone wants you hurt, they might figure out that they could get to you through Morgan."

"I know a place. But she won't know anyone there and she might be frightened. Would you stay with her?"

"I wouldn't mind a safe place to sleep myself. Most nights I wake up every time the wind blows a branch across the roof of the trailer." She brushed her hand along his rib cage. "This wasn't what I had in mind when I wished to sleep with a McCulloch, but I could do it. Any chance Toad will stop and stand guard while I pack up my PJs?"

"You wear them?" he whispered, fully aware that she was still moving her fingers along his side.

"At this rate, you may never know."

At that moment, he would have given half he owned for one hour alone with her. "When this is over," he said close to her ear, "we've got unfinished business."

When she leaned near to kiss him, they both saw Morgan watching and straightened back to a respectable distance.

They were all in Toad's police car before Morgan asked, "Where is this safe place you've found?"

"You'll see." Mike didn't want to tell them too early or he knew he'd have a mutiny on his hands.

They dropped Lorie at the hospital, then drove to his house. While Toad stood guard out front, Pepper helped Morgan pack. Mike had called May from the hospital and told her to take the rest of the week off. The housekeeper kept a bag packed for weekends, so she had probably left within minutes after he talked to her.

Mike sat at his desk. He thumbed through week-old mail, then pulled his journal from his briefcase. He wrote the first thing that came to mind.

> *Journal Entry: If I am smart enough to reason out all the 'should have done's' in my life, why do I have so many regrets? Wisdom, for me, is only seen in the rearview mirror.*

He paused, thinking of all he would change if he could go backward: He would have come home more in college and gotten to know his father better. He would have handled his brother's lying differently. He would have been more honest about his feelings toward Pepper from the first day. He would have tried harder to reason with the insane man in the basement.

If he could go backward . . . Mike tapped the pen on the paper. He wouldn't have to know how great a man his father was from stories others told. Pepper would know how much she affected him. The alley man might be behind bars or headed toward the asylum.

He leaned back and closed his eyes. Maybe the time had come to stop waiting to see what the alley man had planned next and start acting. Mike was tired of being the hunted. Somehow he had to turn the table. But action wasn't in his nature. Watching was. If he was going to act, he could think of only one person who could help him—the agent.

"Ready," Morgan said from behind him. "Pepper said I could pack my laptop and my iPod."

"Sure." He stood and lifted her huge bag. "You really need all this for one night, kid?"

"I'm going into the unknown," she answered. "I don't know what I'll need. Lack of details leads to overpacking."

Mike noticed that Pepper also carried a bag. They

moved through the house, turning off lights. He made sure he locked all the doors before he left, but in truth he knew the house was a sieve. No one in small towns worried about locking doors or whether windows were burglar proof. If someone really wanted in his place, there would be a dozen ways.

When they climbed into the police car, Pepper asked, "How'd the guy get in the basement?"

"Through an old air shaft. When I was a kid I went down it once. It vents into the alley. I about scared my dad to death, so he made sure the hatch was hammered closed, but pulling the nails free couldn't have been much trouble. What I can't figure out is why?"

Mike looked at Morgan. "Your grandfather printed his own papers on the old press down there; he didn't source them out. Dave and I had to give up our Saturday mornings to fold papers. Your dad was always faster than me."

"You talk like my dad was better at everything than you."

"He was. It seemed like from the time I could walk he was hurrying me along. He could run faster, talk faster, type faster, read faster. I was always the slow little brother."

Mike almost added *drive faster* to the list. By the time he'd gotten out of the bar that night ten years ago, Dave and his friends were already driving off the parking lot, yelling that the race back to town was on. Dave's car had been in the lead. When he didn't make the curve at the tracks the other cars pulled off, some tumbling down the soft shoulders of the two-lane road.

Dave's friends had backed away, afraid of being arrested for being drunk and on drugs. Only Mike ran through all the smoke to try to save his brother.

If I could go back, Mike almost said aloud. *If I could go back and relive one moment.*

Morgan leaned her head on his shoulder. They'd never talked about it, but he guessed she knew his moods and had figured out long ago that there was no way to help but to be there.

"You're a perfect uncle," she whispered. "You're my Dops."

Pepper turned to stare out the back window, probably making sure they weren't being followed.

When they pulled up to the trailer, Morgan stayed in the car with Toad while Mike followed Pepper in to get her things.

It crossed his mind to grab her the minute they were inside and kiss her senseless, but he'd done that last night. One kiss wasn't enough. He'd lost half a night's sleep wishing for more. Loving Pepper was something he planned to take his time doing. Speed wasn't always an advantage.

"I'm going to miss this place," she said as she stuffed clothes into a bag about the same size as her purse. "Unlike Morgan, I don't care where we're going. Anywhere is bound to be better."

He didn't comment as he dumped half a bag of cat food in Herbert's bowl by the back door.

A few minutes later when they pulled up to the nursing home, Pepper glared at him. "You've got to be kidding."

He shrugged. "It's safe and no one will look for Morgan here. I've called ahead. You two will have your own room. It'll be just like a hotel room."

Morgan giggled. "You're locking us up in the old folks' home."

Mike looked at the kid. "You're not upset?"

She shook her head so hard her hair flew around her face. "Why should I be? You don't need to worry about the guy in the basement. Pepper's going to kill you."

Mike swore Pepper looked like she might.

"You tricked me," she whispered between clenched teeth.

"It can't be that bad. I'll come by later and check on you."

"The smell of bedpans. A hundred people snoring once they take their teeth out. Food that tastes like it's already been chewed."

"One night. I'll try to think of something else," Mike promised.

"You'll bring chocolate when you come back?"

"I will." He smiled, knowing food would win her over.

"One night."

Chapter 36

Heath sat in Lorie's silent apartment and tried to relax. He had no idea where she was, and that bothered him far more than the stranger in the basement or the bandage taped to his forehead. The sheriff had dropped him off at the alley entrance to her place. He'd passed her car gathering dust in the carport, then walked up the stairs dreading having to face her with blood on his shirt.

But the bakery lights were off and she wasn't in the apartment. The place was so small he would have smelled her the moment he walked through the unlocked door if she'd been there. Both Mike's and Pepper's cars were still parked at the paper and, for some strange reason, the old man who worked for the *Bugle* was sitting out front on a bench. The shadows of the tree almost hid him from view, but Heath had noticed. Webster's fedora set him apart from everyone in town.

But he had other problems to worry about besides Webster.

Heath tugged off the bloody shirt and threw it in the trash along with the bottle of pain pills he knew he wouldn't be taking. He dug a black long-sleeve sweatshirt from his bag and swore as he tried to get it on over his head.

The night hadn't turned out like it should have. He'd thought all his experience would have warned him of trouble coming, but it hadn't. The madman in the basement of the paper didn't make sense. He obviously hadn't come to rob the place, and Heath had a hard time believing that a man like Mike McCulloch had pissed off anybody enough to have them try to kill him.

Lorie must be scared to death. She was an only child of two only children. She'd been sheltered and overprotected all her life. He wouldn't be surprised if she packed and ran. Her parents had left her enough money to live anywhere she liked.

He looked around at all the clutter of treasures. No. She hadn't left. She would have taken all her junk.

He frowned at the knowledge that she'd cut him from her life but kept the plaster bookends of kittens. She decorated in warm colors and things that made her smile. He hadn't fit in either category.

He heard someone coming up the steps but didn't move. His shoulder holster and Glock were within easy reach, but he'd take his chances. If an intruder opened the door, Heath could have the weapon in his hand before the guy spotted him on the couch. If it was Lorie, Heath didn't want to meet her armed. She'd probably been frightened enough for one night.

She opened the door and just stood there without turning on the light. The light from her landing sliced across him. "You're here," she whispered. "I went to the hospital but you'd already left, so I walked home."

He didn't move. "I'm sorry," he said, for lack of anything else he could think to say.

She set her purse down and tugged off her coat. "How bad are you hurt?"

"Not bad," he answered. "Little more than a scratch."

"They said seven stitches."

"I didn't count."

She turned her back to him as if to close the door. Leaning against the frame, he could see her pulling into herself like a child trying to get smaller so hurt wouldn't find her.

"Are you all right?" He fought the urge to cross the room and hold her. The need, the ache to comfort her, hurt more than any wound.

"I came here because I thought this town was safe. I need to live in a quiet place where I don't have to worry about anyone being hurt. I'm not brave. I'm not strong. I can't thrive in chaos."

"Lorie," he said in a voice so low it didn't sound like his, "come over here."

He knew he'd frighten her if he made one move toward her. Even when they'd been happy he'd sometimes startled her with his quick movements.

She faced him, her hands clinging to the door frame as if it were holding her up.

He raised his arms. "Let me hold you."

When she didn't move, he added, "I just need to hold you, that's all."

She took one step, then ran into his embrace.

He cradled her close and whispered, "It's all right, Lorie Girl. It's all right. You're safe now."

Her tears dampened his shoulder. He'd known from the first that they lived in two completely different worlds, but he'd loved her so much he'd thought they could survive. When they were married, he'd kept his work at work. He'd protected her. He'd sheltered her.

For a long while, he just held her, feeling her cold body warm against his. He didn't say a word as she cried. His big hands moved over her body in comforting strokes. He breathed in the scent of her and the weight of her against his heart. He wanted to tell her how much he loved holding her, but he was afraid he'd say the wrong thing and she'd pull away from him again. Maybe tonight all she needed for a few minutes was a safe harbor. He could be that for her.

The wind from the open door blew in a cold breeze, and she moved closer against him. He tugged the quilt from the back of her couch and covered her.

To his surprise, she giggled. "We should just close the door."

"I'm fine," he said as he shifted her so that her body rested on his good leg. He wanted to see her face. His Lorie had a great face, not beautiful, not made up, but honest with eyes that could see right through a man.

She closed those eyes and moved her cheek against his arm. Maybe she didn't want to see the truth tonight. Maybe she just wanted to relax.

He tucked the covers around her, remembering the feel of her every curve. She was his soft spot, he thought, recalling a freshman English lecture once about how every warrior in history had something he cared about more than life. Sometimes that passion, the teacher had said, led the warrior to do great things, and sometimes it broke him. For the first time, Heath understood that it didn't matter which. The warrior couldn't and wouldn't have changed his fate even if he'd known the ending.

"Why'd you leave that day?" she said softly.

He didn't pretend not to know what day she spoke

about. "I was afraid," he said, hating himself a little more as he spoke the words. "I couldn't stand to see you in so much pain. You were hurting. Your heart was breaking and I couldn't do anything. I couldn't protect you."

"I thought you didn't want the baby."

"I didn't want you hurt. The doctors said it was a long shot. You didn't seem to care that you could die, but I did. If you'd died that day, I would have too."

They were silent for a long while. She didn't move out of his arms, but he knew she was not fully there either. He might be holding her body, but she'd closed off her heart. He thought of telling her that he'd wished a thousand times that he'd stayed with her, but even a million wishes can't cover one action. He'd convinced himself that what they both needed was time apart, so he'd taken an assignment that no one wanted and when he'd returned, the divorce papers were waiting on his desk.

He'd wanted to wait until they could talk, maybe work it out, but the longer he waited, the more he realized what a fool he'd been.

"I thought you were mad at me." She breathed the words softly.

He cupped the back of her head and kissed her forehead in answer. He'd meant the action to be gentler, but she didn't seem to mind.

"What did you name our baby?" he said, feeling the loss of his child for the first time.

"Hope," she whispered. "I named her Hope. I still miss her. Once in a while I ask the age of a little girl and think, my Hope would have been that old."

He had no idea how to tell her how sorry he was. All his life he'd wanted to fight bad guys and make the world a safer place. He'd been raised by a divorced father who'd been a cop with no tolerance for weakness. He'd never learned how to handle tears, but if she'd just let him hold her, he could manage it. If only that would be enough for her.

He brushed his thumb across her cheek. "I've missed you so much." He spoke his thoughts.

She smiled and brushed her soft hand over the stubble along his jaw.

Goggles barked from somewhere near the bottom of the stairs.

Heath heard Mike's voice greeting the dog and then footsteps taking the stairs two at a time. He knew he should pull away from Lorie, but he wanted one more second with her. She must have felt the same, for she made no move to leave.

"Later," he whispered, his lips almost touching hers. "We have to find time."

"Later," she echoed.

Mike stepped into the doorway. "Heath, if you're still up I—"

The editor froze.

Raising his head, Heath smiled at the man, then gently lifted Lorie off his lap. "Come on in, McCulloch."

Mike looked like a man who'd been slapped with a two-by-four. He took a step inside and pushed the door closed as Lorie passed him and flipped on the light.

"Did I miss something here?" Mike seemed to be picking his words carefully. "Were you just cuddling with my baker?" When neither of them said anything, he added, "Maybe it's none of my business . . ."

"It's not." Heath frowned, thinking he'd just as soon slug the editor as explain.

"But weren't you just . . . aren't you two related . . ." Mike didn't seem to want to leave it alone.

Lorie had moved over to the kitchen, her back to them both as she put on a pot of coffee.

Heath decided he had to stop Mike or he might go on stammering for hours. "We're related by marriage," he said. "Our own marriage."

Mike made him even madder by looking shocked. "You're kidding." The editor looked like he was witnessing the cross-mating of two species.

"Can I kill him now, Lorie?" Heath asked, like a spoiled giant wanting to step on the ant of a peasant.

"No, dear, let him have his coffee first. He came up here to find you, so he must have something to say."

Heath couldn't hide the smile. She'd called him *dear*.

Chapter 37

Bailee, Texas
Population 15,004
Shades of Time Nursing Home
11:15 P.M.

I sat cross-legged on my bed and giggled at Morgan. We'd been in the place a little over an hour and she was pretending to age by the minute. First, she'd borrowed one of Aunt Wilma's robes, then she'd asked the night nurse if she could have some of those paper shoes. Now she played with one of the walkers that had been left in our room.

Mike, when he dumped us here, forgot to tell us that the empty room they had available was a storage room. We barely had enough space to unfold the beds. If Morgan wanted to go to the bathroom, she had to walk across my bed.

I was just glad it wasn't the empty made by the resident being picked up by the station wagon with a funeral home logo. I'd seen it parked out back when we arrived but hoped Morgan hadn't noticed.

"This place reminds me of where Dr. Frankenstein

must store his equipment." She pushed buttons on a dead machine and acted like it shocked her. "Maybe we could look around for spare parts and make something? What did they do with your aunt Wilma's hip? The original one."

I laughed. "I'll have to ask her."

"She's a cool old lady. I'll bet she knows where all kinds of skeletons are buried." Morgan giggled. "Of course, Mr. Gray probably buried them all for her. Are they dating? Do old people date? Not old people like you and Dops, but real old people."

I smiled. The kid was like a question machine. Answers not necessary.

"It's only for tonight," I said, as if I believed my own words. In truth, this was probably the safest place in town. We were in the center hallway with a nurses' station in both directions. All the outside doors were locked at nine, and Mr. Gray had organized a night watch, mostly in wheelchairs, to be right outside our door. He'd had so many of the residents wanting to help that he'd divided the shifts into thirty-minute duty. Right now the nine-thirty and ten o'clock guards were still there talking to the ten-thirty guard. Eleven o'clock had shown up early and brought stakeout hot chocolate and a box of Girl Scout cookies.

"I don't mind." Morgan smiled. "As long as I'm not alone. This place must be what a dorm at college is like."

I could hear someone throwing up down the hall. "Almost exactly," I said and flicked off my night light. "We should get some sleep."

"Wait. I want to show you something." She hopped off the bed and dug in her bag. "Dops doesn't know I have this. I've never shown it to anyone before."

I smiled as I saw the scrapbook decorated with construction paper and ribbons.

She crawled up on my bed and opened the book. "It's a

book about my dad. He died when I was three. I didn't have a single memory of him so I thought I'd make them up," She began to turn the pages covered with clippings from the newspaper. "Audrey helped me copy some of them. Here's when he played football in high school. They went to state his senior year." She turned page after page of pictures captioned *McCulloch scores* and *Dave McCulloch leads the team to victory.* "And this is him signing to play for Baylor, but he had an injury and didn't get to finish college."

She laughed as she turned the next page. "Here is my dad in the school play. He looks funny as an old man in *Fiddler on the Roof.* He was the star in the school play both his junior and senior year. Everybody says he could have been an actor."

I stared at the picture of a young man painted up to look old. He looked familiar somehow. Like someone I'd met years ago and couldn't place. Or maybe he just looked familiar because I'd seen him as a soldier on the wall in the office. "What about your uncle? Didn't he play football or act in the school play?"

Morgan laughed. "I asked him that once and he said he was in the library."

I smiled. I could see Michael saying just that.

She flipped the page again. "And these are his letters home when he went to war. He wrote home every month. I was already born by then. See, he put a note to me at the end of every letter."

"This is wonderful," I told her. "It'll be something you can treasure all your life. I lost my father when I was little too. I have a few memories, I think. It's been so many years I'm not sure if they're real memories or just things I wish I could remember."

Morgan suddenly looked older than thirteen. "I know

what you mean. I think I remember the day Dops came and got me, but I'm not sure if it's memories or May telling me about all the things that happened. She says she'd never seen him so angry when he brought me home all dirty. It was like the minute he found me, I was his kid and she says he could have easily gone right back over to that baby-sitter's dirty old house and beat the tar out of her and her drunk husband."

I couldn't imagine Michael that angry, but I was glad Morgan had the story. She might have collected all the clippings of her father, but this one "almost memory" told her how much Michael loved her.

"You know why we're here, don't you?" she asked.

"Why?"

She closed the book and put it aside. "Because I heard Dops say he's going after the alley man but he has to know we're safe first, 'cause we're the ones he loves."

I smiled, tempted to tell her I was just along to watch over her, but I guessed that might hurt her feelings. She seemed to think here with her was the place I truly wanted to be.

Thirty minutes later she was sound asleep and I was wide awake. Could the kid really have heard Michael say he was going after the bad guy? I could see the logic in it, but there would also be danger. Michael knew nothing of what to do. He'd already almost gotten himself killed tonight.

Without me there was no telling what kind of trouble he'd get into.

Suddenly, it hit me. I was worried about him.

Note to self: Never get involved emotionally with any-one. Never worry, it causes premature wrinkles.

I hit my fist against my forehead. It was too late for that note. I should have thought of it earlier.

I already cared about these people. I worried about Michael getting killed and Lorie getting hurt and Toad forgetting to load his gun. "Hell," I said aloud. I was even worried about that bear of an agent being hurt tonight. Who would I have to pick fights with if he died?

Something was seriously wrong with me. I was losing my edge. I needed my three Starbucks fixes a day. I needed big-city nightly news where you could see the end of the world coming. I needed to get out of this town before I started worrying about the population sign being accurate.

Oh, too late. I was already worrying about that.

I might as well sign up for a permanent room here. I was losing my mind.

The light tapping on the door came twice before it registered in my tired brain. I slipped from my bed and tiptoed to the door.

Michael stood in the hall holding a bag. "Sorry it took me so long," he apologized. "It's not easy finding chocolate this time of night."

Mr. Gray and one of my wheelchair dates from bingo were sitting two feet away listening.

"Morgan is asleep," I whispered. "She danced around the room until she finally gave out."

He nodded once. "Any way I could talk to you for a minute?"

I tugged the blanket off my bed to use as a robe and stepped into the hall. "Sure, what's up?"

Mike looked back at the two guards. "Alone."

The two guards shook their heads as if it wasn't part of the top-security code, but the night nurse pointed with her pencil toward a door across from her station. Mike followed me into what looked like an abandoned office and closed the door. Neither of us turned on the lights. The parking lot lights coming in from two long windows gave the air a thin, milky color.

"Are you all right?" he whispered as he leaned against the door to make sure we weren't disturbed.

"I'm fine. Morgan had fun tonight, I think." He looked so sad, I added, "She understands, you know. She's not mad at you or anything."

"I know."

"I'm okay with it too." I studied him, trying to guess what he needed to hear. "You didn't have to bring the candy. I would have survived."

He nodded. "I know. That's not why I dropped by." He raked his fingers through his hair and straightened slightly. "I know this isn't the right time and this definitely isn't the right place, but I need to know where we stand. You and me."

"Why?" He had the look of a man writing his will.

"Because it matters, and I don't want all that is going on to smother what we have . . . what we might have . . . what we almost have."

"Involvement with a woman doesn't come easy for you, does it?"

"No." He smiled. "It usually doesn't come at all."

"We're a pair. You don't want any involvement and I don't want any commitment. Maybe there should be a bar someplace where we could go and *not* meet."

He looked down as if I'd given him his answer. "Sure," he said. "We'll have to look for that place sometime."

I rested my arm on his shoulder and leaned into him. "Why don't we stop talking and try *showing* how we feel."

He leaned his head against the door and closed his eyes. We both knew we only had minutes before someone came looking for us, and time alone seemed almost impossible.

I didn't kiss him right away. I let my body warm against his first. I waited until I felt his heart pounding, then I kissed him feather soft with my mouth open. "Maybe we could get away some weekend when everything settles down."

He pulled me close and ended the hesitation.

Chapter 38

Bailee, Texas
Population 15,006
Wednesday, April 2, 2008
McCulloch house
1:15 A.M.

Mike flipped open his journal and dug for a pen in his desk.

Journal Entry: Tonight I faced my own death and kept wondering why I'm alive in the first place.

He chewed on the pen a while, then closed the book. He'd been trying to think deep thoughts for a year and all he'd come up with was a mulch made of nonsense. All his life he'd fooled himself into believing he was a deep thinker, only to wake up and find he didn't have a thought that mattered in his entire head. He wasn't going to write the Great American Novel or even a so-so novel. He was going to live and die right here and be nothing more than an editor of a small-town paper.

He'd be depressed right now if he had the time. That was the silver lining to knowing someone was trying to kill him. He'd spent his whole life hiding from life, and now he was hiding from death.

He smiled slowly. He might not have a life right now, but he had the hope of a weekend in the future. A weekend alone with Pepper would probably kill him.

A car pulled into his drive, and he got up to let Heath Fuller inside. Mike was still having trouble wrapping his mind around the idea that the tough agent and sweet Lorie had been married, but he'd seen them with his own eyes. Heath wasn't torturing her; he was holding her like a man holds a woman he knows well and loves.

Mike would ask a few questions about their relationship if he didn't firmly believe Heath would gladly murder him before he could get even one answer out of the man.

The way his life was going, Mike wouldn't be surprised if folks started forming a line to kill him.

"This better be important," Heath hissed as he walked into the living area, where the sheriff and Toad already waited.

Watson looked tired, and Toad looked nervous.

"It is," Mike answered as he motioned for Heath to take the other half of the couch. "I've got an idea and I wanted you all to hear it. I'm tired of waiting for the next time this clown shows up to send my life to hell. I think we should set a trap and see if he comes to the party."

"You've been watching too many crime stories on TV, McCulloch," Heath mumbled.

Sheriff Watson shook his head. "I don't like it. Someone could get hurt."

"Someone's already been hurt." Mike glanced at Heath, expecting him to object next, but the agent was too busy going through the mail Mike had tossed on the coffee table. Apparently, because he'd been invited in, he thought no search warrant was necessary.

Watson tried again. "Our job is to protect you, not to go hunting. These kinds of criminals are restless. We won't have to wait long for his next move. In the meantime, Toad will drive you and Morgan around just as a precaution."

Toad straightened. "I won't mind at all. I'll even do it when I'm clocked out."

"I can't have someone following me all the time." Mike wanted to get on with it.

"We might be able to draw him out." Heath finally joined the conversation. "Only if we do this, we do it by my rules. We keep you wired at all times and you wear a vest."

Watson stood. "Now look here, Fuller, we're not using Mike as the bait in a trap. I want no part of it. We'll double the guard around both his office and this house. I'll call in deputies from every county around if I have to, but I'm not setting him in the park with a wire and a vest so he can wait to get shot with one of his grandfather's guns."

Mike rubbed his scalp. "All right, we don't set a trap, but we 'accidentally' leave one time, one place where the guy thinks he can catch me alone. If he happens to show up then, it's not my fault."

"That's a worse idea." The sheriff frowned. "If he finds you alone we might not be close enough to get to you in time. No, Mike, I'm flat-out against this."

Mike glanced at Heath. The agent didn't move a muscle, but he had the feeling the man was with him on this. "All right. We play it your way, Sheriff." Mike swore he saw a slight nod from the agent.

They talked on for a while, piecing the facts together. Most of the trouble had happened at the paper, so there was a good chance the stranger wanted the paper to suffer as well as McCulloch. They also agreed that he had to be familiar with the town to move so freely without anyone noticing him.

"I don't like the possibility," the sheriff said, "but we've got to consider that one of Bailee's own hates you."

"Probably more than one," Heath added, as if to cheer Mike up. "Just one that wants you out of business and plans to help the process along."

"Thanks for the insight." Mike stared at the agent.

Finally, the sheriff and Toad left. Mike held the door for Heath, but when he turned back he noticed the agent moving the coffee table away from the couch.

"What do you think you're doing?"

"My job," Heath answered. "I've decided to sleep here tonight and I'm running a wire across the main hallway. If anyone moves toward the stairs, I'll know it, so don't walk in your sleep unless you have a death wish."

"Why don't you go home to your wife?" Mike said.

To his surprise, Heath smiled. "I would, but for some reason she thinks you're her friend and she wants you to stay alive. I plan to make sure that happens if for no other reason than to make her happy."

"So you're only doing this because of her?"

"You guessed it. Officially, I'm on vacation. Keeping you alive seems to have developed into a hobby of mine." Heath held his hand out. "Give me your keys."

Mike hesitated.

"I'll give them right back. I promise."

Mike passed him the keys and watched Heath latch a small keychain the size of a thumbprint onto his keys. "Never go anywhere without your keys." He handed them back.

"It's a tracking device," Mike guessed. "So you'll know where to find the body."

Heath didn't comment; he just turned back to the couch and started stacking pillows.

"Make yourself at home," Mike mumbled as he walked up the stairs.

"I already have," Heath answered. "Got any beer in the fridge?"

"Sure," Mike answered. "Help yourself." He paused on the landing but couldn't hear the agent moving around below. It crossed his mind that the beer question might have been Heath's idea of a joke.

When he came back down the next morning, he wasn't surprised to find the agent gone. He opened the front door and waved at a deputy parked in the drive, then grabbed his briefcase and caught a ride with his shadow to work.

Before the cop let him off at the *Bugle*, he asked to drive by and pick up Pepper and Morgan.

His niece came out to the car. "I am going to get to go to school. Right, Dops?"

"Right, but you stay in the building or with your usual friends. Don't leave the grounds and don't even go to the bathroom alone."

"Great!" She climbed in with her backpack. "Pepper said to tell you she caught a ride to the *Bugle* so she could start work on a story early."

Mike wished Malone had waited for him, but she'd done him a favor last night. Maybe he owed her a little peace and quiet today.

The cop dropped him off at the *Bugle* and drove on with Morgan waving at everyone like she was the queen of a parade.

He walked into the office and didn't see Pepper. Maybe she'd decided to go over to Lorie's for breakfast.

Morgan called him on her way to school and told him she'd had a blast last night. She even agreed to stay another night if one of her friends could stay over too. "The night nurse said it's all right if we're quiet."

"This isn't a slumber party," Mike said.

"I know, but I don't think Pepper slept at all. Staying up at my age is fun, but once you're thirty, it's hard on you. She had shadows under her eyes this morning and she didn't even try a bite of her pancakes."

"Maybe the cop should have taken her home so she can sleep a few hours."

"Oh, she didn't go with the cop. She went with that big guy you said was an FBI agent. He came by and ate breakfast with me."

A few minutes after he hung up, Pepper came in, but she went straight to her desk. She looked tired and worried.

All morning Mike kept waiting for something to happen, but it was just an ordinary day. Fred and Dora Henderson had twin boys around noon. A couple of sophomores, with drivers' licenses less than a month old, decided to race and wrecked both their fathers' cars out on Claude Road. The price of gas went up five cents again.

Pepper barely spoke to him when he bumped into her at the coffeepot. She looked exhausted. He had no idea whether she was mad or busy. He'd never been able to read women's moods, so if he'd guessed hers right Mike would have seen it as near miraculous.

Last night she'd pressed her finger to his lips and slipped from the room without a word. The few heated moments they'd shared might have meant little to her.

Journal Entry: God made women to confuse men. If He'd never taken the rib, men would never have discussions like, "Where do you want to eat?" or "How do you feel?"

"Chief." Audrey poked her head in his door. "Have you seen Webster this morning?"

Mike closed his journal. "No."

"He wasn't at breakfast, and that's not like him." She folded her thin arms over her chest. "I've been worried about him since he was hit in the head. He could have bleeding on the brain and be dead in his house. Or he could have fallen last night and not be able to get up. Folks that age are always falling and breaking something. Or he might have—"

"Stop." Mike didn't want to hear more. "I just saw him pass the window. He should be coming in the door."

Sure enough, Webster walked in, his cane in one hand and his fedora in the other. "Sorry I'm late," he said to all. "It appears I overslept."

Before Audrey could catch him and give him advice on how to wake up in the morning, Webster slipped into Mike's office and said as he closed the door, "Mind if I have a word with you?"

Mike swiveled his chair around and motioned for Webster to take the only other seat.

The old man got right to the point. "I couldn't sleep last night because I think I may be the cause of all this trouble. You see, I don't like folks to know this, but I was a guard at a prison down in Huntsville for years and I didn't make many friends. I've thought about it and I think one of those men may have been released and came here to pester me. Maybe he wants to close down the paper so I'll be out of a job."

"I don't think—"

Web continued, "Besides the agent who got in the way, I'm the only other one who has been hit."

Mike wished it were that simple. Just like he wished the

stranger were a mad ex-husband his brother had bothered or a half dozen others the town had come up with. None of them fit. The shooter had made it plain in the blackness of the basement last night that he hated Mike. What had he said? "I want you to disappear." Mike could still hear the words whispered in that raspy voice across the darkness.

"It's not you the guy is after, Web, but thanks for trying to help."

Webster looked disappointed that he hadn't solved the mystery.

"Agent Fuller is down in the basement now. He said he needed to see you when you came in."

"I'm on my way," Webster cheered up at the thought of having a mission.

As the old man walked out, Pepper came in with a handful of copy.

"How about a date tonight?" Mike asked. "I know a place where the food's served on trays and you can play bingo while you eat."

She leaned against the file cabinet. "No thanks. I think I'll go back to Wilma's trailer tonight and pack. This weekend I'll be moving on."

Mike fought the urge to yell that she couldn't go. She belonged here. They hadn't had their "going out" dates and first weekend getaway. They hadn't played their *if we get married* game.

He wanted to tell her that she was one of them. She mattered to lots of people in town even if they didn't matter to her. He turned away, not wanting her to see the confusion and rage in his face. "Where you headed?" he asked in as normal a voice as he could muster.

"Dallas maybe." She took a step toward the door. "I want to finish a few stories about the people in town and the history of a few buildings. Do you think the agent is finished digging bullets out of the walls of the basement? I'd like to check a few of my facts."

"Fine," he said, then listened as her heels clicked when she walked away. She'd told him a dozen times she wouldn't be around long. She'd even said she was a one-night-stand kind of girl, but he hadn't expected she'd leave so soon. All they'd done was flirt a little, kiss a few times, fight more often than not. Since that first night when they'd seen the alley man running toward them, he'd thought they were somehow in this mess together.

Now he realized they weren't. He was in the mess. She could walk away any time she wanted to. Who knows, she might even be going to join that guy in the fancy suit and car. He was more her type anyway.

Pepper Malone had surprised him at every turn, and finally, much as he hated to admit it, she'd hurt him, just as he knew she would.

Chapter 39

"Did you do it?" Heath asked as I reached the basement.

"I did it." I wanted to add that I hated myself but the agent wouldn't have cared. Webster looked like he felt sorry for me. The old man was obviously in on whatever game the agent was playing.

Heath moved to the back of the basement. "The more people we get away from Mike right now, the better. If I'm going to protect him I have to know where he is at all times."

Webster patted me on the shoulder. "Promise you'll come back when this is all over."

I couldn't lie. "I don't know that he'll hire me back. I wish I'd had time to think of some great excuse." When Heath had caught me this morning at breakfast, he'd suggested I take myself not only out of danger, but out of Mike's life. I'd worked enough crime beats to know that

Watson and Toad would never be able to keep Mike from getting killed. Last night made it plain that his life was in real danger. If I was complicating the problem, it made sense that I leave.

I tried to smile at Heath. "You know, you're ruining my love life."

The corner of the agent's mouth lifted in the hint of a smile. "Join the club, Malone."

"Well, no one is going to ruin mine," Webster protested. "I'm heading upstairs to my e-mail darlings. We've got a discussion going on dreams, and one of the girls has some you wouldn't believe." He winked. "I have to use a surge protector just to read them."

When Webster left, I turned back to Heath and was surprised to see him looking as if he felt sorry for me.

"You're doing the right thing, you know," he said.

"I know. I'm one less person he has to worry about, but this town grows on you. I'm going to miss it."

I went back to the table where I'd been doing research. I had one last story to write. I saw it as my parting gift. Morgan would have one more clipping to put in her scrapbook. A story about Dave McCulloch. I even planned to dig up pictures of his football days and maybe one in his uniform.

One of the first stories I'd done out of college had been on Desert Strike, a military operation in September 1996. The United States had no troops fighting, but we dumped enough firepower down to make a difference. I'd rewritten the story so many times I could almost quote the entire thing. It wouldn't take me long to blend the strike and the beginning of the war with Dave McCulloch's military service. He'd provided enough information in his letters that I could piece together his years in the army. Then, tomorrow I'd go out to the cemetery and get a shot of his grave. The football hero and the war hero would make a nice parallel.

I'd just gotten into the research when Audrey ran halfway down the stairs. "Chief wants you," she chirped like some kind of deranged cuckoo clock and ran back up the steps.

I stuffed my research in my bag, grabbed my pad, and headed for his office.

"Malone!" Michael yelled, unaware that I was standing at his door.

"Yes," I answered, but he didn't turn around.

"Dispatch just called and they arrested a burglar that's been pestering this town for years. Go over and get the details."

"Right, Chief," I said, wishing Michael would look at me. I wouldn't mind seeing those baby blues one more time.

"You need a ride?" he asked when I didn't move away.

"No. I'll walk. By the end of the day I'll have new tires on my Saturn. Howard found me some good retreads for half of what I thought I'd have to pay. He said he'd get me all fixed up and leave the car out front."

"Howard?"

"You know, the bearded guy who hangs out at the bakery. Everyone calls him Shorty. He worried so much over my slit tires that he finally found a way I could afford to get them fixed."

"Malone." He sounded bothered. "The story."

I jumped. "Right. The story." I couldn't believe I was rambling on about tires when he'd actually given me an assignment.

I grabbed my jacket and bag, then headed to the courthouse. From there I could cut through the building and be at the sheriff's back door in nothing flat.

Rain blew in the air as I stepped outside. I could taste spring. The town had changed in the few weeks I'd been here. Winter had vanished and the signs of spring were everywhere. Lorie had planted flower boxes beneath her windows. The old elms were dusting the ground with so many seeds it looked like snow. I couldn't help but wonder if I'd be back in time to see everything green. I bet this town would look like a postcard of small-town America.

For the first time ever, deep down I wanted to stay in one place long enough to watch the seasons change. The weather to me had been nothing else but a factor in considering what to wear. Here the people seemed to live closer to it. They planned things around the seasons. They looked forward to the changing. They even talked in terms like *come spring* and *next fall* as if measuring time that way instead of by days and months.

I walked into the back of the sheriff's offices and noticed Toad eating the leftover doughnuts. "What's happening?" I asked, deciding I liked the barrel of a man. He tried hard at his job. I used to think I admired people who were successful, but lately I'd switched to respecting folks who gave it their all. Toad was one of those. He'd never be rich or famous, but he gave all he had.

He pouted. "Nothing's happening at all, I'm afraid. Sorry that you wasted your time coming over. I thought I caught the panty burglar, but my uncle says we can't prove anything. You'd think a thousand pair of panties would prove something."

I sat down. "Start at the beginning."

He relaxed as if he had nothing else to do. "Women all over town have been complaining to each other for years about finding their underwear drawers open with all their panties missing. None of them actually filed a complaint, but the sheriff knew about it. Someone was sneaking in their houses and stealing underwear."

"Really." I pulled out my notepad.

"Sometimes he'd steal them when someone had a big party. Sometimes he'd take them off a clothesline at night. We knew about him, but we didn't figure we'd ever be able to catch him," Toad said. "Unless we caught him red-handed coming out of a house. But my uncle said we couldn't start frisking people to see if they had extra panties stuffed in their pockets."

I tried to keep a straight face. "How did you catch him?"

"He called 911 this morning thinking he was having a heart attack. I went out with the ambulance to help with the call. There were stacks of panties everywhere. I thought I had a case for sure."

"And you don't?"

Toad shook his head. "Sheriff says one of the ladies has to come down and claim the panties as hers and say they were stolen. He's made a dozen calls and not one woman's willing to do it."

"Where is this bandit?"

"He's over at the hospital getting checked out. The doc doesn't think it was a heart attack. He thinks it may be one of the hundred beers the guy drank since the Rangers lost Sunday in preseason."

I patted Toad on the shoulder as I stood. "You tried to do the right thing. I'm proud of you."

He smiled. "Thanks."

I walked into the sheriff's office, but he wasn't in. When I looked outside I noticed the rain had started pouring. "Doesn't it ever sprinkle in this town?" I asked.

"Nope," his secretary answered as if she thought I was talking to her. "When we get rain, we get major rain.

There's even been a tornado alert for tonight. The sheriff's out now spotting."

"You want me to give you a ride back to the office, Miss Malone?" Toad asked from the back.

"I'd appreciate it."

He put on a slicker and a plastic cover for his hat. "I don't mind at all."

He drove me around to my car. My old Saturn sparkled in the rain. I thought of running in to say good night to everyone, but decided to just call in my story that wasn't a story to Audrey.

Parked in my car, I talked to her and stared at the *Bugle* through the rain. They'd fixed the big window, but the painter hadn't been out to redo the lettering across the top. I could see Michael working at his desk. I wondered if he'd ever stop pretending to live.

Bob Earl darted from the *Bugle* and ran across the street. Lorie met him at the door with a towel. The bakery looked empty. I guessed the downpour kept even the regulars away.

I caught the last few words Audrey was saying. ". . . tornado warnings."

"What did you say?" I shouted into the phone as thunder rumbled above.

"We're getting reports from all over about tornado warnings. You better get out of that car."

"I think I'm heading home," I answered.

"We're closing up here, too. It's not five o'clock but the clouds make it look almost dark. Nobody wants to go to the basement after what happened last night, so I guess we're all going to run like rats when the rain lets up a little."

I said good-bye and started my car. It felt good to be in the Saturn again, like wearing an old sweater you love.

I drove to Wilma's trailer and ran for the door, but I still managed to get soaked. For a change I didn't worry about lightning striking me. I figured I'd had my quota of bad luck lately.

After locking myself in, I changed into a T-shirt and pajama bottoms. Flipping on the news, I grabbed the last of the ice cream from the freezer and sat down to watch the storm tracking. The local weather map looked like some kid had watercolored all over it, but the weather girl kept saying that the worst had missed us.

Herbert jumped up beside me and started licking the lid of the ice cream carton.

I listened to the thunder rattling above me. It didn't sound like I was missing a thing. Curling up in my favorite blanket of Aunt Wilma's, I covered my head and fell asleep, thankful I didn't have to listen to snoring at the home tonight.

A little after eleven, a sound awoke me. For a second I couldn't figure out what it was. The rain had stopped. The world had been silent for a while.

Then I remembered my cell phone inside the bag I'd brought full of research papers. I pulled out the phone but didn't recognize the number.

"Hello?" I said, preparing to hang up if the low voice of the alley man was on the other line.

"Malone, about time you answered."

"Michael?"

"Yes."

"Where are you calling from?"

"My house. I found the housekeeper's phone in the kitchen and figured I could talk to you for a minute without worrying about it being tapped."

"Has there been more trouble?" My brain was finally pulling out of the fog of sleep I'd so enjoyed.

"It's been so quiet, I'm starting to worry. Twenty-six

hours ago some guy was trying to club me in the dark and now he's vanished again. Morgan's happy entertaining her friend at the nursing home. They called in to say they were learning to play poker"—he paused—"but I don't know how many nights I can stand Heath Fuller sleeping on my couch downstairs."

"You figured out he's Lorie's husband?"

"Yeah."

I could almost hear him plowing his fingers through his hair. Michael liked everything in sensible little categories, and Lorie and the agent didn't fit. "I saw something the first time they were together. He's crazy about her."

"Whereas, she's just crazy," Michael added.

I yawned. "It's nice you called, but I really need some sleep."

He cleared his throat. "I had another reason for calling."

"Well if you want to come over and attack me, you're a little late. I've already made the offer and you've already turned it down."

"I didn't call about that, but I'm glad to know the offer is still on the menu." He laughed. "I want to tell you how I feel about you. Feel free to hang up at any point if I start making a fool of myself, but I'm not letting you leave without knowing. I'm not spending another minute in this life wishing I'd done something besides hesitating."

"Michael, say what you called to say."

"All right. I don't like the idea you're leaving. You didn't even give two weeks' notice." He stopped.

I waited, guessing this had nothing to do with giving notice. He was such an adorable klutz of a person. An editor who couldn't find the right words. Far sexier than some smooth guy rolling off a line. Any girl can fall for a sweet talker, but when she falls for a shy man, she'll fall hard every time.

He started again. "There are some people who just listen to music and there are some who make it. I'm a listener and you make the music."

"Michael, say what you want to say. I'm too sleepy for metaphors."

His words came out low and honest. "Without you I can't hear the music."

No one had ever said something so beautiful to me. I felt tears running down my face as I gripped the phone so hard my knuckles turned white. For the first time some guy wasn't asking for my number and promising to call; he was asking for me.

"I know leaving is in your nature," he whispered. "I know you don't do strings, and friends all come with expiration dates. But this time stay. Even if I don't see you alone until this trouble is over, I need to know you're there, waiting."

I knew I was blowing the FBI agent's plan to hell, but I couldn't help it. Michael was the one man—the first man I couldn't leave. "I'll be here," I answered.

I wish I could have seen his smile.

Chapter 40

Thursday, April 3, 2008
Lorie's apartment
6:00 A.M.

Heath let himself into Lorie's apartment with the key he knew would be over the light fixture. He tugged off his boots and left them by the door, then lowered himself slowly down on the couch.

He'd stood watch all night and hadn't heard a sound out of Mike. It was almost dawn and still the madman hadn't made a play. Heath knew it was just a matter of time, and he planned to be there when it happened.

The patrol car was already in front of the McCulloch house. Heath's shift was over. He needed a few hours of sleep.

His body slowly relaxed, surrounded by the smells of Lorie's home. The wound on his forehead was no more than a dull ache he could block. The worry lines across his face eased as his muscles slowly relaxed.

Something moved in the shadow near the bedroom door.

He didn't open his eyes. He knew it was Lorie. Her bare feet padded softly across the wood floor.

"You awake?" she whispered from the end of the couch.

He didn't answer.

"I just haven't seen you much and now I have to go to work." She moved closer. "I just wanted to tell you thanks for holding me the other night."

She knelt beside him and brushed her fingers over his cheek.

He fought the urge to grab her and pull her to him.

Her hand moved tenderly to his hair and then along the side of his jaw. "There is a kindness in you, Heath, that no one sees but me."

When her lips brushed against his mouth, he lost the battle and pulled her on top of him.

She squealed and laughed. "I just thought we'd talk," she said without making any effort to pull away. "I hear things all day at the bakery, but you don't drop by to say a word."

"Nothing happened. We're just waiting. Mike is trying to go about as normal, and I'm keeping a close eye on him."

"We don't have to talk about that, Heath, we could talk about anything." Her body relaxed against him.

"I don't want to talk," he answered and returned her light kiss.

"But we have to." She giggled as if they were teenagers. "We have to get to know each other again."

All the fatigue left his body as she cuddled against him. When he moved his hand beneath her gown, she made a little sound that always told him he was welcome.

"I love the way you feel," he whispered. "And the way you smell and the way you taste." He bit her throat gently just below her ear as his hand moved over her bare hip.

"I've changed my mind," she answered. "I don't want to talk."

He didn't argue.

Chapter 41

Bailee, Texas
Population 15,007
8:00 A.M.

I decided to sit by myself and read during breakfast at the bakery. You would have thought I'd put a sign over my head that read *Terminally Ill*. Half the people who came in stopped by to talk to me and most asked me to join them for breakfast. In any other town in the world a person could enjoy a quiet meal alone, but in Bailee it seemed to be a crime.

I finally gave up halfway through one of the articles about Desert Strike I'd been trying to read and moved my coffee over to the table with Webster and Audrey. Apparently Michael hadn't mentioned my resignation to anyone, so I didn't have to explain to Audrey, who would see my quitting as nothing more than extra accounting for her to do.

"We've got a ton of work to do today," Audrey said as she took mouse bites of her muffin. "It seems the minute the fruit trees start blooming everybody wants to plan a wedding. And, did you hear, the Donavans' daughter moved back late yesterday. D-I-V-O-R-C-E." She spelled out the word. "Her big-city husband didn't turn out to be so grand. I remember when she married she wanted me to put a note in the paper that if any man attending didn't show up in a tie, he shouldn't bother walking into the church."

I tried to listen to Audrey as I watched Heath Fuller walk in and move directly over to the counter nearest the kitchen. Lorie smiled at him, and he frowned but nodded once to her as he ignored everyone else.

Note to self: Talk to friend about her choice in men.

"Oh, look." Audrey poked me in the arm. "There's Mr. Monday and it's Thursday."

We all watched the stranger in his expensive black suit cross the room and sit next to Heath.

"What do you think that means, having Mr. Monday show up today?" Audrey leaned in as if we were discussing a plot to blow up the courthouse. "I've never seen that before. I don't know what to think of it, do you, Web? It's not natural."

"Maybe," I jumped in, "we should think about calling him something else besides Mr. Monday? Maybe just Mr. Weekday would work."

Webster chuckled behind his napkin, and Audrey looked at me as if I were a spy in their midst.

I decided to straighten up and get in on this game Audrey was playing. "Keep eating just like normal. I can see him over your shoulder, Audrey. I'll keep an eye on him and he won't even know."

They agreed to my plan and we went back to eating breakfast.

Mr. Monday did nothing but order coffee and a bear claw. He seemed to be making small talk with Heath, which I wouldn't have thought the agent capable of doing. I saw nothing unusual with Mr. Monday, but Heath, on the other hand, shocked me.

Every time Lorie passed through the space in the counter, he touched her. A finger brushing her arm. A touch at her waist. A light pat on her hip. It was so slight, so quick I'm sure no one noticed except me.

It didn't take me long to figure out that Lorie was making far more trips out into the café part than necessary.

Note to self: Forget prior note.

Mr. Monday pulled an envelope from the inside of his suit jacket and placed it on the counter. He stood, dropped a five by his coffee for his breakfast, and left.

"Well," Audrey said. "What did you notice about our man?"

I watched Heath pick up the envelope and slide it into his paper. To my surprise, he left through the kitchen.

"Well!" Audrey waved her hands as if flagging down a trucker. "What?"

"I think your Mr. Monday knows the FBI agent," I answered.

"I'm not surprised," Audrey said. "He's bound to be an important man, wearing a suit on Monday. And did you notice his white hair is styled, not just cut? I can tell the difference."

I stood. "I'll meet you back at the office. I want to check on that dog that was shot."

I didn't give them time to disagree. I slipped past the counter and moved into the kitchen. "I thought I'd check on Goggles," I said to Lorie, who only had time to nod.

When I reached the back porch, I found Heath feeding the mutt bacon. "How's the wounded?"

"We're fine," Heath answered. "When do you leave?"

"I'm not. I've decided to stay."

He looked like he might try to talk me out of it.

"Deal with it," I said before he could answer. "I'm staying. I got Aunt Wilma to worry about. I got a root in this place." I held my chin high, daring him to argue.

He grinned. "I've seen air ferns with more roots than you've got, Malone. You're just hanging around because you think there's going to be a story come out of this."

A few weeks ago his words would have rung true, but now they clanged in my ears. I wasn't about to tell him the details of Michael's phone call last night or about any of my feelings. He wouldn't understand. So I smiled and said, "It's a free country, Agent Fuller. Don't even think about harassing me."

"Don't even consider going there, Malone. It's not something I do. Stay if you want to, but don't come bleeding all over me when you get caught in the middle of a gunfight."

"Deal," I said and turned to the walk. "See you in the war zone."

I was so angry I stepped out in the street without looking. A pickup swerved and honked. I jumped to the curb, breaking the heel off my favorite pair of Anne Kleins. When I glanced back, Heath was smiling at me as he carried a huge box up the steps to Loric's place.

I hoped he wasn't moving in, but I was too busy dodging traffic to worry about him.

When I finally made it across, I glanced up at the *Bugle* window to find Michael frowning at me. Great start to the day. One guy waiting for me to die and the other looks like he might kill me.

I walked in, realizing I'd beat the others to work. Crossing to the sink at the coffee station, I tugged off my shoe and began trying to make repairs. I'd never be able to afford another pair on my salary now.

Michael came up behind me. "You seem a lot shorter

without those on." He moved his right hand along my waist, guessing that I'd welcome his touch.

"I'm adjustable," I said and turned around, liking the feel of him brushing against me.

He leaned down and planted a hesitant kiss on my mouth. The kind of front-porch kiss a sixteen-year-old gives his date because he knows she won't go in until he does. "Good morning," he said. "I'm glad you decided to stay."

"I'm not promising anything. I'm just not running like usual."

"Fair enough." He moved to the coffeepot as the others stormed the door, all talking at once.

I picked up my shoes and wandered to my desk. Audrey was right. It was Thursday and we had work to do.

By late morning something in my research on the Desert Strike article bothered me. I couldn't put my finger on what, but it was like I was looking at one of those pictures within a picture and everyone could see the second one but me.

I checked my facts again, then reread each of the letters the *Bugle* had published. Something about Dave McCulloch's story didn't fit. I stared at the pictures of him in the army uniform, him in a football helmet, him dressed for the play. I'd spent so much time looking at him I felt like I knew him. Anyone could tell Michael and Dave were brothers, but there was something very different about them. Dave was self-assured and confident, like he was at the top of his game no matter what—almost arrogant. Michael rarely seemed to be sure of what he was doing. He was constantly checking himself, trying to make his work better.

Again and again I tried to make Dave's story go together, but it wouldn't. I checked a second source for the dates and places of Desert Strike, and then I went to Michael's office.

"Chief," I said as I walked in.

"Malone," he answered without turning around.

"I've been working on an article about your brother. You know, local football hero becomes war hero, but the dates and places don't exactly match."

Michael swiveled around and stared at me as if I were the ghost of Halloween come to call. "Close the door, will you?"

I did and perched on the chair across from him. He looked tired. I almost wished I hadn't bothered him. Then he took a deep breath and smiled. The kind of smile someone has when nothing in the world is funny but he has nothing else he can do.

"I don't suppose you'd just drop the story, no questions asked."

"No." The reporter in me wouldn't let me. "Something's wrong. Either the records have the wrong dates or . . ."

"The records are right; the letters are a week off from the time line. I noticed the discrepancy when my father sent me the *Bugle* with Dave's letters printed on the first page. It didn't take much digging to find out that my brother lied. He'd had to wait until the news of the attack came out before he could write the letters. He'd done it so fast, or been so careless, it didn't look like he bothered to backdate the letters."

"Did he lie about being wounded also?"

"About it all. He never went to Desert Strike. He washed out of the army after eight weeks. But I guess he couldn't just come home, not the town's star son. He had to invent this elaborate lie. The letters. The medals. Even the part about being wounded. My father supported his wife and kid while Dave bummed around the world, stoned on whatever drug was cheap. He told my dad he was in recovery, and every letter my dad didn't print asked for more money to help with extra doctor bills."

"I'm sorry," I said, thinking of Morgan and her scrapbook of lies.

"I'm glad you found out. I've been waiting for ten years for someone to notice. That was what we fought about that night at the bar. I wanted him to come clean and tell Dad the truth. Dave told me to go to hell. He knew the old man would believe him over me; he had all our lives. He also knew Dad's heart was wearing out. All he had to do was wait and he'd have all Dad's money as well as his title as editor. Dave had always wanted the power he thought came with owning the paper. I always figured it was his, but I didn't want him taking over with all the lies behind him."

"But he died?"

Michael plowed his fingers through his hair. "I think he did. I couldn't be sure that was my brother in the car that night, but all his friends said it was. Twenty people saw him and Anna leave together. It had to be him in that car. Dave wouldn't have walked away, not when he knew he was the one Dad planned on giving everything to."

"But what about you?"

"I'd made it plain I wanted to be somewhere else. Dad planned to leave me the land so I could supplement my teaching with the leases. Dave got the paper and the house. It was only fair; he had the family."

Mike stared down at his hand. "So I agreed he was in the car, and when he didn't show up to claim what was his when Dad died, I knew I'd been right to bury the burned body in the family plot. If I had any doubts, I kept them to myself."

"Why?" I whispered.

"For Morgan. For my dad. For the town." He pressed

his palms against his eye sockets. "For me, I guess. If Dave hadn't been killed, that meant he would go to jail. He'd already had DWIs in three states. His drinking had killed Anna." He let out a long breath. "And that was my fault too. If I hadn't started the fight, he would probably have stayed at the bar and drunk until he passed out. So I told no one about what I'd found."

He sighed as if bone tired of it all—the lies, the heritage of the paper, the job he'd been forced to take. "The town still talks about him. I let my doubt stand as well. I was angry that night about all the lies, and yet I never wanted him dead."

"What about the other things I've heard? That he went to college in England for a year while he was recovering. That he could have been a writer or maybe even editor at the *New York Times* if he hadn't decided to come home and take over the *Bugle*."

"I don't know. The only stories I think were true are the ones about his high school football career. All the others were made up. I played along when we were kids and he stretched the truth. I thought the stories were harmless. But the war hero was too much. I thought I'd stop him that night. When the accident happened, I decided it didn't matter any longer. I let all the lies stand."

I saw it then; the real hero, the one who'd stepped in and raised Morgan and kept the paper running, had stood in the shadow of a fool all these years.

Michael looked at me. "I know it's a lot to ask from a writer, but could you kill the story? It doesn't matter anymore. The only one who cares about Dave McCulloch is Morgan."

I smiled. "What story?"

It took a moment for my words to sink in, and then he grinned. "Thanks, Malone." I saw the relief in his face. Admitting the truth about Dave hadn't been as bad as he'd feared.

He stared at me as if he were fully seeing me for the first time. He'd finally let someone in, and it hadn't hurt as bad as he thought it might.

"You all right?" I asked.

He nodded. "How about I take you to lunch?"

"Does the food come on trays?"

"No, the last time I asked you there, you quit. I was thinking more like a place where the food comes in a cardboard basket with fries in the bottom and steak fingers with gravy on top."

"Do cows have fingers?"

"Not anymore. They cut them off for the meals at the DQ."

"Can I have one of those ice creams dipped in chocolate?"

"Babe, you can have anything you want." He stood, grabbed his keys, set my notes on his desk, then put his arm around me and hurried me out of his office.

I thought about telling him no man today calls a woman *babe* since that Disney movie, but educating him might turn out to be a full-time job. His clothes, his hair, the way he talked, the way he kissed good morning.

Note to self: Start a list.

The office phone rang, and we looked at each other. For a moment we'd stepped away from reality, and neither of us wanted to go back. I could feel the fingers of his hand tighten around me as if he couldn't bear to let go again.

Another few steps and we would have been gone. I saw the questions in his eyes. The hesitance. The need to get away.

"Answer it," I said, knowing he would. No matter what I'd learned, this was still his paper, his job, his responsibility.

I watched as he stepped back into his office.

"*Bailee Bugle*," he said, turning so he could watch me.

After a pulse, he frowned and said, "Where?" Then, "I'll be right there."

He hung up the phone and looked up. I saw all the pain in the world in his eyes. He reached for the holster with his Colt that had been hanging on his chair all morning.

"What is it?" I asked as Audrey and Webster moved up beside me.

Something had changed in Michael. A rage in the way he moved and recklessness in his jerking actions as he checked the gun. The smiling man from thirty seconds ago had vanished.

"Michael, what's wrong? Was that the caller?" There was no need for me to say more.

He looked directly at us. "Yes, and he's got Morgan."

Moving through the office, he ignored all our questions. At the door he stopped and turned back. "I'm going alone. Tell the sheriff and Heath that he'll hurt her if anyone else comes up the road. I have to go alone."

He was gone before we could even try to stop him.

Audrey started crying.

Webster dialed the sheriff.

I ran for Heath.

He met me at the bottom of the stairs beside the bakery. "What's wrong? I could barely hear the call."

"The alley man has Morgan."

He turned toward his car parked behind the bakery carport. "I heard the call, but all the whispered voice said was, 'The kid is with me' and 'Come alone to Lookout Point by the old Indian trail if you want to say good-bye to her.'"

I followed, opening the passenger side as he slid behind the wheel.

"Stay here, Malone!" He snapped an order he expected to be followed. "You're not going with me."

"I know who the alley man is," I shouted, as if I thought the agent suddenly hard of hearing. I climbed in. "And I know where they are."

He stopped fiddling with a box on the dash. "You do? Where?"

"I'll tell you as you drive."

He swore and started the car.

Chapter 42

**North Road, heading out of town
104 miles per hour**

Heath drove like an Indy race car driver along the back roads toward the section of Michael's land that had been burned.

He flipped open his phone and hit one number. "Frank," he said. "It's going down. I'm headed toward McCulloch. You cover the *Bugle* just in case. Call in Luke from Twisted Creek to cover the old house. He might hit them all."

If the man on the other end answered, it couldn't have been more than a chirp before Heath snapped the phone closed.

"Who is Frank?" I asked.

"He used to be my partner. He retired and bought a house down south, but he drives in every Monday just to talk through cases with me. Says it keeps his mind fresh."

I finished the puzzle. "And he just happens to pass through here and pick up a paper for you."

"Brilliant, Malone." He didn't say it like he meant it.

"Next question. In case of what?" I asked. "Why do you think someone kidnapping Morgan might be using her as the bait to lure us away from where trouble's really happening?"

"Because," he said, sounding angry at even having to talk to me. "We found all the makings for a bomb in one of the abandoned houses a few miles out of town this morning. It must have been the thirtieth house Toad went through. He's been working his shift at night and then searching most of the day. He said he couldn't stand the idea of a bad guy hiding out in his town."

"What does the find mean?" I wasn't sure I wanted to know.

"It means that the plan, or at least one of them, is to blow up something. The *Bugle* and Mike's house are suspected to be targets. The fire the other night on the McCulloch land was set by small bombs tied to timers. It didn't have to be big, just big enough to spark a fire. We think the barn fire was our bad guy's practice run."

I remembered the barn fire. It had gone from a flicker to an explosion of flames within minutes. The *Bugle* with all its stacks of newspapers and files would do the same.

"How did you know the 'old Indian Trail' is out here by the McCulloch homestead? I don't remember it referred to on any map."

"Mike told me."

"It's a big area. Mike inherited close to ten thousand acres around here from both sides of his family tree."

"I know where the Indian trail is because he took me there."

"I guess he took you to the point along the trail as well?" He swerved, sending rocks and dirt flying higher than the car.

I braced myself for a crash that was bound to come at this speed. "Look, Agent Fuller, do you think you could interrogate me sometime when we're going less than a hundred miles an hour?"

"Why?"

"Shut up."

He glared at me as if trying to decide whether to arrest me now or just toss me out of his car.

"We've got a short hike, but"—I tugged the broken shoe off my foot—"I've got a bigger problem than you at the moment."

"What size do you wear?"

I'd always hated that question. "A ten."

"Hold the wheel."

"What?"

"Hold the wheel!" he shouted as if my only problem at the moment were hearing.

I gripped the side of the wheel as he leaned back without slowing down and pulled a duffel bag into the front seat.

While we weaved he pulled out a pair of boots and two pairs of socks and tossed them in my lap.

"There," he said, taking back control of the car. "Wear two pairs of socks. They'll fit."

I examined the boots, which looked like they'd been bought at the army surplus store on the "used but still good" rack.

"You've got to be kidding," I said.

"We'll be there in two minutes. If you're not ready and able to keep up, I'll go alone."

I had no doubt he meant it. I pulled on the socks and shoved my feet into the ugliest boots in the universe. My brain said what did it matter, getting to Michael and Morgan was a thousand times more important, but my fashion sense still groaned in protest. Once we found them, I'd climb back down the mountain barefooted.

He pulled up to the ruins of the homestead and barns. Heath was out of the car unloading a rifle before I could find the door handle. He strapped on a halter that held one big weapon on his back and another two on each side of his chest. If he hadn't been so big and frightening I would have sworn he was an action figure.

"Stay behind me, and if I order you down, hit the ground and stay there. Do you understand?"

"Yes." He'd finally frightened me speechless. There was no need to yell at me at this point.

"Now I can track this without you, but we'll make better time if you know the way. If you go, it's following orders."

"Got it," I said as he finished strapping on enough weapons to be a one-man army.

"Go!"

I didn't hesitate. I circled the old dugout and crossed between the elms, then picked my way along a forgotten trail Michael swore Indians used hundreds of years ago. I didn't take the time to look south. I knew Michael's Jeep would be parked deep into the weeds.

Heath was right behind me, eating up the ground at twice my rate.

When we reached the place where Michael had turned off toward the rocks and the cliff just beyond, I heard voices.

Heath touched my shoulder. "Get down," he whispered and almost shoved me into the brush.

For once, I followed orders. He climbed silently up the rocks.

I remained still until he disappeared, and then I remembered the brush that bordered the downhill side of the rocks. Tall, three-foot-high weeds Michael had slipped between to cut me off when I headed back. If he could slice through them going down, maybe I could at least get close enough to see what was happening.

I moved to the left and saw the line of sagebrush that had been brown and dead only a week ago. It now glistened with tiny silver leaves. He had told me it would turn soft as the brush of feathers.

Moving slowly, an inch at a time, I maneuvered until I could see the ledge. Lookout Point. The alley man stood near the edge of the cliff, his big hand digging into Morgan's shoulder. His clothes were dirty and old, his face and body looked like he hadn't washed in weeks, and his teeth were the yellow of a druggie, but I knew without a doubt who he was.

I'd seen him dressed almost exactly as he was now in a picture during a school play. His shoulders were rounder. His eyes were bloodshot and wild, unlike the confident stare of a hero. He looked mad. A madman with a hunting knife gripped in one hand and a frightened child in the other.

All the things Michael had said about his brother drifted back to me. Dave was good with a rifle. We found this ledge and played Lewis and Clark. Dave should have been the editor. Dave lived in his own world of lies, believing them himself.

I stared at the McCulloch brothers. Life had changed them both until they no longer looked like they could be related.

"Tell her!" Dave McCulloch hissed at his brother. "Tell her who I am."

Michael stood ten feet away. His Colt rested on a rock behind him. His hands were raised in the air, the scars pink in the sun. "Why?" Michael's words came low, almost calm.

"Because she's mine," the madman screamed.

Michael took a slow step toward him. "You never wanted her. You never cared."

"But she's mine just like the paper is mine, and the house. All mine."

I fought the urge to rush in, but fear that the alley man might take one step backward and send both Morgan and himself off the cliff kept me huddled in the sage.

Michael moved again. "Then why didn't you claim them after the accident?"

Dave waved the knife. "I was too drunk or high that night to think. I just ran, but then by the time I realized what had happened you'd buried some bum, sleeping off a bad trip in my car, as me." He grinned. "I thought I was free. I took all Dad's guns I could carry and sold them in L.A. About the time the money ran out, I got arrested."

Michael walked closer. "Why didn't you let me know you were alive?"

Dave laughed. "All the time I was locked up, all I thought about was coming back here and ruining your life, like you ruined mine." He patted Morgan's head. "I'm taking it all back, brother. All of it. If I can't have it, neither will you."

Morgan started to cry. I dug my hands into the sandy dirt to keep from moving.

Michael took another step.

Dave warned him away with the knife.

"Shut up." He shook Morgan's shoulder hard. "All I ever remembered you doing was crying."

"You can have the paper, Dave. You can have it all."

I could hear the panic in Michael's voice as he set his only term. "Just let Morgan go."

Insanity flickered in Dave's eyes. For a moment his fried brain thought it was possible.

Michael now stood five feet away. His voice shook as he said, "We both know Dad wanted it that way. The town loves you. They'll welcome you back. You can be the editor."

Dave stood a bit taller. "The old man thought I walked on water."

"Everyone did," Michael added. "It'll be like you never left. Morgan and I will disappear. You can have everything."

"But the kid stays with me." Greed, not love, flickered in his eyes.

Michael shocked me by nodding. "All right, can I hug her good-bye?"

Dave smiled, thinking he'd won. He let go of Morgan. She ran to her uncle.

Michael lifted her off the ground in a hug. "Vanish," he whispered as he set her down behind him.

Dave saw his mistake and rushed Michael as Morgan dropped into the sagebush. Vanishing just like her Dops had told her to.

Chapter 43

I reached for Morgan, wrapping around her in an effort to protect her as we tumbled through the brush.

When we landed at the edge of the path, I got to my feet and offered her my hand. "We've got to run."

"I can't leave Dops," she cried. "He's not a fighter. He'll . . ."

"He's got backup," I said, knowing Heath would step in. With all his guns, a hunting knife shouldn't be all that frightening.

Morgan believed me and headed up the trail farther into the rock hills. I was right behind her. We ran until we couldn't take another step, then hid in the trees at a place where we could see about fifty feet of the trail.

Morgan was a smart kid. She didn't waste time asking me if I thought Michael was all right, or if the bad guy was really her father. She just propped her chin on her knees and waited. I could almost hear her brain sorting out the facts.

I listened, waiting for the sound of gunfire to rattle across the hills. None came.

After a long while, she whispered, "He's my guardian angel, you know."

"Who?"

"My uncle. He doesn't know he has wings, but he does. I saw them the first time I saw him." She thought for a minute, then added, "I don't know, or care who that bad man was. All I know is that he was wrong. I don't belong with him. I belong with Dops."

I stared at her, thinking I wish I could be as smart as this kid when I grow up. She never doubted for one second who loved her.

Chapter 44

Beyond Lookout Point
McCulloch land
1:30 P.M.

The shade from the trees at our back stretched over us, but still we waited. I thought about how brave Michael was. He hadn't hesitated to give up everything for Morgan. My own mother would have tried to talk even a guy with a knife down to half the price.

Morgan stood and walked to the path without saying a word.

She shaded her eyes. "There he is. I knew he'd come to get me."

I turned and saw Michael jogging up the path. When he saw us, he smiled and slowed as if giving his heart time to catch up.

Morgan ran to him and moved easily beneath the wing his jacket made as he opened his arm. "I want to go home," she said. "Not the old folks' home, but our home."

"Sounds good to me." He smiled and kissed her on the forehead. "If I'd lost you, kid . . ."

She laughed. "You're never ever going to lose me, Dops."

He offered me his free hand. "Come on, Pepper. Let's go home."

I took it, barely noticing the scars. His grip made me believe he'd never let go.

Morgan wrapped her arms around Michael's waist. She rattled on about how frightened she'd been when Dave told her that her uncle had been in a wreck and she had to come fast. As she filled in details, she calmed, letting fear flow out with her words. Finally, she gave him one last hug, then danced around us like a butterfly.

"What happened back there?" I whispered.

Mike watched her as he answered. "About the time Dave decided to slice me up for the hell of it, Heath came off the rock like a wild man. I thought Dave would have a stroke. He turned to run, but Heath grabbed him. The last I saw of them, Heath was half-dragging him down the hill toward jail. Heath said he and another agent have been collecting information and a list of crimes committed by Dave. They suspected his last name, but didn't know for sure until this morning."

We walked slowly down the path. I felt Michael slowly calming, but his grip remained strong around my fingers.

Morgan circled back to us. "How'd you find us?" she asked.

"Heath's kept me on a tracker for days. I slipped my keys into your pocket when I hugged you. Heath turned on this little machine and it showed me the direction. That's all I needed."

When we reached the Jeep, he put Morgan in the back

and walked around to open my door. "Thanks," he whispered. "For getting her away."

"Maybe she was the one who got me away," I said.

"Then I'll thank her." He opened the door. "Love the boots."

I frowned. I'd been wearing four-hundred-dollar shoes since we met and the only time he noticed was when I wore combat boots way too big.

Chapter 45

North Road
2:00 P.M.

Mike drove toward town. He didn't like the idea that Morgan had to be in the middle of this mess, but he knew Watson would want to talk to her, so they'd stop at the station before heading home.

When he reached town, he pulled in at the Dairy Queen for a round of drinks. Pepper and Morgan both ordered fries, and he smiled. He didn't want to get to the station before they had Dave safely locked away. The last thing Morgan needed was to see her father in cuffs.

Morgan hopped out to get more ketchup, and Pepper asked, "How'd you know it was your brother?"

"I never told anyone we called it Lookout Point, except you. When he said, 'I'll be at Lookout Point,' I knew who it was. If I'd known he was alive, I still never would have guessed he'd come back. When we were growing up, he hated this place. Dave swore if he ever broke free, he'd run and never look back." He frowned. "Only it seemed not much of him did return. Not even a recognizable shell. I feel like I buried him a long time ago and his ghost is trying to haunt me."

"What are you going to tell Morgan?"

"The truth. I've had enough lies to last this lifetime. No matter how she takes it, I'll be there with her."

Morgan climbed back in the car. "Dops," she said, "when we finish at the sheriff's office, can we go for pizza? I'm starving."

"Sure." He glanced at Pepper. "I'm surrounded." He winked. "Maybe if I feed you, you'll grow into your boots."

They drove to the station. Pepper went in, but Mike wanted a moment alone with Morgan. If he could take this pain away from her, he would. It wasn't fair that she had to learn the truth about her father. Not this way.

"I thought he was dead," Mike began, wanting her to understand that he hadn't lied about everything. "But I knew Dave wasn't all the things the paper said he was. I was waiting for the right time to tell you. I guess I waited too long."

Morgan took his big hand in both of hers. "He can't ever get me, can he? I don't like that man. He said he could take me away and there was nothing anyone could do about it. That's not true, is it?"

"No. Never." Mike realized she didn't even think of him as her father.

"And I'll always live with you?"

"Of course." He doubted Dave would live long enough to get out of jail. Heath said he'd been racking up crimes since he got out of jail.

She smiled as if she'd figured out everything she needed to know. "Then, don't worry. I'll be with you through this.

It must have been hard for you seeing your big brother like that."

He touched her nose. "Since when did you become the adult?"

"I always have been, Dops, you're just now figuring it out."

He hugged her. "From the day I found you, kid, you've always been mine."

"No, Dops." She laughed. "You were mine."

Mike looked up to see the sheriff, Toad, and two other deputies running toward him. "McCulloch, get Morgan inside and both of you stay there."

"What's happened?" Trouble, he guessed. Big trouble.

"Bob Earl found a bomb in a pile of papers in the basement of the *Bugle*."

"What?"

The sheriff yelled for his men to close off the street and get everyone back at least a block. Then he turned to Mike. "If he planted one bomb, he may have planted more."

Mike grabbed Morgan's hand and headed up the steps. "Where's Heath?"

"He took off out the back door when he heard. I'm sure he's already at the bakery pulling Lorie out."

Mike pushed Morgan inside the building. "What about the others?"

"Webster said he got everyone outside the minute Bob Earl showed him what he found." Watson opened his trunk and pulled out a bulletproof vest Mike had never seen the sheriff wear. "I got the girls inside calling around trying to find a bomb squad team that can come. In the meantime, we'll keep everyone away. If it's one of those homemade jobs like Toad found in an abandoned house this morning, it'll be unstable and unpredictable, but not all that powerful."

Mike wanted to go with them. It was his paper. Four generations of McCullochs. But he knew this time the sheriff wouldn't let him near the *Bugle*. This time he needed to be here with Morgan.

He opened his phone and dialed the agent.

Chapter 46

Heath strapped on the padded equipment he'd never worn before. When they found the bombs in the barn, he'd had Frank bring the special suit over from Dallas, never believing he'd have to use it. A bomb squad would take an hour or more to get here. Dave McCulloch could have set the timer to go off any minute.

It made sense. Dave wanted his brother away from the paper when he blew the *Bugle*, and the only way he could think of was to grab Morgan. The only thing Heath wasn't sure of was why. Did Dave fear the fire wouldn't be grand enough to kill his brother, so he had them meet where no one would see him do the job? If Mike had been stabbed and tossed off the cliff, no one would ever find his body among the rocks.

Or did he want Mike to suffer watching his world crumble? That might explain why Dave bothered Pepper. He thought she meant something to his brother.

Heath swore. He was giving the drugged-out criminal too much credit. On the way back to town Dave couldn't stop talking, and most of the time he didn't make sense. He named several crimes he'd committed as if proving what a tough guy he was and how he'd never be caught. Dave blamed everything on Mike. His life, his crimes, even his habit.

"What are you doing?" Lorie's voice drew his attention. He couldn't believe he hadn't heard her come in.

Heath opened his mouth to lie, but knew he couldn't. Not anymore, no matter how much he wanted to shelter her. He'd given his word. "I'm gearing up to go in after a bomb left at the *Bugle*."

He hated seeing Lorie's eyes fill with panic. "Oh no, Heath. You might be hurt."

"I might be," he admitted as he continued to work. "But this gear is made to protect me. It's what I do, Lorie Girl. It's what I've always done. Yes, there's danger involved, but I take every precaution." He had to tell it all. She'd know if he was holding back. "It's what I was born to do."

She looked like she was about to cry, but she nodded. "When you finish," she said, standing very still as if she might fall apart if she moved, "when you finish, will you come back to me?"

He grabbed the headgear and closed the distance between them. "Do you mean that?"

She nodded and let a single tear fall. "Come back to me."

He brushed the tear away with his thumb, wishing he had time to tell her how much he loved her and how brave he thought she was at this moment. For the first time since they met, she was accepting him just as he was, flaws and all.

"I'll come back, Lorie Girl, and when I do, I'm never leaving again. Never."

She smiled. "I know."

He wanted to kiss her, but if he did he knew one kiss wouldn't be enough. "I'll be back," he said as he stormed out of her apartment. "Stay away from the windows. If a bomb goes off it might blow some of your glass out."

He didn't look back. He couldn't. His Lorie would be waiting and that was all he needed to know.

His cell rang and he tapped the earpiece. "What?" he snapped as he moved across the street.

Mike's voice. "Heath?"

"I'm going in now," Heath answered, knowing the question. "He must have hidden them in the basement when he broke in. I'll look there first."

"I know every inch. I'll walk you through where to look." Mike's voice sounded almost calm.

"Sounds good, partner, let's go to work." Heath pulled on the headgear and moved into the building.

An hour later, thanks to Mike, Heath located three more of the small bombs. They'd all been set to go off at three forty-five p.m—the time all the *Bugle* employees were usually at their desks working.

"Get out of the building," Mike shouted in his ear. "If there's one we didn't find, chances are it will go off within minutes."

"But—" Heath wanted to keep searching. The bombs would do little more than damage his suit. Then he realized that if he was inside and Lorie heard a bomb, she might not realize he'd be fine.

"I don't care about the paper," Mike answered. "We can rebuild. I don't want you taking any more risk."

Heath climbed the stairs. "All right, Chief. I'm coming out."

A few minutes later, Mike met him behind the barricade. "What do we do now?"

Heath pulled off the cover. "We wait."

Lorie pushed her way through all the folks standing around and jumped into his arms. Heath held her tight. "I told you I'd come back," he whispered. Then he grinned at Mike. "Can you believe this woman loves me?"

"No," Mike answered with total honesty.

They all stood waiting. Five minutes, ten, fifteen. No explosion.

Sheriff Watson finally faced the crowd. "It's all over, folks. You can go home." He turned to Heath. "The bomb squad will be here in a few minutes. They'll go over the *Bugle* with a fine-toothed comb. After that, I'll take the barricade down and you can go back in."

Heath nodded. "I'll be home with my wife if you need me. As long as the street's blocked off, the bakery will have to stay closed." He looked at Watson. "Don't be in any hurry taking them down."

Watson laughed. "It's a favor I owe you."

Chapter 47

Wilma's trailer
6:15 P.M.

I'd delivered Wilma's car to her and walked back to mine. In a few days she'd be out of rehab and home.

Now it was time for me to pack.

I didn't belong in a small town. Who was I kidding? I'd needed a place to hide out. I'd found more than I could handle.

Note to self. Note to self. Note to self. I couldn't think of any notes.

Maybe my self and I weren't talking. I hadn't been listening anyway. I'd been too busy falling in love with the wrong guy. He could never make me happy. Who was I kidding?

I needed my three cups of Starbucks and . . . and . . . I couldn't even remember. The best thing I could do for everyone was to step out of their lives.

A tap rattled the metal door. Herbert showed no interest in answering it, so I crossed the room.

I wasn't surprised to see Michael standing there when I opened it.

He pushed me gently out of his way and walked inside. The only person I'd told I was leaving was Wilma and surely news doesn't travel that fast, even in a small town.

He looked directly at me with those adorable blue eyes and said simply, "Pack."

"That's what I was doing," I said, thinking that for the first time in our history, we were on the same page.

"I know it's not Friday, but I can't wait any longer and Morgan agrees with me. She's over at Kami's, so I don't have to worry about her. Kami's mom will see that she gets to school on time tomorrow. I also called her grandparents in Fort Worth, and they said it would be okay if she didn't come this weekend. Orrie is taking charge of the final edit on the paper, so I'm already free and packed."

"What are you talking about?" I asked when I could get a word in.

He smiled as if asking for a first date. "I thought we'd do a weekend in Dallas. Just me and you. Then when we come back we'll start turning *if we get married* into *when we get married.*"

I tossed the clothes in my hands at him. "You've got to be kidding. You've known me two weeks and every bad thing that could possibly happen has. You almost got killed. You nearly lost Morgan. The paper was wired to be bombed. At what point were you planning to stop and consider that maybe I was bad news in your life, not good?"

He moved his hands as if he could wipe away my words. "I know it's been hell, but the one good thing about the past few weeks is I found you."

"I'm not that great a prize." I could think of a dozen reasons he should think about *not* marrying me.

He took my hand and tugged me to the couch. We sat down, almost touching.

"Maybe I should tell you something. This week ranks up there as one of the worst in my life, but I wouldn't change one minute of it, because if I did there wouldn't be you."

"It wouldn't work. We're too different."

"You're not even going to give it a shot?"

I didn't know what to say. I was nuts about him. Even if we didn't fit together, our life would never be dull. But I didn't belong here. I could never fill the mother role and I couldn't stand not having hard news to report. "I can't."

"Can't what? Can't love me? Can't stay?"

I tried being honest. "I think I might—could love you, except that it's not something I do. I wouldn't be any good at it."

He stood slowly. "Look, Malone, maybe you should think about it. I love you. I don't think I might or could, I know. I love you and it doesn't come with an expiration date. It's forever."

He walked to the door, then turned back, and I saw the hurt in his eyes. "We could make it, Pepper. We could. When we're old and gray I'd tell our grandchildren about how we met, and I'd say that I would change nothing about the days that brought you to me. You stormed into my life and I learned to breathe."

I wanted the weekend with him. I needed the loving way he touched me. But I'd known from the beginning this was only temporary. Everything, everyone in my life had always been temporary.

He walked out the door and took the first step. "If you don't give us a shot, Pepper, you'll regret it the rest of your life. You'll dream about what might have been. If we try, we'll fight and love and live but we'll never be empty with only regrets to sleep with."

I watched as he stepped off the porch. He was so right my heart hurt. I'd never thought about wanting someone forever because I didn't believe in forever. He was willing to say out loud that he loved me even after knowing I wasn't sure.

Herbert jumped into my lap and looked at me as he usually did, like I was definitely the lower life form in the room.

"You're right," I said. For once in my life I needed to run toward something, not away.

I set the cat on the floor and ran out the door.

Michael was leaning against his Jeep, his legs and arms crossed as if he planned to wait all day. When I walked up, he met me, sliding his arms around my waist and pulling me against him.

For a minute I just let the warmth of him move over me. He was a gentle, complicated, loving man whose biggest flaw seemed to be wanting me.

I wrapped my arms around him and held tight to something for the first time in my life.

"Is there any chance I can rewrite that last statement I made, Chief?"

His hand pressed against my back, tugging me closer. "It's a possibility, Malone."

Epilogue

Saturday, July 19, 2008
The orchard behind Wilma's trailer
Sunset

We were married at sunset on the steps of the old manor house behind Wilma's trailer. As far as I could see everyone in town was there, even Orrie.

Morgan and her friend Kami were flower girls. Lorie was my maid of honor, and Aunt Wilma gave me away without using her walker.

As the sun dipped below the horizon, tiny lights came on all across the orchard and the party began. I noticed that Audrey danced almost every dance with her Mr. Monday. Webster had brought a date no one knew, but I had a feeling he'd met her in a chat room.

Heath still stood on the sidelines looking like he was watching for trouble, but folks smiled and talked to him even though he only nodded in response. He'd become a weekend resident of Bailee, and Lorie now closed the bakery on Mondays. The only time the agent smiled was when his wife was near. It was hard not to like a man who loved his woman so much. They were counting the months until he retired and came back full time.

We toasted and danced for hours, then stood on the porch and said good night to our friends. One room on the old house we'd been remodeling was finished. The bedroom. We planned to make good use of it tonight.

The old house was mine. Ours now. It turned out that Wilma had moved out years ago, claiming it was far too big for one. She had left it to me in her will, but decided it would be far more fun to see me enjoy it.

Mike sold his family home to Lorie and Heath. I worried that he'd miss it, but he said it was time. Morgan claimed she'd always thought it was spooky, and by the time Dave got out of prison it would be time for him to move into the Shades.

I looked out the upstairs window as car lights headed back to town. This place was beautiful in summer and the night smelled of peaches.

"What are you thinking?" Mike stood behind me and circled his arms around my waist.

I smiled deep down in my soul. "I'm thinking I have roots."

NOW AVAILABLE FROM
NEW YORK TIMES BESTSELLING AUTHOR

Jodi Thomas

TWISTED CREEK

Bad luck has been biting at Allie Daniels's heels all her life, so when she inherits a café in a small Texas lake community she's sure there's a catch. But Allie decides to move and brings her grandmother along, since the café gives Nana a chance to do what she loves best—cook. As Allie settles in, she soon discovers that she's not alone anymore—and that sometimes, the only cure for bad luck is gaining the courage to love.

penguin.com

More entertaining Texas-style romance
from **USA Today** *bestselling author*

Jodi Thomas
"The Queen of Texas Romance"*

FEATURING THE MCLAIN BROTHERS:

TO KISS A TEXAN
TO WED IN TEXAS

THE WIFE LOTTERY SERIES:

TWO TEXAS HEARTS
THE TEXAN'S DREAM
THE TEXAN'S WAGER
WHEN A TEXAN GAMBLES
A TEXAN'S LUCK
THE TEXAN'S REWARD

"Jodi draws the reader into her stories from the first page...
She's one of my favorites."
—Debbie Macomber

penguin.com

*Midwest Book Review

Enter the rich world of
historical romance
with Berkley Books.

Lynn Kurland

Patricia Potter

Betina Krahn

Jodi Thomas

Anne Gracie

Love is timeless.

penguin.com